*'I'm not about*
*anyone about*

Audra informed Sam
life.'

'Hey, you wouldn't be lying if you said you'd
been in bed with me.'

Her cheeks turned scarlet.

'If pressed, I'd even be able to testify to that tiny
mole you have on the inside of your left thigh.'

*'Sam!'*

'Engaged couples are expected to be hot for each
other. It would seem suspicious if we weren't,
especially considering how fast we fell in love.'

'But we're not—' She pressed her lips together
for a moment. 'Of course. We have to put on a
good act…'

Dear Reader

Welcome to the Sensation™ line-up for October. With winter just around the corner, we're delighted to bring you four passionate, exciting stories guaranteed to keep the chills at bay!

Firstly, Suzanne Brockmann brings us another of her **Tall, Dark and Dangerous** navy SEALs. You may have met hunky Harvard in *Everyday, Average Jones* earlier in the year. But don't worry, even if you missed that one, you'll still love *Harvard's Education*. And talking about dangerous men...don't miss our **Heartbreakers** title this month by rising star Eileen Wilks. Nathan Jones is no Prince Charming—he was once accused of murder—but that isn't going to stop nurse Hannah McBride becoming his *Midnight Cinderella*.

Also this month, Marie Ferrarella brings us a P.I. forced to work with her former lover—a millionaire who once broke her heart. And Ingrid Weaver's heroine embarks on the adventure of a lifetime when an undercover cop asks her to pretend to be his fiancée!

Enjoy them all!

The Editors

# Engaging Sam

## INGRID WEAVER

SILHOUETTE
SENSATION®

*Silhouette, Silhouette Sensation and Colophon are registered trademarks of Harlequin Books S.A., used under licence.*

*First published in Great Britain 1999*
*Silhouette Books, Eton House, 18-24 Paradise Road,*
*Richmond, Surrey TW9 1SR*

© Ingrid Caris 1998

ISBN 0 373 07875 7

*18-9910*

*Printed and bound in Spain*
*by Litografia Rosés S.A., Barcelona*

## INGRID WEAVER

admits to being a compulsive reader who loves a book that can make her cry. A former teacher, now a homemaker and mother, she delights in creating stories that reflect the wonder and adventure of falling in love. When she isn't writing or reading, she enjoys old *Star Trek* re-runs, going on sweater-knitting binges and taking long walks with her husband.

**Other novels by Ingrid Weaver**

*Silhouette Special Edition®*

The Wolf and the Woman's Touch

To Mark, with love.
After three children and twenty-five years,
you're still my hero.

# Chapter 1

Audra McPherson really should have screamed the instant the naked man crawled through her window.

Sure, there were plenty of excuses for her failure to react sensibly. A broken air conditioner, an unrelenting heat wave and simple exhaustion had left her about as sharp as a collapsed soufflé. And on top of the understandable grogginess, there was a paralyzing moment of disbelief because somehow, the man looked...familiar.

Which was ridiculous. After all, a naked man, especially a tall, taut, moonlight-silvered one that could have stepped out of a stud-of-the-month calendar, was not exactly a familiar sight for Audra McPherson. Still, he was enough to make any woman pause, or at least hesitate long enough to wonder if she were dreaming.

But whether she blamed her stunned silence on grogginess, disbelief or an ingrained urge not to disturb the neighbors, it was nevertheless a serious mistake. Because during those precious seconds she lost as her brain tried to grasp what her eyes were seeing, the man lunged across the shadowed bedroom and clamped his hand over her mouth.

Too late, full awareness of her situation crashed over her. This was no fantasy; this was a very real, flesh-and-blood stranger. Despite the fact that there was no balcony or fire escape outside her third-floor window, and the ledge was barely wide enough for a skinny pigeon, somehow this man was really here. And he wasn't here because she'd conjured him out of her imagination. No, he was here because...because...

Oh, God! She wasn't rich. There was nothing in her apartment worth stealing, so what other reason could there be for a man— a *naked* man—to sneak into a single woman's bedroom? Fear tripped her pulse and tensed her body as the answer sprang full-blown into her mind. Desperation giving her a burst of strength, she fought to free her arms from the bedclothes. Her hands collided with a solid, damp, hair-roughened chest and she pushed, but she couldn't budge him. Curling her fingers, she dug her nails into his arm.

Not loosening his hold on her mouth, he caught her wrists in his free hand and pressed them to the pillow above her head. Bedsprings creaked as he knelt beside her. "I'm sorry," he said, his voice a raspy whisper. "I didn't mean to frighten you."

Didn't mean to frighten her? His words didn't make sense. Neither did his apologetic tone. What kind of maniac was this? Audra jerked her arms. The fingers circling her wrists were oddly gentle but as inflexible as living steel. Frantically, she kicked off the sheet, braced one heel against the mattress and struck out at him with the other leg. Her foot thudded against the bare skin beside his spine with a solid smack.

He inhaled sharply and muttered a short oath. Before she could kick him again, he threw his leg over hers and stretched out on top of her, pinning her to the mattress with the weight of his body. "I'm not going to hurt you," he gasped. "I just need to use your phone."

The scream she should have given ten seconds ago thickened her throat, but the broad palm that was pressed against her mouth muffled the sound. She twisted her head, trying to sink her teeth into his hand.

''Dammit, keep still or they'll hear us,'' he muttered, curling his little finger around her chin to keep her jaw shut.

His grip on her jaw was as gently unyielding as his grip on her wrists. Panic joined the fear now as she thrashed and squirmed beneath him. Stark images she had seen on the news, nightmare scenarios of random violence flitted in and out of her mind with every painfully hard beat of her heart. Oh, God! Was this how it happened? Would she be nothing but a statistic by the time the morning finally came? Would there be yellow police-line tape and somber coroners and crowds of reporters—

''Miss McPherson,'' he said. ''Please, don't struggle. You're only going to hurt yourself.''

The sound of her name surprised her into pausing for an instant. If he knew who she was, then he couldn't be some perverted maniac who had chosen her window at random.

No, he was a perverted maniac who had chosen her window *deliberately*.

Another scream gurgled at the back of her throat. She arched her back and twisted, renewing her efforts to dislodge him, but his body was as solid and immovable as a rock.

''Audra, take it easy,'' he whispered, bringing his mouth close to her ear despite her continued thrashing. ''It's me. Sam.''

The name whirled in her head, weaving itself into the fabric of those nightmare images. Sam? *Sam?* She was being attacked by a maniac who not only apologized but wanted to introduce himself? Flexing her jaw, she tried to bite his hand again. To her satisfaction, this time she managed to catch a fold of skin between her teeth.

His breath hissed out on another short oath and he shifted his hand, curling a second finger beneath her chin. ''Audra, for God's sake, quit fighting me. I only want to use your phone.''

Her eyes widened. Her phone? He'd said that before, hadn't he? What was he going to do, use the cord to strangle her? Or tie her up? Or maybe he was going to use it in some other sick, sadistic—

''I need to use your phone,'' he repeated, subduing her struggles by settling his weight more securely on top of her. "I need to call the police."

Her mind must be snapping, she thought, trying to tug her wrists free of his grip. For a second there it sounded as if he said... No, her mind was definitely snapping. Since when did naked maniacs crawl into innocent women's apartments in order to phone the police?

"Listen to me, Audra," he said, his breath hot on the side of her neck. "I'm your neighbor, Sam. I live next door to you in 308. We met when I moved into the building two months ago."

She shook her head against his grip on her jaw and made a noise in her throat.

His chest pressed hard against her breasts as he raised his head. His face was a pale blur in the moonlight that filtered through her curtains. "Look at me," he ordered. "Don't you recognize me?"

Although she didn't deliberately obey him, she couldn't help looking. In the dim lighting, all she could make out were high cheekbones, a square jaw and dark hair that fell over his forehead. There was something vaguely familiar about him, all right. She squinted, trying in vain to pierce the shadows, hoping at least to be able to give the police artist enough for a composite sketch.

Beneath a slash of dark eyebrows, his eyes gleamed with intensity. "I talked to you in the elevator two days ago, remember? You asked me about claiming your library fines as a tax deduction."

His words started to penetrate her panic, but they still didn't make sense. She frowned. She remembered talking to her neighbor in the elevator. And yes, she'd asked him some advice about tax deductions. But could this really be Samuel Tindale? The quiet bookkeeper from next door?

A muggy breeze puffed the curtain aside for a moment, allowing a shaft of moonlight to fall across the bed. The man's features were suddenly revealed, and Audra's frown deepened. She recognized him now. Blue eyes surrounded by spiky lashes, long, straight nose with a hint of a bump in the center, firm lips, dimple in the chin...

Yes, it was Sam, all right. No matter how impossible it seemed, this solid hulk of naked masculinity was actually poor, cute but shy Sam from next door.

"I swear, I don't want to hurt you," he went on. "I know you must be thinking the worst, and I'm sorry for frightening you like this, but I can't afford to waste any more time. I have to call for backup."

Backup? *Backup?* Was there a rabbit hole around here that she had fallen into without realizing it? Another scream scraped her throat. It wasn't a scream of fear this time but of frustration. What on earth was happening here?

"There are two men who have broken into my apartment who were probably sent to kill me, Audra," he said, his low voice vibrating with urgency. "I saw them coming in time and ducked out the window before they could find me. I noticed your window was open, so I took the chance and came over here. I need to call the police before they figure out where I went. Please, the longer you struggle, the more danger you're in."

The stress of adding up those columns of numbers all day must have flipped him out. Two men trying to kill him? What kind of paranoid delusion was he caught in? She jerked upward, trying to ram her knee into some strategic part of his anatomy, but he merely shifted again, curling his legs around hers in some kind of wrestling lock.

"Sorry, Audra," he said tightly. "I don't have time to explain it any further." In a smooth move that was over before she realized what he was doing, Sam shifted his weight to one elbow, twisted his body and rolled so that she was on top of him. He released her wrists and grabbed the sheet in one fluid motion, then flipped her over in his arms as he wrapped her up in the cotton folds. With another swift roll, he had her trapped beneath him, the sheet pinning her arms to her sides as effectively as a straitjacket.

She arched her back, but her effort to dislodge him was futile.

She'd never considered herself a helpless kind of woman, despite what her family believed. She wasn't especially small, either. When she wore heels, she was almost as tall as her oldest nephew. But this man—she still couldn't get over the fact that it was Sam—had the strength and coordination to completely immobilize her.

Still keeping one hand over her mouth, he slid up her body and rotated sideways until his stomach pinned her shoulders. From that position, he was able to stretch out his free arm and reach the phone on her bedside table. He dragged it onto the bed, propped the receiver against the pillow and rapidly punched in a number.

Audra immediately stilled, holding her breath as she strained to listen. If Sam actually did believe that there were killers out to get him, then his paranoia might work in her favor. If he really had called the police...

Without the creaking bedsprings and raspy breathing caused by her struggles, the bedroom was suddenly, deathly silent. Through the phone line came the tinny sound of ringing, then a man's voice.

"Bergstrom?" Sam asked, his voice barely above a whisper. He pulled the phone closer, pressing the receiver to his mouth. "It's Tucker. I'm bailing out. Two of the goons from the warehouse are at my place right now."

Although the way he was lying on top of her made it impossible to see past the side of his ribs, she detected a subtle change in the tension of his body as the telephone conversation progressed. Whoever was on the other end of the phone line was either doing a wonderful job of humoring this crazy man, or...

*Or maybe he wasn't crazy.*

"Yeah, let me talk to Lieutenant Jones while you put out the call," he said. There was a short pause, then a spate of rapid conversation as a new voice came through the phone. Sam sighed before he answered. "I was getting close, Xavier," he said. "We've probably already got enough to shut down the warehouse branch. If not, at least we can bring these sweethearts in for break and enter.... Yeah, good.... All right." There was another pause. "I got out as soon as I saw them in the building. I didn't want to risk a shoot-out with so many civilians around. I'm calling from the apartment next door. 306. Woman named McPherson is letting me use her phone."

The breath Audra had been holding whooshed out against Sam's hand. He'd told her name to the person he was talking to. Why would he do that if he was intending to hurt her? And despite his obviously superior physical strength, he *hadn't* hurt her. As a matter of fact, even now he was keeping some of his weight balanced on his knees and elbows so that he didn't squish her into the mattress.

Good God, could he have been telling her the truth?

Another gasp hissed past his hand as she thought she heard a thump from next door. He'd said there were killers in his apartment! If that was true, then...

"Right," Sam said, still keeping his voice as low as possible. "How soon can you get a unit over? It sounds as if they're still at my place."

Yes, that definitely was a thump from next door, as if someone had just knocked over a heavy piece of furniture.

"No, I'll wait for backup. They won't find anything. I brought the disk with me. And one last thing, Xavier," he said. "I'd appreciate it if you verify my story for Miss McPherson.... Yeah, she was a bit skeptical at first, since she only knows me as Tindale, but she's cooperated beautifully. Just a minute." He slid back down her body until he was face-to-face with her once more. He lowered his head next to hers, angling the telephone receiver so that they could both hear what was being said.

In the hushed shadows, the voice from the telephone was startlingly distinct. "Miss McPherson?" a man asked.

"She's listening," Sam said, his hair brushing her cheek as he spoke into the receiver. "Go ahead."

"Miss McPherson, this is Lieutenant Xavier Jones. I'm Detective Tucker's supervisor. One of our cruisers should be there within a few minutes, and we'll do everything we can to assure your safety. Meanwhile, keep calm. You're in good hands. And on behalf of the Chicago Police I'd like to thank you for your assistance.''

*Tucker?* What happened to Tindale? And he'd called Sam *Detective* Tucker. Was he a cop as well as a bookkeeper? And why were people trying to kill him? This was getting crazier by the second.

And the craziest part was that it also was starting to make a weird kind of sense.

Through the open window came the sound of a distant siren. The grip on her mouth loosened slightly, allowing her to turn her head to meet Sam's gaze.

Now that her initial, stomach-knotting panic was receding, Audra felt her reason slowly return. Either this was one of the most elaborate paranoid hoaxes ever conceived, or... The whirling in her brain steadied as the facts fell into place.

Sam wasn't going to hurt her.

Sam wasn't a bookkeeper, he was a cop.

He'd snuck into her apartment in order to use her phone.

He hadn't let her scream because he hadn't wanted to let the men who were after him know he was over here.

A police lieutenant named Jones had thanked her for her assistance....

So things weren't as bad as she'd feared. She wasn't being accosted in her bedroom by some roving madman. No, instead she was trussed up in a sheet like a cartoon mummy, lying beneath a stark naked cop while criminals bent on murder were clunking around on the other side of her bedroom wall.

Well, that certainly made things all better, right?

Sam terminated the call and stretched to hang up the phone. ''I apologize again for frightening you, Audra,'' he said. ''I hope you understand now that your silence was essential.''

''Mmph!'' she mumbled.

He brought his face close to hers, trying to read her expression. Her eyes weren't as wide anymore, and her breathing was growing steadier, so hopefully she wasn't going to try biting or kicking him again.

Damn, she was a dangerous woman. He'd run into her often enough over the past two months, but he'd never suspected her sensible, no-nonsense exterior concealed such a wildcat.

Then again, she had plenty of provocation for the damage she tried to inflict.

With a chagrined sigh, he carefully eased his weight onto his knees, straddling her hips as he sat back on his heels. "I really am sorry for all of this, Audra."

"Mmph!" she repeated.

"I'm going to remove my hand from your mouth now. For both our sakes, I hope that you won't scream."

Her lips brushed quickly over his palm as she shook her head in an emphatic negative.

"Okay, then." He pulled his hand away slowly, prepared to silence her immediately at the first indication of trouble. Bergstrom had relayed his request for assistance as soon as he'd transferred the phone to Lieutenant Jones, but with those two goons still next door, they weren't in the clear yet. Now that he'd involved Audra, it was more important than ever not to alert anyone to his whereabouts until help arrived.

The moment he dropped his hand, she inhaled sharply. He tensed, but her inhalation turned into several deep, soundless breaths. He eased back farther and watched to make sure she wasn't about to go into hysterics.

To her credit, she didn't. Apart from the way she moistened her lips, and the way the sheet rose and fell with her rapid breathing, she remained motionless, apparently watching him as carefully as he was watching her.

His gaze sharpened as he took in the details he'd done his best to ignore until now. Above the tightly wrapped sheet, her shoulders gleamed in the moonlight, bare except for the lacy straps of her nightgown. Her hair was a mass of pale curls, spread out like a cloud around her head. Sam hadn't realized her hair was that long. Whenever he'd seen her before, she always had it tightly braided along the back of her head. It was soft, too. He'd felt it brush his cheek as he'd angled the telephone receiver so she could listen to Lieutenant Jones.

Although she was handling things better than could be expected, he couldn't afford to assume she was as calm as she appeared. Until help arrived, he wouldn't be able to let himself relax.

Still, there was no longer any excuse for him to keep her pinned to the bed like this. Warily, conscious of the solid kick she'd landed on his kidneys before he'd finally subdued her, he slid off her body to kneel beside her.

She took a few moments to wriggle her arms free, then clutched the crumpled sheet to her breasts and sat up.

"Are you all right?" he asked, concern deepening his voice. "Did I hurt you?"

"No. I mean, yes, I'm all right." She brushed her hair away from her face with unsteady fingers and moved toward the other side of the bed. "You did frighten me for a minute, though."

That had to be the understatement of the century, he thought. Too bad she'd awakened when he'd come through the window. Otherwise, he could have taken the phone into the next room and avoided all this trouble.

But rolling around on a queen-size bed while he held that warm, womanly form hadn't been all that much trouble. Just as he'd never realized how long and delightfully soft her hair was, he'd never suspected what a luscious body she had, either. He'd noticed her walk, though. With her long legs and slim hips, she had a certain grace to her movements that always caught his notice despite the loose clothes she usually wore.

Damn, what was the matter with him? How could he be thinking about her body when he'd just escaped Fitzpatrick's enforcers by nothing but dumb luck and an open window?

"I'm really sorry, Audra," he said, wrenching his thoughts back on track. "I didn't want to involve you, but it was the best option open to me at the time. I'll be out of here as soon as the backup arrives, okay?"

"Is there any chance that those...killers are going to come here?"

"Not as long as we keep quiet."

"But—"

"Shh." He slipped off the bed and padded to the window, listening to the furtive noises coming from next door. From the sound of things, they were searching his apartment, probably looking for the evidence he'd gathered.

Sam squatted down to peer at the floor, frowning as he tried in vain to penetrate the shadows. He extended his hand to run his palm along the baseboard, then smiled grimly when his fingertips brushed the hard, flat edge of the floppy disk he'd dropped when he'd squeezed through the window.

Even though his cover was blown, and he'd have to find a completely new angle to go after Fitzpatrick again, at least he'd managed to save this. Names, dates, dollar figures—all the dry details that hopefully would add up to enough evidence to close down this particular branch of the money-laundering operation. It had been a quick decision, grabbing the disk instead of his gun. He'd had less than a second to consider his alternatives, yet he'd probably made the right choice. With a gun, he could put away only a few of Fitzpatrick's men, but with the evidence on the disk, he still had the chance to build the case that would eventually get them all.

Eventually? It had taken Sam months to establish the Tindale persona and infiltrate the warehouse, a minor operation as far as Fitzpatrick was concerned. What they really needed was a way to cut through the subsidiary companies and get close to the man himself.

"S-Sam?"

At Audra's shaky whisper, he straightened up. Carefully, ready to stop at the first indication of a squeak, he eased the window closed. "What?"

She hesitated. "I've got so many questions, I don't know where to start. Are you really a cop?"

"Yeah, I'm a cop. Sorry, but I don't have my badge on me

right now." Hooking his thumb on the edge of the curtain, he surveyed the street for any signs of movement.

"So you're not a bookkeeper at all?"

"No. That was the cover I was using because of the case I'm working on."

"And your name is Sam Tucker, not Tindale?"

"That's right. Tindale was my cover."

"This is unbelievable. I never would have guessed you weren't...who you said you were."

"Someone did."

"How...how did you get over here?"

"I used the ledge."

"The *ledge?* It's only two inches wide."

More like four inches, he thought, but he didn't want to argue about it. He also didn't want to remember the nerve-wracking, painstaking process of clinging to the cracks in the bricks forty feet above a cement sidewalk. "I was lucky my feet were bare so I could grip with my toes."

There was a long silence before she cleared her throat with a delicate cough. "Yes, I noticed your bare, um, feet."

He glanced down at himself and grimaced. All right. Help was on the way and Audra didn't show any signs of impending hysteria, so for now there was nothing he could do but wait. Maybe he could finally spare the time to take care of one last little detail.

Well, maybe not *that* little.

He always slept in the nude, but tonight it had been too hot to sleep. He'd gone into the kitchen to get a cold beer when he'd heard the footsteps outside his door. One glance through the peephole had been all the warning he'd had. There hadn't been time to get dressed. And he'd never have been able to negotiate that ledge if he'd been burdened down with an armful of clothes. Modesty had been the least of his worries when his case, not to mention his life, was at stake, but now—

God, talk about being caught with your pants down. If the guys at the station ever found out about this...

"Audra, would you mind if I borrowed a towel or something?" he asked.

"A towel?"

He clenched his jaw and gestured, keeping his back toward her.

"Oh. Of course," she said hurriedly. "I'll be right back."

He looked over his shoulder in time to see her shadowy figure move gracefully toward the hall. If this apartment had the same layout as his, then there would be a linen closet just on the other side of that doorway. He crossed the room, but the hall was empty. Shuffling noises came from the direction of the living room, as if someone were dragging something across the floor.

Sam increased his pace, concerned that he'd misread the situation. "Audra?" he called softly.

There was a bump, then a muffled exclamation and the click of a switch. Light flooded the living room from the fixture over the front closet. Audra was standing on a low stool, stretching to grasp a cardboard box that was on the top shelf.

Sam blinked hard, and it wasn't only because of the sudden light. He hadn't been able to see what she was wearing before. He'd known she'd been wearing *something,* since he'd seen the lacy straps and felt the folds of fabric as he'd wrapped her in the sheet. If he'd stopped to think about it, he would have assumed her nightgown would have been as voluminous and concealing as the clothes she wore in the daytime. But it was just as well he hadn't thought about it, because he would have been wrong.

Her nightgown was as pale and sheer as the moonlight that spilled through her window. While she lifted herself up on her toes with her arms over her head, what the raised hemline didn't reveal, the thin fabric did. He tried to tell himself not to look. And for a noble split second, he didn't. But somehow the picture she presented got burned into his brain.

She looked as good as she'd felt. Long, slim legs, pert bottom, slender waist...and a pair of sweetly curved breasts that strained against the front of her nightgown just enough to reveal a hint of dusky rose in the center—

This was nuts. Crazy. What was the matter with him? he wondered for the second time in as many minutes. How could he waste even a split second ogling her body at a time like this? Muttering a curse, Sam strode across the floor before his own body had a chance to display the inevitable reaction.

Audra wrestled the cardboard box off the closet shelf just as Sam reached her side. She sucked in her breath, her gaze darting toward the ceiling, the floor, the box, anywhere except at him.

"What are you doing?" he asked, setting the disk down on a table beside the door so that he could take the box from her arms.

"One of my nephews left some things here when he helped me paint the living room. Jimmy's only fifteen, but he's big for his age. Not as, um, big as you, but..." Her gaze finally steadied on his face. "There might be something in the box you could fit into that would be less embarrassing than a towel."

Before he could think of a reply, there was the sound of screeching tires from the street in front of the building. Car doors slammed. Clearly the cavalry had arrived.

Wasting no more time, Sam put the box on the floor and ripped it open. He rifled past a pair of tennis shoes that looked four sizes too small, a purple baseball cap and a paint-spattered T-shirt. His fingers closed around a pair of jeans, but as soon as he yanked them out, he could see that he'd never be able to get into them.

Audra brushed his hands aside and leaned over the box. "I think there's...yes, here they are." She held up a pair of ragged knee-length gray fleece shorts that looked as if they had begun life as jogging pants.

Without hesitation, Sam took them from her hand. "Thanks, Audra," he said, balancing on one leg as he jammed his foot into the shorts. "You've just saved my life for the second time tonight."

Footsteps sounded from the corridor. Sam sucked in his breath and tugged the shorts over his hips. Despite the stretchy fabric they were a tight squeeze, and he'd be singing soprano if he did any deep knee bends in them, but they were better than nothing. Thrusting Audra behind him protectively, he moved toward the door. "Get back," he ordered firmly.

He felt the warmth of her breath against his skin as she shuffled closer. Frowning, he glanced over his shoulder. "Audra, I think it would be better if you move away from the door."

There was a sudden thud from the direction of his apartment, followed by the sound of splintering wood. Damn, some over-eager rookie must have taken the call. There was no reason to break down his door. The whole point of getting out when he had was to prevent this from happening. There were too many innocent citizens around to risk a confrontation. Regulation ammo wouldn't go through the walls, but—

Muttering a curse under his breath, he spun around and grasped Audra by the arms. Hooking his ankle behind her legs, he pulled her off her feet and carried her down to the floor with him. Before she could draw a breath to protest, Audra was flat on her back with Sam spread-eagled on top of her.

Again.

# Chapter 2

"This evidence almost crossed the line from acceptable to inadmissible, but that's pretty much what I've come to expect from you, Tucker," Xavier said, his fingers a blur as he typed commands into his computer. "As it is, though, I'll be able to pass this disk on to the D.A. as soon as he gets in. Good work," he added gruffly.

Suppressing a yawn, Sam shifted his weight to one leg and leaned back against the office door. Despite the sunrise that was seeping through the venetian blinds, Xavier Jones didn't look like a man who had been up all night. His tie was still neatly knotted, his back was military-straight under his white shirt and not one of his steel-gray hairs was out of place.

That didn't really surprise Sam. During the seventeen years that he'd known him, including the past four when he'd worked on Xavier's special task force on organized crime, he had never seen his superior lose his composure. The man was the epitome of the dedicated career cop—his decisions were swift, his perceptions accurate and his energy endless. He was like a cross between a rock and a pit bull: solid, stubborn, and completely immovable once he sank his teeth into something.

Being assigned to the task force didn't suit everyone. Several other members of the team had burned out or quit because of the havoc that prolonged undercover work could wreak on an officer's personal life—Epstein and O'Hara had transferred to Homicide and Prentice had vanished into some small town in Maine. But this kind of work suited Sam perfectly. He liked the challenge of playing out a deep cover and the adrenaline rush that came from making split second decisions. Although like last night, help was usually a phone call away, as a rule he was on his own.

That was another reason this work suited him. Being on his own was the only way he wanted it. Technically he'd been on his own from the time he'd been sixteen, but in reality it had started years before that. And that was fine with him. There was no one else to answer to or worry about, no one else to let him down. That's the way he did his job, and as he'd learned long ago, that was the best way to live his life.

Audra lived alone, too. During the two months Sam had lived next door, he'd never seen any sign of a boyfriend at her place. Even with the windows open because of this heat wave, he hadn't been disturbed by any noise from her apartment. Yet he could tell when she was home, since from time to time the smell of her cooking would drift into the hall. There would be homey, mouth-watering aromas like fresh bread, or sometimes the scents were tantalizing and exotic, conjuring up images of foreign markets and rich, dark chocolate....

A faint gurgle came from his stomach, and he reminded himself yet again not to have any more of the sludge that passed for coffee at the station. He rubbed his hand over his jaw, feeling the rasp of whiskers against his palm. He needed a shave and a shower, but he'd settle for an hour of uninterrupted sleep. Maybe then his concentration would improve and his thoughts wouldn't keep straying back to Audra McPherson and the smell of her cooking...and her baby-soft hair, and her wide blue eyes...and the unforgettable sensation of having her lying beneath him.

She had felt good. Damn good. And if she'd made such a lasting impression on him when there had been so many more important things going on, what would it be like to feel her pressed so close to him when he could give her his full attention?

That was one question he'd probably never be able to answer. No matter how good she had felt, it was unlikely that they'd get the chance to try it again. He was in the middle of an investigation—until Fitzpatrick was put away, Sam didn't have time for distractions. Besides, Audra didn't date. And if she ever did, it sure wouldn't be a quick, no-strings fling with a man like him. Despite the dynamite body he'd glimpsed through her filmy nightgown, judging by her appearance and her behavior the rest of the time, she probably was as wholesome as the bread she baked.

Forcing his attention back to the conversation, Sam straightened up. "So what do we do now?" he asked.

"We'll have the warehouse shut down by the end of the day," Xavier said, clicking to another screen.

"Then what?"

There was a pause as he read the list of addresses in front of him. "Bergstrom's in charge of mopping up. You've been in deep for sixty-one days now. I'll expect your report by tomorrow morning."

Sam scowled as he thought about the hours of paperwork ahead of him—that was one part of this job that *didn't* suit him. As much as he hated to admit it, from the way things were shaping up there wasn't much left to do except try to make the best of the evidence they already had and hope they'd get luckier next time.

And when it came to this case, they were long overdue for some good luck.

Crossing his arms over his chest, he settled more comfortably against the door. His gaze moved to the surveillance snapshot of Fitzpatrick that had been tacked to one corner of Xavier's orderly bulletin board. The round-faced, middle-aged businessman who smiled back at him looked like a benign, red-haired Santa Claus. "There has to be a better way than chipping away at Fitzpatrick one subsidiary operation at a time. We still don't have anything on the man himself that'll stand up in court.''

"I'm aware of that.''

"He's doing too good a job of insulating himself from the dirty end of his business. We need to get closer, gather more data.''

"We already have data,'' Xavier said, tipping his head toward the computer.

"I would have got more if that jerk on the forklift hadn't seen me pocket the disk.''

"You would have needed to pull out soon anyway. Your cover wasn't solid enough to last much longer.''

"Next time I'll make sure it's airtight.''

The chair squeaked as Xavier swiveled to face Sam. "What do you have in mind?''

Good question, Sam thought. The reason they'd had to go after a branch operation in the first place was that Fitzpatrick was unbelievably careful about the people he surrounded himself with. The man verged on paranoia when it came to his personal security. "There's got to be an angle.''

"We'll be stepping up our surveillance of his estate at the end of the month.''

"That'll be, what, two weeks before his daughter's wedding?''

"Right.''

"You're hoping he'll get careless?''

"Judging by his track record, I doubt if that will happen. But we'll be watching him anyway, and if an opportunity comes up, we'll be sure to use it.''

Sam muttered a curse under his breath. When they'd first heard about the impending marriage of Fitzpatrick's only daughter, Marion, they'd hoped it would provide them with a chance to penetrate his security, but so far they'd had no luck. When it came to organizing protection, Fitzpatrick could give the Secret Service some pointers. "What I wouldn't do for a look at the guest list.''

Xavier pressed his lips into a tight line of frustration before he turned back to his computer. "We have to work within the law, Tucker. We'll know who's attending when they get there.''

"I know, I know. But I doubt if the majority of the guests will be there because of his daughter. There's going to be a hell of a lot of business done. Nothing like weddings and funerals to gather the clan."

"There's no denying that having a man inside would be an advantage, but at this point there's no possibility of that."

"Still no luck placing anyone?"

"Not yet. I doubt if a bee could hitch a ride on the florist's van without some level of security clearance."

"But with all the extra traffic that's going to go on at his estate and the outside help he's going to need—"

"We're still in the process of checking out everyone he's hired, but so far we don't have any good possibilities. He's being his usual sly self, not firming up the contracts until the last minute. We didn't learn which caterer he'd chosen until the day before yesterday…" He paused. "Hang on. Your neighbor."

"What about her?"

"You said her name was McPherson, right?"

Sam nodded. It wasn't really necessary to answer Xavier's question—the man was as good at remembering details as his computer. "What about her?" he repeated.

Xavier was leaning forward, clicking purposefully at his keyboard until a new list appeared on the screen. "There it is," he murmured. "I knew I'd seen that name recently. McPherson Catering is the firm that's doing the Fitzpatrick wedding. It's owned by an individual named John McPherson."

"There must be hundreds of McPhersons in the city. The chances of Audra being related to him are pretty slim."

"Like I said, they only got the job two days ago, so we haven't had much chance to check them out. I'll let you know if there's any connection with your neighbor."

Sam rubbed his chin while he forced his weary brain to think it through. Audra? Being involved with someone of Fitzpatrick's ilk? He'd guess that she was too sweetly innocent for that.

On the other hand, one of the reasons Fitzpatrick had managed to escape prosecution so far was by making sure that the companies he dealt with directly were so clean they squeaked. He kept himself well removed from the sleazy side of his business. And when it came to something like his daughter's wedding, he'd probably be more careful than ever to choose a catering company that was above reproach.

Straightening up, he turned around to open the door. There wasn't much point wondering about it at this stage. Sure, it would be great to have already established contact with someone connected with the Fitzpatrick wedding, but the odds were that Audra's having the same last name as the head of the catering firm was nothing but coincidence.

Considering the way their luck had been going on this case so far, it would be foolish to hope otherwise, right?

"Okay," he muttered. "Maybe I should check on Bergstrom's progress—"

"Leave him alone," Xavier ordered. "We both know he's fully capable of tying up the loose ends. You have a report to write."

Sam restrained himself from groaning. "Yeah, I know."

"And one last thing, Tucker."

"Yeah?" he asked, pausing in the doorway.

Xavier brushed an imaginary wrinkle from his tie as he bent toward his computer once more. "I know the city's in the middle of a heat wave, but try to put on a few more clothes before you come down here again. This is a police station, not a beach."

"...and it looks like another hot Sunday, people, so crank up the old air conditioner and put an extra beer on ice for me," the voice of the morning show announcer chirped through the radio.

Audra yawned as she poured herself another cup of coffee, then reached out to adjust the fan that whirred softly back and forth on her counter. In one way the night had seemed endless. In another, it seemed as if no time at all had passed before the first rays of another hot, sticky sunrise had crept through her well-used window.

"...with the predicted high around ninety-seven and humidity close to eighty percent, that brings the humidex to around three million, I'd say. Makes moving to Canada almost look good, don't you think?''

Rolling her eyes, Audra switched off the radio. Normally she didn't subject herself to this kind of annoyingly cheerful patter so early in the morning, but she'd wanted to hear the news. Not surprisingly, there hadn't been any mention of the arrests of those two men who had been in Sam's apartment. Apart from the broken door, it had all gone too smoothly to attract the notice of the media. That's what Sam had predicted before he'd left—she turned her head groggily to peer at the clock—five hours ago.

Choosing a chair that would put her in front of the fan, she placed her cup on the kitchen table and carefully eased herself down. If it weren't for the residual tenderness in her backside— a result of hitting the floor with Sam on top of her—she would have a hard time believing that the events of the previous night had really happened.

Getting mixed up with an undercover operation, a pair of thugs, a swiftly organized arrest...well, things like that might be commonplace in the books she liked to read, but they simply didn't happen to Audra McPherson. No, as a rule there wasn't a whole lot of excitement in her day-to-day life, unless she counted that time last year when the cherries jubilee had set fire to the drapes at the Steadman's house.

That job had been trouble from the start. With her mother and three of the nephews down with the flu, and Jake and Geraldine off on their honeymoon, she'd warned her father that they needed more help, but he'd stubbornly insisted that he wasn't going to start hiring outside the family. So McPherson Catering had gone short-staffed to the Steadman anniversary party, and disaster had struck in the form of open patio doors, a sudden breeze and too much brandy on the cherries. Luckily, Audra had managed to tear down the drapes and toss them through the doors into the swimming pool before any major damage was done. Her quick thinking had saved the party—and the much-needed bonus the client had promised them.

But what had happened to her usual quick thinking last night?

If the circumstances had been different, if it hadn't been Sam who had taken her by surprise like that in her bedroom... Oh, God, the prospect was too horrible to contemplate. Alone and completely overpowered by a naked stranger—

She gulped a mouthful of coffee, fighting off an echo of last night's initial panic. It was okay now; it was all over. At least, it had better be over. She had work to do today, a job to plan, a new dessert sauce to test, suppliers to contact. The usual everyday details that filled her time. She shouldn't be worrying about what *could* have occurred if the man who had crawled through her window had been anyone except Sam.

If her family ever found out what had happened here last night, they would insist that she move back home. It wouldn't matter to them that no reasonable person would have considered it a risk to leave that third-floor window open. No, the McPherson males would say that she should have realized that someone could inch their way along that narrow ledge from the neighboring apartment and accost her in her bedroom. They would say it wasn't natural for a woman to want to live alone without the protection of at least one big strong man. They would ignore the fact that she had been managing just fine by herself for more than five years.

They were good at ignoring what they didn't want to hear.

Sighing, she lifted her face into the breeze from the fan. It was too early and too hot to get into all that again. The main thing to keep in mind was that no matter what they said, she was well on her way to doing what she wanted, anyway. Her savings account was continuing to grow, and once she received her share of the bonus from the next catering job, she'd be that much closer to her dream of opening her own restaurant.

It wasn't as if she didn't love her family. Underneath their overprotective attitudes they really were wonderful, warm, supportive people. The problem was, they couldn't understand her desire for independence, for something more than the life they'd planned for her. Her father wanted her to stay within the shelter of the family business instead of striking out on her own. Her mother wanted her to do what she had done herself: find a good man to take care of her, settle down and get married and spend the next twenty years barefoot, pregnant and in the kitchen.

While Audra enjoyed the creativity involved during her work in the kitchen, she had no desire for the rest. Once, back when she was first engaged to Ryan, she might have thought so. But that was before she'd learned the flip side of love, that terrible, unfathomable vulnerability that went along with committing your heart.

Her family insisted it was high time to try again. They all were so satisfied with their stable, loving marriages, they couldn't understand her desire for independence. But if Audra had learned anything during those years with Ryan, it was that she didn't need a man to take care of her or to make her life complete. She was doing just fine on her own. Besides, in spite of well-meaning but misguided attempts at matchmaking by her mother and her sisters-in-law, she hadn't yet met another man who had sparked her interest....

Unbidden, the image of Sam Tucker appeared in her mind, in particular the image of Sam as he had looked standing beside her window with the moonlight gleaming on his naked skin.

Audra set her coffee cup down on the table with a thud. All right, once she had realized that Sam wasn't going to hurt her, there was no denying that he had sparked more than her interest. That was no surprise, considering his...appearance. With his broad shoulders, sculpted biceps and those subtle ripples over his washboard stomach, he would kindle a spark or two in any healthy woman.

Not that he had anything she hadn't seen before. After growing up in a house with six brothers, and then doing her share of baby-sitting as her sisters-in-law produced at least one nephew a year... Well, suffice it to say that the masculine form had lost its mystery for her well before the time she'd first changed a diaper.

Of course, there was a considerable difference between the baby McPherson boys and a full-grown—a *very* full-grown—man.

She chewed her lower lip, her memory supplying yet another

vivid image. Lord, who would have suspected what was really underneath that self-effacing bookkeeper she'd known—or thought she'd known—for two months? When it came to acting out a part for his undercover work, Sam must be one of the best.

And if he ever got tired of working for the police department, he would make a fortune as a male centerfold. From what she'd glimpsed last night before he'd squeezed himself into Jimmy's shorts...

"Oh, for heaven's sake," she muttered, disgusted with herself. How could she be dwelling on Sam's nudity like some kind of, well, virgin?

From what he'd explained afterward, apparently his nudity had been unavoidable. And apart from when he'd asked her for something to cover himself with, it hadn't seemed to bother him. Until she'd mentioned it, he hadn't seemed to be aware he was naked. Even then, he'd treated his lack of clothing as nothing more than a minor inconvenience, certainly not something to be ashamed or embarrassed about. For all she knew, strutting around a woman's bedroom without any clothes on might be a common occurrence for Sam.

And that was all the more reason why she shouldn't be dwelling on it. As far as experience went, they were worlds apart. A man like Sam, a macho, take-charge cop who dealt with life-and-death situations on a regular basis, would probably pursue the same kind of excitement in his personal relationships. If he could inspire sparks when he was only trying to make a phone call, what kind of heat would he generate when he turned his attention to lovemaking?

"Enough," she said, rising to her feet. Speculating about Sam's sex life was as pointless as speculating about spending the winnings from a lottery ticket that she had no intention of buying.

Over the whirr of the fan, she heard a quiet knock on her apartment door. She glanced at the clock. Her mother was supposed to drop by sometime this morning so they could start the planning for the next job, but seven o'clock was early even for someone with Constance McPherson's energy level. Sighing, Audra tugged the edges of her robe together and walked toward the door.

It was just as well her mother was early—Audra could use a distraction to alter the course of her thoughts. It wasn't like her to be so preoccupied with a man, no matter what he looked like.

"Good morning," she said, sliding off the chain and pulling open the door. "You're..." Her greeting trailed off as her gaze encountered a familiar—and very masculine—chest. "Oh, it's you."

"Good morning, Audra," said a voice that was several octaves lower than her mother's. "Expecting someone else?"

She tightened her grip on the door and on her robe. Obviously Sam hadn't slept any more than she had. He was still wearing her nephew's shorts and the beat-up jogging shoes and wildly colored Hawaiian print shirt he'd retrieved from his apartment before he'd followed the other policemen down to the station last night. The shadow of his beard was darker, and his eyes were tinged with fatigue, but he was still a disconcertingly handsome man.

Even with some clothes on.

"Yes, I was expecting my mother," she answered finally.

He looked at her robe, then glanced at the corridor behind him. "Audra, you should check to see who it is before you open your door."

The twinge of irritation she felt at his comment was automatic, in spite of the fact that he was right. "I was expecting my mother, but now I get one of my brothers."

"What?"

"The protectiveness spiel."

"In my line of work, caution is a good habit to get into." One corner of his mouth lifted in a wry smile. "On the other hand, I hate to think what would have happened if you'd been cautious enough to sleep with your window closed last night."

"Is everything all settled with those men who were after you?"

"Uh-huh. No problems. I just thought I'd thank you again for your help."

"You're welcome." Her irritation faded as she focused on his smile. It was unexpectedly boyish, deepening the lines beside his mouth and crinkling the corners of his eyes. It hinted that there was more to this man than the cop she had seen last night.

Of course, last night she had already seen everything there was to see....

*Just stop it,* she told herself firmly. "So what happens now? Do I need to do anything, like make a statement or testify?"

"No, we've got it covered." His jaw tightened and his nostrils flared as he suppressed a yawn. "I apologize again for frightening you last night."

"It's okay. Really."

"Audra, even though we won't need your testimony, there are a few things about the case that I'd like to straighten out with you. Do you have a few minutes to talk about it now?"

"Well, I suppose so."

"Do you mind if we talk about this inside?"

After a brief hesitation, she let go of the door and stepped back. She moved aside as he entered, trying to give him more space, acutely aware of his size and the aura of masculine strength that surrounded him. And along with the awareness came a belated self-consciousness.

She tightened the belt on her robe before smoothing her hair impatiently. There was no reason for her to feel self-conscious about her appearance—he'd seen her in a lot less. And as far as the propriety of entertaining a man in her apartment at this hour of the morning, after last night they were really beyond that, weren't they?

Sam stood in the center of the living room to wait as Audra mumbled something about getting coffee and detoured to the kitchen. He watched her until she was out of sight, then let out his breath in a long, slow exhalation.

How could a woman look so innocent and so tempting at the same time? Today she was covered from her neck to her ankles. Her robe was peach-colored cotton, as modest and practical as the clothes she usually wore. Yet the way her tousled hair brushed

softly across her shoulders when she walked, and the way her
pulse had fluttered delicately at the side of her throat when she'd
seen him on her doorstep, made him think yet again of the de-
lectable body he'd held beneath him last night.

Rubbing his face briskly, he forced himself to get his mind
back on business. He'd planned to postpone this visit until after
he'd had a chance to rest. It was over a day and a half since he'd
gotten any sleep, but then as he was passing by Audra's door,
he'd caught a whiff of that chocolate-laced coffee she made every
morning and his plans had changed.

He turned in a slow circle, taking a more thorough look at the
room he'd only glimpsed the night before. Like his place, the
apartment was small, but Audra had made the most of the space
available. Books and potted plants crammed the shelf on the far
wall, along with an array of framed photographs of smiling children. Between a pillow-strewn sofa and a deep rose armchair
there was a basket stuffed full of colorful yarn balls, the topmost
ball skewered by a pair of knitting needles. The pale rose curtains
on the front window and the fringed rug in the center of the floor
completed an overall impression that was warm and homey.

Her bedroom was decorated with the same kind of cozy, feminine touches. He hadn't been able to see many details in the
dark, and he'd been too occupied with subduing Audra's struggles
to pay close attention to the decor, but he remembered the flower-
patterned sheets and the gracefully glinting curves of the brass
headboard. And he'd never forget that short, gauzy nightgown
she'd been wearing that had revealed even more feminine details....

But he *should* try to forget about that. He already knew she
wasn't his type of woman, and seeing this place only reinforced
that fact. Flowered sheets. Pictures of kids. A basket of knitting.
She might live alone, but everything about her screamed family,
home and commitment.

A book lay discarded facedown on a polished wood side table,
a tasselled bookmark peeking out from the pages. Sam moved
over to pick it up, expecting to see something like a Jane Austen

novel. His eyebrows rose as he saw the blood-spattered corpse on the cover. He wouldn't have guessed that Audra's taste in reading material included this kind of murder mystery.

But then, until a few hours ago, he wouldn't have guessed that her hair would have felt so soft or her body would have felt so good....

At the clink of cutlery, Sam set the book down and turned around. Audra had returned, and the tray she placed on the coffee table was loaded with two steaming mugs, a pottery bowl full of sugar, a small pitcher of cream and a plate piled with icing-drizzled Danishes. The sharp aroma of coffee blended with the delicate fragrance of cinnamon, and Sam inhaled appreciatively as he crossed the room to join her.

"I didn't want you to go to any trouble," he said, eyeing the nearest Danish.

"I was about to have breakfast anyway. You're welcome to join me, Sam."

He took the armchair across from her, watching as she carefully arranged the folds of her robe to cover her legs. He wondered whether she still wore that short, practically transparent night-gown beneath the robe. Or did she wear nothing? Either alternative was equally distracting.

Wrenching his gaze back to hers, he reached for the mug she offered. The coffee was as dark and delicious as he'd imagined when he'd smelled it in the corridor. The pastry was warm, bursting into buttery flakes the moment he bit into it. He chewed slowly, prolonging the pleasure as long as he could before he finally got down to business. "Audra, I'd like to ask you a favor."

She licked a flake of pastry from the corner of her mouth and met his gaze. "Oh?"

For a crazy moment he thought about kissing her. What would she do? How would she taste? What would it feel like to lean across the space between them and lick the trace of icing from her lower lip—

"Sam?"

He gulped a mouthful of coffee and set the mug down on the

tray. "It's about last night. Most of my work is done under-cover."

"Yes, you mentioned that already. That's why you were mas-querading as that wim—um, bookkeeper."

"Generally, I try to keep the number of people who know about my investigations to a minimum."

She nodded. "For security, right? You don't want anyone to be able to blow your cover if you're on a case."

"Right. While you're not under any legal obligation to keep what happened here confidential, I'd really appreciate it if you didn't tell anyone what you know about me."

"Of course," she answered immediately. "The fewer people who know you're a cop, the safer your undercover work is."

He was pleasantly surprised by her quick grasp of the situation, but he should have expected it after seeing the crime novel she'd been reading. "I'm glad you understand. That should simplify things when it comes to my next assignment."

"What about the other people in the building? Someone must have noticed the commotion when those men were arrested."

"That won't be a problem. The Sawchuks across the hall are away on vacation, and Rohan in 307 is on graveyard shift this week, so you were the only person who was home at this end of the hall. The building superintendent thinks it was just a break-in—he doesn't know I work with the police, either."

"So I'm the only one who knows what really happened?"

"Yeah."

"Well, I hadn't intended to tell anyone, Sam."

"Thanks. I appreciate that, Audra."

"Oh, I understand your concern, but I have my own reasons for keeping all of this to myself. My family can be a little over-protective, and if they ever found out about the way you got into my apartment—" She shifted on the couch and cleared her throat. "Well, it would be better for both of us if no one knew."

"More protectiveness spiels from your brothers?"

"To put it mildly."

"You must be a close family."

"You could say that." She glanced at the pictures on the book-shelf. "Besides my parents and my grandmother, I have aunts, uncles and cousins. Adding to that, all six of my brothers are married and have been very diligent about providing me with nieces and nephews. Seventeen at last count."

"Including Jimmy the painter?"

"Yes, including Jimmy." Her gaze darted to the borrowed fleece shorts he was wearing and her lips twitched. "Lucky for you it wasn't his sister who helped me paint."

He smiled. "And here I thought I'd had nothing but bad luck on this case."

"My family is quite...unique." She tilted her head as she looked at him. "We don't always see eye to eye, and they drive me crazy every now and then, but I love them anyway. You know how it is."

Sam felt his smile fade. No, he didn't know how it was. He had never loved his family; he'd never even had one. A memory flashed across his mind, an image of a closed door, echoes of drunken laughter...a child's quiet sobs as he finally understood he was completely alone.... He forced the memory away, surprised that it had stirred at all. He'd buried his past the day he'd earned his badge, so why was he thinking about it now?

It must be fatigue. Or maybe it was this place, with its homey warmth, and Audra with her arousing innocence. She was so different from him. He didn't belong here, sitting on her flowered chair, enjoying her coffee and her company. Now that she had agreed not to broadcast his identity, he had no legitimate reason for prolonging this visit. He should go home, get some sleep and leave innocent young women to innocent young men. Sam lost out on both counts—he had never been innocent or young.

Bracing his hands on his knees, he pushed himself to his feet. "Thanks for the breakfast, Audra, but I have to go. My boss needs my report by tomorrow."

"Oh." She wiped her fingers on a napkin and stood up quickly. "Of course. I really should get to work, too. My mother's coming over to help plan the next wedding."

He moved toward the door. "Is someone in your family getting married?"

"Good Lord, no. Aside from my underage nieces and nephews, I'm the only single one left, and I certainly don't have any plans to get married."

He was surprised by the firmness in her tone. Given her love of family, and her homey apartment, and that wholesome air of innocence around her, he'd assumed that she was the permanent commitment type. "Then why are you and your mother planning a wedding?"

"It's our next job. Usually my sister-in-law Geraldine draws up the preliminary menus, but her pregnancy is really tiring her out lately, so Mom and I are pitching in."

Sam paused before he could grasp the doorknob, her words suddenly registering. Next job? Menus? *Wedding?*

Maybe this was a trick of his sleep-deprived brain. He hadn't considered the possibility seriously when Xavier had mentioned it earlier because it was such a long shot.

*But long shot didn't mean impossible.* "Did you say 'menus'?" he asked.

She nodded. "It's one of the first steps in any catering job."

He felt his pulse thud. A spurt of adrenaline blew away his fatigue as his entire body went on alert. "So you work for a catering company. What made you choose that for a career?"

"Well, since my father owns the company, the choice seemed natural. I'm sure it must seem pretty tame compared to the kind of work you do, but it has its moments."

Her father? Could he be John McPherson? "Do you do a lot of weddings?" he asked, struggling to keep his growing excitement out of his voice.

"Usually spring is our busiest time. We only got the contract for this one two days ago, which is awfully short notice. It's going to be a scramble to get organized by next month."

Fitzpatrick had chosen the caterer two days ago. The Fitzpatrick wedding was next month. Sam propped his arm on the door frame above Audra's head and leaned closer. "Audra, what's the name of your father's company?"

Her gaze touched the gap in his open shirt, then slowly rose to his face. "McPherson Catering."

Impulsively, Sam smiled and slid his hand into her hair.

He'd thought they were due for some good luck, but *this?* It was like winning a lottery when he hadn't bothered to buy a ticket.

## Chapter 3

For one insane second, Audra was sure that Sam was going to kiss her. His fingers cradled the back of her head, his eyes were shining with a combination of surprise and pleasure and his lips were parted in another one of his charmingly boyish smiles. He leaned closer, his face so near, she could feel the warmth of his breath on her skin.

But the insanity lasted less than a heartbeat, because in the next second, there was a sharp rapping on the door beside her head.

Sam withdrew his hand and straightened up, his smile disappearing.

She pressed her lips together, trying to make sense out of what had just happened. Or hadn't happened, depending on how you looked at it.

The knock came again. "Audra?"

Her gaze still on Sam, she reached for the door. "It's my mother," she said.

He covered her hand with his before she could twist the doorknob. "Don't tell her anything, okay?"

"I said I wouldn't," she whispered.

"I'll call you later. We need to talk."

"I thought we already did. Sam—"

He squeezed her hand once, then before she could stop him, he opened the door.

Constance McPherson, her arms full of loose-leaf binders, was already talking as she stepped over the threshold. "Audra, dear, I brought Geraldine's notes from the last ten weddings—" She came to an abrupt halt inches before she would have collided with Sam. "Oh!"

"Mom, this is Sam Tucker," Audra said, taking the precariously stacked binders out of her mother's arms. "Sam, my mother, Constance McPherson."

Constance tipped her head forward to peer at him over the rims of her glasses as she offered him her hand. "Well hello, Sam. I hadn't realized that my daughter had company," she added, giving him a thorough, head-to-toe inspection before she transferred her gaze to Audra.

"Sam's my neighbor," Audra said. "He's...um..." She hesitated, fumbling for an explanation. "He just stopped by for coffee."

"Oh?" Constance's gaze sharpened as she glanced back at Sam. "Am I interrupting something?"

It didn't take any special detective skills to recognize that speculative look in her mother's eyes. With Sam's shirt unbuttoned and his jaw shadowed by a night's growth of beard, and Audra looking as if she'd just gotten out of bed... She swallowed a sigh. "You're not interrupting anything, Mom. Would you like some breakfast?"

"No thanks, dear. So, Sam, I don't remember seeing you before. How long have you lived in this building?"

"Only a few months, Mrs. McPherson."

"Call me Constance. And what is it you do, Sam?"

"Mom, how about some coffee?" Audra said before the inquisition got into full swing.

Sam took a step toward the corridor. "It was nice meeting you, Constance," he said, "but I can see you two have a lot of work to do, so I'd better get going. Audra,'' he added, pausing to give her a long, intense look. ''I'll call you later.''

With a distracted nod, she watched him walk to his apartment. He had held her hand, he had smiled and had leaned near enough to almost kiss her and now he said he'd call.

What on earth had that been about?

Or maybe she should be asking herself what she *wanted* it to be about.

Nothing. The look, the touch, the almost-kiss, she wanted them to mean absolutely nothing. A man as sexy and good-looking as Sam was fine as fodder for fantasies, but that's as far as it would go. She wasn't about to get involved with any man again, especially when she was so close to achieving her dream of complete independence. Right. So she'd simply ignore the way her pulse was still racing.

''Well,'' Constance said. That was all. But like mothers everywhere, she was able to inject a wealth of meaning into that one syllable.

Audra shifted the binders in her arms and closed the door. ''We'll have more space to work in the living room,'' she said, carrying the binders to the couch. She quickly scooped up the tray with the breakfast she and Sam had shared and carried it toward the kitchen. ''I'll just move the fan closer so we get a breeze. The air conditioner is still on the fritz,'' she chattered on, hoping to avoid the inevitable. ''The repairman said he's too busy to get to it until tomorrow. He's had more business than he can handle because of the heat wave.''

''What an extremely attractive young man,'' her mother said, following her. ''Why haven't you mentioned him before?''

''Who? The air conditioner guy?''

Constance made a clucking sound with her tongue. ''No, your neighbor.''

''You mean Sam?''

''How long have you been seeing him?''

''Mom, I'm not *seeing* him. We're just neighbors.''

''Mmm.''

Audra grimaced and set the tray down on the counter. That was another one of those syllables that mothers could inject with all kinds of meaning.

Constance picked up one of the Danish pastries that was left on the tray and took a small bite. "Cinnamon. I can never quite manage to get mine as tender as yours. You have a wonderfully light touch with pastry, Audra."

"Thanks," she said, switching off the fan and tugging the cord out of the socket.

"Just last month I read about a study that was done on men's reactions to certain scents. Did you know that cinnamon scored the highest when it came to arousing a man's interest?"

"Mo-om..."

"Evidently, it's much more effective than perfume. It works directly on the appetite center of a man's brain."

Appetite center? Is that why Sam had shown such a sudden interest in her when she'd mentioned the catering business?

*Idiot,* she chided herself. Someone as sexy as Sam wouldn't be interested in her even if she smeared herself with cinnamon and dangled strips of bacon from her ears. Besides, she didn't want him to be interested, right? "Mom, please. I know how this looks, but Sam and I are just neighbors, that's all."

"Fine," Constance said. Smiling, she patted Audra's cheek. "I won't pry. Just be careful that none of your brothers see your young man leaving in the mornings. You know how they can get."

"Thanks for the advice, but he's not my 'young man.'"

"Of course, dear."

Gritting her teeth, Audra carried the fan to the table under the front window and turned the motor to its highest setting. Even if Sam hadn't asked for her silence, she had already decided it would be a disaster if she told her mother the truth about him.

But letting her jump to all the wrong conclusions might prove to be almost as bad.

Sam had just finished repairing his broken door frame when Xavier finally got back to him with the results of his background check on the McPhersons. Propping the telephone against his shoulder, he opened a can of cola and took a long, cool swig while he listened. The air-conditioning unit in his living room window was running full out, chugging valiantly, but it was barely holding its own against the muggy afternoon heat.

"McPherson Catering," Xavier said. "Established thirty-five years ago by John McPherson. Privately owned and operated, employs a permanent staff of ten, hires temporary part-timers on a contract basis."

Sam rolled the can of cola against his forehead and thought longingly about the new heavy-duty unit that kept Xavier's office a constant seventy-two degrees. "They hire temporary help?" he asked. "How do you know that?"

"They did the graduation party for the mayor's son a few months ago. I was able to obtain a detailed copy of their final bill. It had an itemized breakdown of the costs incurred, including the addition of some last-minute help."

"This just keeps getting better and better. If they needed extra help for a graduation party, they'll need it for something as big as the Fitzpatrick wedding."

"The situation does appear to have potential." The *snick-tap* of a computer keyboard sounded in the background before Xavier continued. "John McPherson has no criminal record, no traffic convictions, not even an outstanding parking fine. He's been married for thirty-six years, supports his widowed mother-in-law, lives in the childhood home he inherited from his father and always pays his taxes on time. On top of all that, he donates his catering company's services to homeless shelters every Thanksgiving and Christmas."

"So clean he squeaks," Sam murmured.

"Apparently. McPherson Catering has an excellent reputation. The mayor recommended them highly."

"Which is why Fitzpatrick would choose them for the kid's wedding."

"Exactly."

As usual, Sam was impressed by the ease with which Xavier had been able to gather information, but from the sound of it, John McPherson had nothing he was trying to hide. Sam drained the rest of the cola, then carried the phone to the window and stood so that the stream of cooled air played over his back. "What about Audra? Did she check out?"

"Same solid citizen as her father. No convictions, no arrests. She turned twenty-eight in April, never been married, has been working in the family business for the past five years." He paused.

"Anything else?"

"I don't have as much information on her as I'd like."

"That doesn't mean she'll be a risk."

"Give me a chance to keep digging before you approach her."

"Odds are you won't find anything significant. I have to move fast if we're going to take advantage of this opportunity. The sooner I get myself into the company—"

"You're not going in. If we can put a man inside, I'd prefer Bergstrom or Middleton to take the assignment."

"Why? I already know her. She's bound to be more cooperative with me."

"Too risky," Xavier said. "Your Tindale cover was breached."

"The men you arrested for breaking into my place don't know for sure Tindale was a cop. I didn't confront them, and I didn't play a part in their arrest. For all they know, I was a bookkeeper who wanted to take his work home."

There was a brief silence. "That's true. Disappearing the way you did was a good move."

"Besides, they'll be busy for a few months at least, won't they?"

"In all probability, yes. Both of them had a string of priors, so chances are they'll be doing time. But it's still too risky."

"Fitzpatrick's habit of separating himself from the dirty end of his business works to our advantage," Sam persisted. "No one will recognize me, since he's not going to invite any of his underlings to his daughter's wedding. That's not how he operates.''

"We'll see how it plays out. I'm not making any decisions until I have all the facts.''

"Audra's been cooperating with me so far, so it wouldn't hurt to feel her out about the family catering business. I'll find out their hiring policies, things like that.''

"I'm aware of how you like to work without a script, but I don't want you going off on your own with this, Tucker. Groundwork, that's all you're doing.''

"Right.''

Groundwork, Sam thought with a tinge of impatience as he hung up the phone. Most of Xavier's job was done within reach of a computer where everything functioned according to a logical sequence. He was one of the best cops Sam had worked with when it came to planning strategy and coordinating information. And on a personal level, there wasn't anyone Sam respected more. But unlike his superior, Sam had to rely on the ability to adapt quickly to unforeseen situations, to make up a plan as he went along. While he usually tried to follow Xavier's advice, Sam never discounted his instincts. He trusted his gut as often as he trusted his brain.

And in this case, both were in agreement as far as Audra McPherson went. She could be the key that would get them close to Fitzpatrick. And now that her involvement with the wedding was confirmed, Sam had a legitimate reason for seeing her again.

He flipped open the phone book, running his finger down the column of McPhersons. He found Audra's number and punched it in, then listened to it ring.

How much more should he tell her? How far could he trust her? Ideally, he'd keep her as far removed from the case as possible. All she needed to do was to put in a good word with her father, or whoever did the hiring for McPherson Catering. As long as she smoothed the way to place someone inside, he could take it from there. Or Bergstrom or Middleton would take it.

The ringing continued. He turned around, bracing one hand

against the window frame so that the outflow from the air conditioner cooled his chest. Xavier might be right about assigning someone else to go undercover. Ever since he'd landed in her bedroom, Sam hadn't been able to get Audra off his mind. And the more he learned about her and her family, the clearer it was that he had no business thinking about her in anything other than a professional capacity. Considering her background, she definitely wasn't the type of woman he usually sought out.

A movement on the street in front of the apartment building caught his eye, a flash of blond hair and blue fabric. He leaned closer to the window and squinted through the wavering heat. That was Audra down there, her hair pulled into a bun on the top of her head, her figure skimmed by a loose-fitting sleeveless dress that nevertheless managed to look almost as enticing as her filmy nightgown.

She'd looked enticing in an old robe, too. He couldn't believe he'd almost kissed her when they'd been standing at the door together. He'd been pleased about getting a break in the case, but that didn't excuse what he'd almost done. She was one distracting woman, he decided, focusing on the appealing sway of her hips as she crossed to the other side of the street...

*As she crossed to the other side of the street?*

"Damn," he muttered, slamming the receiver into its cradle. Scowling, he grabbed his shirt and headed for the door.

Audra could feel her dress sticking to her back by the time she reached the lot where she'd parked the van. She let the engine idle for a few minutes until the interior started to cool down, then backed out of her spot and steered the van toward the curb. She was waiting for a chance to pull onto the street when she noticed a tall, dark-haired man walking toward her.

Her pulse jumped when she realized the man was Sam. Of course, it hadn't completely slowed down from the last time she'd seen him.

He waved, moving directly to the side of her door. "Hi," he said as soon as she rolled down her window. He propped his forearms on the lower edge. "I was just trying to call you."

Audra felt the warmth in her cheeks and knew she was blushing like a schoolgirl. She hoped he'd attribute it to the heat. "Oh, yes, you mentioned something about that."

"Nice van," he said, leaning back to look at the sign on the side. "Is it yours?"

"It belongs to the company, but I use it from time to time. Jimmy painted the sign a few weeks ago."

"Did he do the background painting too?"

She nodded.

"Talented kid, your nephew. Are you on your way to work?"

"Not really. I just need to deliver an extra carton of champagne flutes to the office where we're doing a retirement party tomorrow."

He twisted his wrist to check his watch, then lifted his gaze to hers. "Mind if I come along for the ride?"

"Why?"

"I just wanted to talk to you, but if you have other plans after you deliver those glasses, I'd understand."

She chewed her lip for a moment. Other plans? Hardly. Just an evening of drawing up lists from the menus she and her mother had worked out this morning. What harm could it do to have company on the trip downtown? She might not want to have a man in her life, but he only wanted to be in her van.

Here in the sunlight, his eyes were a vibrant blue, making his spiky lashes look long and lush. The skin on his jaw was taut and smooth from a fresh shave, accentuating his square jaw and dimpled chin. He'd changed his shirt, and although all the buttons except the top two were fastened, she could see a hint of the dark hair that covered his chest. Muscles corded his arms below his short sleeves, reminding her of the gentle strength he'd used the night before when he'd held her on her bed.

But then, everything seemed to remind her of how it had felt to have him lying on top of her in her bed.

A car horn sounded from behind her. She checked her side mirror and saw that a red station wagon was waiting on her bumper.

"Audra?"

Without stopping to analyze her decision further, she flipped the switch to unlock the passenger door. "All right," she said.

He rounded the hood and slipped into the seat beside her. "Thanks."

Awareness of his size and his proximity tingled over Audra's nerves. She tried to concentrate on her driving as she eased the van onto the street. "If you're still concerned that I'm going to tell people about your undercover work," she said finally, "I'd like to assure you that I won't."

"I believe you, Audra. You seemed to have handled the situation with your mother just fine."

She sighed. "My mom got the wrong impression about us."

"I kind of figured that, considering the time of day and the fact that you weren't yet dressed. Is it going to be a problem for you?"

"I don't know. She considers herself modern, so she wasn't scandalized when she saw you in my apartment. If anything, it's the other way around. It might have been easier on me if she *had* been scandalized."

"What do you mean?"

"She's not as modern as she thinks. Mom still believes that no one can be really happy unless they're married with at least half a dozen kids. She's been trying to match me up with someone for the past few years. She's even managed to get my sisters-in-law in on it. Now that she saw what she thinks she saw, she's going to get her hopes up for nothing."

"I take it from what you said earlier that you're not eager to get married."

"No."

"I guess this means I won't be visited by a shotgun-toting papa?"

The thought of the proper, respectable John McPherson forcing a shotgun wedding to preserve his daughter's honor was so incongruous it made Audra chuckle. "I don't think so. Not Dad. The twins are the hotheads in the family."

"Two of your brothers, I assume?"

"Jake and Christopher." She glanced at Sam. "I hope if my mother goes into full matchmaking mode it won't cause problems for you. You're not married, are you?"

"No. My job keeps me busy enough already." He shifted on the seat, leaning against the door so he could angle his legs under the dashboard. "Great air conditioning in this van."

Obviously, he wanted to change the subject. That was fine with her—marriage wasn't something she liked to think about, anyway. "Sometimes we use the vans for transporting food, so we need good temperature control."

"Do you do any of the food preparation?"

"I've done all the jobs at one time or another, but I do enjoy the hands-on creativity in the kitchen. Sometimes I work at home, testing new recipes or developing my own."

"That explains the smells."

"What smells?"

He tapped his nose with his index finger. "From the day I moved next door to you I've been noticing all kinds of delicious aromas coming from your apartment. That's how I knew you were already up when I passed by this morning."

The idea of Sam appreciating the smell of her cooking was oddly...intimate. And what had her mother said about certain scents working directly on the appetite center of a man's brain? "I suppose in your profession you're trained to be observant."

"You never know when some supposedly insignificant fact might lead to a breakthrough on a case."

"What's it like to work undercover?"

"It suits me, I suppose. Except for the paperwork. What about you? What's it like working for your father?"

"All right. Intense at times. Dad's a perfectionist, and he's very dedicated to the success of the company. Still, he's fair about paying all of his employees what their work is worth."

"Sounds like an ideal employer."

"Oh, he is. It's just that—" She hesitated.

"What's wrong?"

"Nothing really. The only drawback of working for my father is that it's difficult to *stop* working for him." She glanced sideways at Sam. "I'll be breaking a long family tradition when I quit the company, but I plan to start my own business one day."

"What kind of business?"

While she drove, Audra found herself telling him about her dream of opening her own restaurant. He was a good listener, prompting her with pertinent questions and appearing genuinely interested in everything she said.

It would be easy to feel flattered by Sam's attention. It would be even easier to let his sexy good looks affect her good sense. Still, she barely knew him, so she didn't drop her caution entirely. He'd told her he wanted to talk to her, but so far he'd been doing most of the listening.

"Well, this is the place," she said, flicking on her signal as she turned into the entrance of a parking garage. The carton of glasses clinked softly as she eased the van over a speed bump in the concrete. Since it was Sunday, it was easy to find a vacant space near the freight elevator. She pointed to the gleaming green van in the adjacent parking spot. A trompe l'oeil painting of fruit and pastries, courtesy of her talented nephew, took up most of the van's side. "That belongs to my brother Norm, Jimmy's dad. He's meeting me in the forty-fifth floor conference room. I shouldn't be long, so if you'd like to wait in the van—"

"I'll carry the box for you," Sam said, opening his door. He walked to the back of the van and waited for her to unlock the rear doors, then reached in to pick up the carton.

Audra glanced at the wheeled dolly she'd used yesterday when she'd picked the heavy box up from the equipment rental company, then moved her gaze to Sam. The muscles she'd noticed earlier bulged against his sleeves, but otherwise, he showed no signs of strain. "Um, thanks."

"No problem," he said, falling into step beside her as she walked to the elevator.

She pressed the button and watched as the floor indicator lights glowed in descending sequence. "Normally one of my other brothers handles the equipment, but we've been swamped with work lately.''

"Maybe your father should hire some extra help."

"I wish he would. Especially with that big wedding coming up next month, we could use all the help we could get."

Sam shifted the box to his shoulder. "I know a couple of guys who are looking for work. How about if I tell them to call your father?"

"There wouldn't be any point."

"They're not experienced caterers, but they could handle deliveries like this one."

"I'm sure they would be a great help, but they don't stand a chance of being hired by my father unless their last names happen to be McPherson."

"What?"

"It's a family company, and my dad has a firm policy of only hiring relatives. Lord knows, we normally have enough around to do most jobs, but we've run into trouble more than once when some family crisis has left us short-staffed." The elevator doors finally slid open. She stepped inside, then waited until Sam followed before she pressed the button for the forty-fifth floor. "I know it's old-fashioned, but that's the way my family is. Our clients don't seem to mind. Actually, a lot of them like the fact that we don't hire strangers."

"I don't believe this," he said slowly. "Your catering company has its own built-in security system."

"I've never heard it put that way, but yes, I suppose so."

"And your clients know your hiring policy?"

"That's right. I'm sorry we can't help your friends. Maybe I could ask around with some of our suppliers to see if they have any job openings."

Sam put the box down and turned to face her. He watched her in silence while the elevator sped upward. "Audra," he said finally. "Are you sure there's no way anyone who isn't related to you can work for McPherson Catering?"

She shook her head. "Not unless they marry into the family,

and since Thomas—that's my youngest brother—got married at Easter, there aren't any eligible McPhersons around.''

His gaze sharpened. ''Except for you.''

''Technically, yes, but—''

He slapped the side of his fist against the emergency stop button. Gears clunked and the cable whined as the elevator jerked to a halt.

With a startled gasp, Audra stumbled against the box of glasses. ''My God, Sam! What are you doing?''

He stepped around the box and grasped her arms to steady her. ''If you married someone, he'd be guaranteed a job in your father's company, right?''

''What's going on? Why did you stop us?''

He pulled her closer. ''Answer me and I'll tell you.''

''Okay, yes, if he wanted. Sam, what—''

''A marriage would be too sudden and too complicated,'' he said, his eyebrows drawing together in a frown. ''What about an engagement? Would he be able to work if you were engaged?''

''I suppose so. One of my sisters-in-law took over designing the table settings right after their engagement party....'' She flattened her palms against his shirtfront. ''But this is ridiculous. Why should it matter—''

''Audra, I didn't want to involve you any further in this investigation, but it seems unavoidable.'' He searched her face, his jaw tightening until a muscle jumped in his cheek. Finally he looked directly into her eyes. ''I'm going out on a limb here, but I believe I can trust you. I need your help.''

Audra shook her head, trying to make sense out of what he was saying. It was like last night all over again. The sudden shock, the confusion, Sam's grip holding her motionless.

''I need your help,'' he repeated. ''We need to place a member of my team undercover in McPherson Catering.''

His words were so unexpected, it took a few seconds for his meaning to penetrate. Place a member of his team undercover? *In her family's catering company?* ''What!''

"You won't need to do anything, just tell your family that you're engaged. We'll take it from there."

With a sudden twist, she yanked her hands free and shoved hard against his chest. "You're crazy. My father is the most honest man in the world. You have no business spying on him!"

Sam swore under his breath. "No, you misunderstood me. Your father has nothing to do with this. We simply want to place someone in the catering company so that we can gather information on one of your clients."

She backed away until her shoulders struck the side of the elevator. "So that's what this is all about. This is why you wanted to call me, and why you came with me, and why you were so darn interested in my work. You want to use me as part of your next cover."

He spread his hands, holding them palms up in a gesture of appeasement. "It will only be temporary. And there'll be no danger to you or your family as long as no one knows the truth. Once we have what we need, your involvement will end."

"I can't possibly—"

"Audra, hear me out before you decide. We're in the process of gathering evidence against a man who is responsible for the growth of everything from drug smuggling to racketeering. Because of his organization—"

"Organization?" she repeated, her voice rising. "As in organized crime? You mean one of our clients is some kind of...godfather?"

"Calm down. He's not involved directly in the dirty end—he's in the business of laundering money. He uses a complex chain of transactions to legitimize the proceeds from other people's crimes. To put it simply, without him, crime wouldn't pay."

"This is unbelievable."

"I'll ask Xavier to brief you before we get started. He's the lieutenant you heard on the phone last night."

"Which client is it?"

"Are you agreeing to help us?"

She ignored his question, frowning as she tried to concentrate.

"If this...this money launderer is that important, he must be rich," she muttered. So that ruled out the Dubcheks who hired them for their family reunion. She could rule out the insurance company's vice president who was organizing this retirement party, because he was an old friend of Norm's. And they'd already finished the job for the mayor. So besides that class reunion next week and the summer camp parents' night and the charity concert, that left...

She pressed her hands to her cheeks. "Of course. It's the Fitzpatrick wedding."

Sam remained silent.

"Larry Fitzpatrick. He's your criminal, isn't he?"

More silence.

Yes, it had to be the Fitzpatrick wedding Sam wanted to crash. It was right after she mentioned it that Sam had shown such a sudden interest in her.

No, he had never been interested in *her*. He'd been interested in his case all along.

The twinge of disappointment she felt was an unwelcome surprise.

"The Fitzpatrick wedding," she said unsteadily. "It's supposed to be big and splashy, with money no object. It's going to be held at his estate. My mother was there yesterday. She said it was huge and luxurious and isolated enough to have guards at the iron gates.... Oh, no." She moved toward the elevator controls. "I have to warn my family. They'll have to cancel the job."

Sam stepped in front of her to block her path. "No, Audra. They're in no danger as long as everyone acts normally. You'll only arouse suspicion if McPherson Catering backs out of a profitable job like that now."

She squeezed past him and reached for the restart button. Before her finger made contact, Sam caught her around the waist and hauled her back against his chest. Lifting her off her feet, he spun around and carried her to the opposite corner, then set her down and turned her to face him.

He braced his hands on either side of her to prevent her from slipping past again. "Audra, please listen to me," he said. "We wouldn't do anything to put you or your family at risk. This is strictly a reconnaissance kind of operation. But if you reveal what I've told you, you'll be endangering the members of my team."

"But—"

"I apologize for approaching you like this, but time is of the essence. The sooner we place someone in McPherson Catering, the more solid his cover will be."

She was vividly aware of Sam's size, and his nearness and her own racing pulse. Forcing herself to take several deep breaths, Audra tried to think. "Are you sure my family will be all right?"

"Positive. We only want to observe. We won't be confronting anyone at this stage. All you need to do would be to make it possible for one of us to attend Marion Fitzpatrick's wedding."

"You're not denying I was right about which of our clients you're after."

"What's the point? You're obviously intelligent enough to figure it out on your own," he stated.

"If it's that important to get into the wedding, surely there must be some other way."

"We've tried. This is the only opportunity that's come up."

"And if I still say no?"

He dropped his hands and stepped back. "If seeing justice done isn't enough of a motive for you, then there's something else to consider. One of the biggest insurance companies in the country has put up a fifty-thousand-dollar reward for information that leads to Fitzpatrick's arrest."

"What?"

"If you help us, you could claim the reward. It would give you a good start on that restaurant of yours that you were telling me about."

Fifty-thousand dollars. With that kind of money, she'd be able to quit the family company and open up her own place within the year. She took another deep breath and tipped back her head to meet his gaze. "This is all so...unbelievable."

"Last night once you understood the situation, you handled

yourself better than I could have hoped. You don't panic and you think fast. That's why I went with my instincts and trusted you enough to ask for your help now. Audra, I'm sure you can handle this.''

Good Lord, was she actually starting to consider it? "Even if I agreed,'' she said finally, ''I don't think it would work.''

''Why not?''

''My family will never believe me if I suddenly announce my engagement to a complete stranger.''

''Your mother seemed ready enough to match you up with me when she saw me at your place.''

''Yes, but—''

''Then the groundwork's already established,'' he said, his gaze unwavering. ''Xavier wanted to send in someone else, but we have no choice if we want this to work. It'll have to be me, that's all.''

''You?''

''I'll be your fiancé.'' Sam reached out to take her hands and coaxed her forward. ''Considering the compromising situation your mother witnessed this morning, it shouldn't be too hard to convince her we're serious about each other. What do you think?''

''I'd hate lying to them.''

''It's only temporary. We'll tell them the truth when the case is over.''

''I need more time to think about—'' Before she could finish her sentence, the elevator jerked. The motor hummed as it began to ascend once more.

''Someone overrode the controls,'' Sam said.

She tilted her head to see past him. The numbers over the door were lighting up in rapid succession. ''Norm. He must have noticed something happened to the elevator.''

''Your brother? You said he was meeting you here?''

''That's right.''

''There's no more time, Audra. I need your answer. Are we engaged or not?''

"There's no danger to my family?"

"None."

"And you'd help me collect that reward?"

"Definitely."

"And this engagement is completely fake?"

His grip on her fingers tightened briefly. "Absolutely," he confirmed as the elevator eased to a stop. "Audra? Yes or no? I have to know now."

Could she pull this off? Until last night, the closest she'd gotten to a criminal investigation was through the pages of the books she liked to read. There was a big difference between reading about it and actually being part of it, but for the sake of justice...and the fifty thousand dollars that would ensure her independence...

The doors slid open. Audra glimpsed her brother's face, then focused on Sam. She had hesitated last night, when she'd first seen him come through her window. Her mind had been dulled by heat and fatigue then, but she was thinking clearly now, wasn't she?

"Yes," she whispered.

Sam leaned closer, releasing her hands to cradle her cheeks in his palms.

"Sam," she hissed. "What are you doing?"

"More groundwork," he murmured against her lips.

# Chapter 4

The shock of Sam's mouth on hers scattered Audra's protest before it could form. His lips were warm and supple, gliding in a teasing caress that was there one second and gone the next. It was a brief promise, merely a hint of a kiss. But it was potent enough to send awareness surging through her body.

She hadn't thought his kiss would feel like that. He was so...big, so tough, so determined, she would have thought he'd kiss with the same take-charge straight-ahead assertiveness that characterized everything else he did. She hadn't guessed he'd be capable of gentleness. It touched her in the same way as the boyishness she'd glimpsed in his smile.

Drawing in a shaky breath, she lifted her hand to his face. Her fingers were unsteady as she feathered them across his cheek, tracing the long groove beside his mouth before she pressed lightly against his lips. "I hadn't expected this, Sam."

He caught her hand in his and kissed her fingertips, his eyes sparkling with pleasure.

At the sweetly romantic gesture, she swayed toward him. Her breasts brushed his warm, solid chest and another jolt of awareness sent her pulse racing. Echoes of sensations she'd done her best to forget tingled along her nerves. She remembered his weight stretched out on top of her, pressing her into the mattress. And the feel of his hair against her cheek, and the slide of his knee against her thigh, and—

There was a quiet cough from the doorway of the elevator.

Audra blinked and glanced past Sam's shoulder. Norm was standing less than a yard away, his arms crossed, his eyebrows drawn together in a frown.

Sam dipped his head to the side of her neck. "Keep it up," he whispered. He flicked his tongue against her earlobe. "You're doing fine."

Reality crashed over her in a belated, humiliating rush. "Oh, my God," she muttered. Her cheeks heating up with a blush, she braced her hands against Sam's chest and pushed herself away.

This was fake. Fake. How could she have forgotten that, even for an instant? Sam wasn't being gentle and romantic, he was playing a part.

Thank God he thought she was acting.

Unable to meet his gaze, she brushed at the wrinkles in her dress and took another step backward. "Um, hi Norm."

The elevator door started to slide shut. Norm slapped his hand against it to hold it open. "Audra," he said.

He had their mother's talent for infusing a realm of meaning into a single word.

Audra's blush deepened. It wasn't really any of her brother's business if she chose to kiss a man in an elevator. Even if the kiss wasn't real. And she hated the way she felt as if she should apologize. She was twenty-eight years old, for God's sake. She had a right to kiss a man wherever she chose, didn't she?

In some ways, her brothers were worse than her parents when it came to their attitude toward her. At least her parents wanted to see her married. Norm would probably prefer to keep her forever sheltered and protected, the quintessential maiden locked in a tower.

If he was shocked because of that brief kiss, what would he

think if he knew the rest? How would her well-meaning, over-protective family react if they learned she had just agreed to participate in an undercover police operation? If she thought having them find out about Sam's unconventional entrance through her window would be bad, that would be nothing compared to the furor that would ensue over her involvement in Sam's scheme.

Oddly enough, thinking about their reaction didn't discourage her. On the contrary, it only reinforced Audra's determination to see this through.

"You must be Audra's brother," Sam said, breaking the awkward silence. He thrust out his right hand. "I'm Sam Tucker."

Norm hesitated, his expression guarded. After a pause just short of rude, he shook Sam's hand. "Norm McPherson," he said.

Sam picked up the carton from the floor of the elevator and hoisted it smoothly to his shoulder, then settled his free hand at the small of Audra's back and guided her through the door. "Where do you want these glasses, Norm?"

Norm tipped his head toward the semicircular desk that was across from the elevators. "Just set them down on the reception desk. I'll take it from there."

"Sure thing." Sam strode to the desk and put the carton down in the center. "Anything else I can do?"

"No, thanks." Norm glanced from Audra to Sam. "Did you have some trouble with the elevator?"

Sam grinned and moved back to Audra's side. "I must have hit the stop button accidentally."

She pushed a strand of loose hair back into her bun. "Sam came along to help me deliver the extra glasses."

"I see." He gave Sam a long, thorough look. "I don't recall Audra mentioning you before, Mr. Tucker."

"Call me Sam. Under the circumstances, there's no need to be formal."

"Oh? And what circumstances would those be?"

Sam slipped his arm around Audra's shoulders and pulled her securely against him. "I think our secret is out, darling. Do you want to tell your brother, or should I?"

Well, this was it. The first lie.

No, that kiss had been the first lie.

He leaned down to brush another tantalizing kiss across her lips, then straightened up and smiled at Norm. "You'll be the first to know. Audra has just agreed to marry me."

As much as she steeled herself not to feel anything this time, she couldn't prevent the renewed rush of sensations that tingled through her at Sam's touch. She started to ease away from him but his arm tightened around her shoulders, anchoring her to his side.

Norm's jaw dropped. He stared at her, his eyebrows practically meeting his hairline. "I don't believe it," he said finally. "Audra, is this true?"

She felt Sam tense. Lifting her chin, she met her brother's gaze. "It's—"

"Hi, Audra. I was wondering when you'd get here."

Audra turned her head. Her sister-in-law Judy, Norm's wife, was walking toward them, crepe paper streamers trailing behind her from the huge bow in her hands. She stopped beside Norm, her warm brown gaze sparkling with curiosity as she regarded Sam. "Well, hello," she said.

"Hi, Judy." Audra made another attempt to pull away from Sam but he squeezed her upper arm with his fingertips in warning. "I'd like you to meet Sam Tucker." She glanced up at him. "Sam, this is my sister-in-law Judy."

Sam extended his free hand and smiled. "You wouldn't have any spare champagne around to go with those glasses we brought, would you?"

Judy juggled the bow into the crook of her elbow and clasped his hand. Her forehead furrowed with a question. "Spare champagne?"

"Audra and I have just become engaged."

For a moment, Judy looked as stunned as her husband. Still holding Sam's hand, she swung her gaze to Audra. "Really? You're getting married?"

This was it, the point of no return. Once she told the lie to

Judy, it would only be a matter of minutes before every one of her relatives knew. As she had expected, her conscience stirred.

But so did a budding sense of...excitement.

Sam's fingers stroked her arm in a caress that she felt all the way to her toes. "Go ahead, sweetheart," he murmured.

Norm's eyes narrowed.

Taking a deep breath, Audra nodded. "Yes, we're engaged."

The crepe paper bow fluttered to the floor as Judy released Sam's hand to throw her arms around Audra. "Oh, honey," she said, kissing her cheek. "I'm so happy for you."

Audra slipped out from underneath Sam's arm to return her sister-in-law's embrace. "Thanks, Judy."

"This is wonderful," Judy said. "Just wonderful."

"And so unexpected," Norm added, making no move to congratulate either one of them.

"Oh, cut it out," Judy said, shooting him a stern look. "If anyone deserves a bit of happiness, it's your sister. After everything she went through—" She turned back to Audra, her face beaming. "You sly devil. You never said a word."

"Well, we've all been so busy lately," she began, fumbling for a reasonable excuse.

"It must have been love at first sight," Judy said. "That's the way it was for me and Norm. One look and I knew he was the one for me."

Love at first sight? A vivid image of Sam naked in the moonlight sprang into Audra's head. She started. "Yes, it was something like that."

Sam grinned. "I guess you could say that I swept her off her feet."

Judy turned her attention to Sam. "So you're Audra's neighbor."

"How did you know?"

"Constance told me all about you."

"What's this?" Norm demanded. "Why didn't anyone tell me?"

"Big brothers don't need to know everything," Judy answered, winking at Audra. "Your mom mentioned that you were seeing someone. I got the impression it was serious."

She didn't know whether to be amused or annoyed. She should have known her mother wouldn't have remained silent about meeting Sam this morning.

"I knew you'd change your mind about marriage eventually," Judy went on. "You have too much love inside you to stay single forever. You're a lucky man, Sam Tucker," she said. "Audra's quite a catch."

"Absolutely." He reached for Audra's hand and twined his fingers with hers. "You have no idea how happy she made me when she said yes."

Only Audra was aware of the real meaning behind Sam's words. "Sam can be very convincing," she said. "Until a few minutes ago, I hadn't decided one way or the other."

"Hey Mom, when are we going to eat? Oh hi, Aunt Audra."

She glanced down the hall. Jimmy was walking toward them, his gangling height curved into a characteristic teenage slouch. His eyebrows drew together as he squinted suspiciously at Sam—he was resembling his father more every day.

Judy ruffled her son's hair. She grinned at his pained expression and repeated the gesture. "Aunt Audra has just become engaged," she said.

"Yeah?" he muttered, crossing his arms.

"Ignore him, it's in the genes," Judy said, rolling her eyes. "When's the wedding going to be?"

"We haven't set a date yet," Sam replied, lifting Audra's hand to press a soft kiss to her knuckles. "Soon, I hope."

"Where's that crate of champagne, Norm?" Judy asked. "This certainly calls for a toast or two."

"It's for tomorrow's job. We can't open it for ourselves."

"Oh, pooh. I'll replace it in the morning." She scooped up the decoration she'd been working on and started down the hall in the direction she'd come from. "There are already some glasses set out in the conference room. Oh, I can't wait to tell the rest of the family."

Jimmy shoved his hands into his pockets and slouched after his mother. Pausing long enough to give Sam a cool, assessing look, Norm followed.

Sam brought his mouth close to Audra's ear. "Your sister-in-law's no problem, but I don't think your brother buys it."

"My brothers are all a bit overprotective. Judy will bring him around eventually."

"Who does the hiring?"

"Hiring? Oh, of course. The hiring. My father and Norm."

"Then we'll have to put some more effort into convincing Norm we're for real. Hang on," he said, leaning over.

"What—" She gasped when she felt Sam's hand slide behind her knees. "Sam!"

Without any warning, he scooped her up in his arms.

She gave a startled shriek. "Sam! What are you doing?"

He grinned. "Demonstrating how I swept you off your feet."

"For heaven's sake, put me down. You don't have to—"

"Put your arm around my neck," he said through his smile. "And try to pretend you're enjoying this."

Norm and Judy had stopped at the doorway of the conference room. While her sister-in-law's face was all smiles, her brother was still regarding them with a look of wary appraisal.

Audra clasped her hands behind Sam's neck, leaned her head against his shoulder and forced her body to relax into his arms as he started to move forward. With each step he took, she felt the muscles of his arms flex behind her back and under her thighs, felt the side of her breast rub against his chest and felt his warmth and the clean tang of his aftershave tease her senses.

*Pretend you're enjoying this.*

She summoned up a smile for the sake of their audience and hoped she had the acting ability to make it look genuine. Because although the smile might be fake, the enjoyment she felt at being carried in Sam's arms was all too real.

Sam gave the waitress their orders, then leaned back against the cushioned booth, rubbed his hand over his face and watched

Audra continue to shred her paper napkin.

She'd been uncharacteristically silent on the drive to the restaurant. And apart from her quick cooperation with that kiss in the elevator, she was more distant now than she'd been before she'd agreed to help him.

Concern tightened his gut. Damn, had he been wrong to trust her? Was she thinking of backing out? "Having second thoughts?"

She glanced up quickly. "No, I agreed to this. I'll see it through."

He breathed a silent sigh of relief. "It seems to be working out fine so far."

"So far."

"Your sister-in-law really took to the idea."

"Yes, Judy would. She's been doing her best to match me up with people for years."

He stretched his arm out to pick up the cup in front of him and took a long swallow of coffee, hoping to drown out the aftertaste of champagne. He'd never liked the stuff, but it had seemed like an appropriate suggestion at the time. Cracking open a bottle of the champagne that had been meant for that retirement party had worked exactly as he'd hoped it would, focusing Audra's family's attention on celebrating the engagement instead of questioning it.

For this cover to work, there were two major goals he had to achieve. First, he had to get the McPhersons to accept the engagement. Second, and most important, he still had to join the company. "Your brother didn't seem to share his wife's enthusiasm."

"No. Norm's not exactly what I'd call a romantic. He's the oldest, and he's always had a strong sense of responsibility. Of all my brothers, he's the one who's most like my father."

Sam remembered what Xavier had told him about John McPherson, the upstanding citizen who supported his widowed mother-in-law and donated his services to a homeless shelter. "Terrific."

Her lips twitched into a quick smile. "Judy will bring him around eventually."

"We don't have a lot of time here. The Fitzpatrick wedding's next month. My cover has to be solid enough for me to join the company before that."

"That's right," she said, her smile faltering.

"We were lucky today that your family was too surprised to ask for many details, but we're going to have to get our story straight."

"I hate deceiving them."

"It's only temporary."

"I know. It's just that—" She paused. "I guess I hadn't thought we would start so quickly. I wasn't really prepared for...having to act."

"All the more reason to get things straight before we go any further." He leaned forward, crossing his arms on the edge of the table. "Okay. What will your family want to know?"

"Oh, God. Are you serious? Everything. How we met, how long we've been dating, when the wedding's going to be."

"We'll keep it simple. We met two months ago when I was moving in and we struck up a conversation in the elevator. Like Judy said, it was love at first sight. We don't need to set a date for the wedding, just say you're too busy to plan it right now. What else would they ask?"

She hesitated, toying with her water glass. "They'll want to know about you. What you're like, what you do for a living."

"I can't be currently employed, or I wouldn't be wanting a job with McPherson Catering. You can say I'm a computer programmer who just got downsized."

"Do you know anything about computers?"

"Enough so I won't have to fake my expertise. Why? Would you prefer me to be something else?"

"No, that should be all right." She ran her finger down the side of her glass, leaving a trail in the condensation. "They'll also expect me to know where you come from and what your family's like."

His shoulders tensed. This was a cover, the same as countless others that he'd made up. The whole idea was to get her family to accept him, and there was no way they'd do that if they knew the truth.

So why did he have this desire not to lie?

"We'll keep that simple, too," he said. "I'm from Cleveland. Never been married. No close relatives, parents died in a car accident when I was a kid."

Her face softened. "Oh, Sam. I'm sorry."

Even though her sympathy was misplaced, it felt unexpectedly good. "It's only a cover story, Audra."

"Oh."

"What else would they need to know?"

"Well, if you and I are supposed to be engaged, we'd be expected to know...personal things about each other."

He lifted an eyebrow. "Such as?"

"Your taste in music, your hobbies, what kind of movies you like, your favorite color, things like that."

"Garth Brooks, no time for hobbies, and action movies." His gaze dropped to the delicate blue shades that patterned the dress she was wearing. "And if I had to choose, I'd say I like blue."

"Is that only a cover story, too?"

"Not this time. I only lie when it's absolutely necessary." He fell silent as the waitress reappeared with the food they'd ordered. When she'd left them alone again, he drew Audra's attention to the plate in front of him. "We'll straighten out more details as we go along, but you already know a fair amount. For instance, you can see I like my steak rare. And you know I like your coffee and those cinnamon Danishes you make."

She looked at his steak, then glanced at her own order of sole almondine with steamed rice. "Yes, I guessed that you have a good appetite."

"So what about you? Besides knitting, reading crime novels, cooking up new recipes and spending time with your family, is there anything else I should know?"

"Well, I suppose that pretty well sums it up."

"Fine." He sliced into his steak. "If a situation comes up that we can't fake our way through, we can always imply that we were too busy making love to do much talking."

Her fork clattered against her plate. "Sam!"

"What's wrong? We're engaged."

"I'm not about to start telling anyone about our love life. I mean, our supposed love life."

"Hey, you wouldn't be lying if you said you'd been in bed with me."

Her cheeks turned scarlet.

"If pressed, I'd even be able to testify to that tiny mole you have on the inside of your left thigh."

*"Sam!"*

"Engaged couples are expected to be hot for each other. It would seem suspicious if we weren't, especially considering how fast we fell in love."

"But we're not—" She pressed her lips together for a moment. "Of course. We have to put on a good act."

"You played along just fine in front of Norm and Judy this afternoon. All you have to do is keep it up, and no one's going to doubt our story."

"About this afternoon, I don't think it's necessary for you to be so...demonstrative, is it?"

He probably *had* been more demonstrative than necessary. At the time, he'd told himself it was just for show. The light kisses, the lingering touches, all those gestures of affection were merely part of the groundwork, right? It had felt so natural, and it had come so easily, that he hadn't wanted to think about it too deeply.

He should have thought about it. How many times did he have to remind himself that she wasn't the type of woman who would be interested in a man like him? Her shy response to his first kiss in the elevator, her sighs, the way she'd leaned against him and let her softness mold to his body...it was all for show. If it had seemed real, it was probably because he'd spent so much time thinking about it since he'd held her in his arms last night.

"I mean, I know we're supposed to be engaged," she continued. "But this is only a...a business arrangement. We're working together to get what we each want, but we're not going to get personally involved."

"I thought I made that clear at the start."

She nodded. "You did. And I agree with you. I just want to make sure you understand that I'm not looking for any kind of relationship."

"Neither am I."

"Especially marriage."

"Same here."

"Fine."

"Good," he said, his tone harsher than he'd intended. "I'll be sure to keep my hands off you unless absolutely necessary."

She lifted her gaze to his. "I didn't mean to hurt your feelings, Sam. It has nothing to do with you personally. I simply don't want to get seriously involved with any man again."

"Again?"

"I was engaged once before."

He couldn't miss the sadness in her eyes. For a moment he had an urge to reach out and cover her hand where it rested on the table. He'd actually lifted his hand before he realized what he was doing and changed the movement into picking up his water glass. "Maybe you'd better tell me about it. Your family would expect me to know."

"His name was Ryan Beresford. We were friends from the time we were kids and planned to marry as soon as I finished college, but he..." She swallowed. "I'm sorry. I should have realized how pretending to be engaged again would stir all of this up."

"What happened?"

"We had just put a down payment on our house when he had an accident. He was a championship diver all through college and was trying out for a spot on the Olympic team. He struck the edge of the pool on his last dive and broke his neck."

"I'm sorry. That must have been horrible to lose him that way."

"The fall didn't kill him. It left him paralyzed."

"Oh, God."

"He cancelled our engagement because he said it wasn't fair for me to be bound to an invalid. I loved him anyway, so when he was released from the hospital, I moved into the house with him. I stayed with him until he died two years later."

The pain in her voice was well disguised, buried under the stark, matter-of-fact words. She had revealed a nightmare. And she probably didn't realize what her words revealed about herself. She'd loved him anyway. She'd stuck by him. What strength that must have taken, what loyalty.

What would it be like to be loved like that?

This time he did touch her. A brief stroke of his fingertips on the back of her wrist.

She started at the contact, but she didn't pull away. "It was at his funeral that I promised myself I would never get married. My family knows it. That's the main reason Norm is having trouble believing I've suddenly changed my mind."

"I can understand that."

"They were all so worried about me after Ryan died, they practically smothered me with their good intentions. They couldn't seem to accept the fact that I was handling it in my own way. I didn't need to be sheltered and protected. I needed to be independent."

"I can understand that, too," he murmured. "If you're on your own, no one can hurt you."

"That's right. Love makes a person too vulnerable. It's better to—" Pausing, she tilted her head as she watched him. "You *do* understand. What happened to you, Sam? Were you ever married?"

He pulled back, withdrawing his hand. "No."

"Were you engaged?"

"No. Settling down with one woman isn't for me, that's all. With the kind of work I do, I don't want to be tied down." Sam turned his attention back to his steak. "How much do I need to know about the catering business to get hired on?"

The abrupt change of topic effectively snuffed out the spark of closeness that had sprung up between them. And that was good, Sam told himself. Hadn't they both agreed that this relationship was strictly a business arrangement? That they didn't want to get personally involved?

The only person in Chicago who knew about Sam's past was Xavier, and even then, there were still some things that Sam had kept to himself. But in the space of less than a day, Audra had threatened to slip past the defenses that had served him well for over thirty years. Why? Was it only because he found her attractive?

She wasn't flashy, and she was too delicately wholesome to be called beautiful. She hid her body's curves under loose clothes and restrained her sensuously soft hair, so obviously she wasn't setting out to entice anyone. It must have been because of the circumstances last night—after lying naked on top of a semi-clothed woman, any normal man would feel something. Lust. That's all it was. No need to start analyzing his feelings any further.

*If you're on your own, no one can hurt you.*

She was a necessary part of his cover, that was all. If he'd had any other way to get close to Fitzpatrick, he would have used it.

# Chapter 5

"If I'd had any other way to get close to Fitzpatrick, I would have used it."

Xavier gripped the steering wheel and swore under his breath, a sure sign of his mounting anger. Normally nothing ruffled him. He took sleepless nights and cross-departmental raids in stride. But ever since Sam had slipped into the unmarked sedan, the atmosphere had been simmering with tension.

"There was no other choice at the time," Sam persisted. "If I hadn't acted immediately, we would have missed the opportunity."

"Middleton could have done it."

"Middleton's a good cop, but he's about as subtle as a grizzly. He's twice Audra's height and three times her weight. And apart from the fact they'd be physically mismatched, you know he's not the romantic type. He'd never be able to convince anyone their engagement was real."

"He can play out a cover as well as anyone else on the team."

"I know, but—" Sam tugged on the knees of his jeans and

slumped lower in the passenger seat. "Her brother's going to be a hard sell. And he's one of the people in charge of the hiring."

"Then you should have left it to Bergstrom. He would have been perfectly convincing in the role of fiancé."

Sam's jaw hardened as he thought about Bergstrom's magazine-model good looks. The man's love 'em and leave 'em reputation was legendary around the station, but the idea of the slick-talking Romeo getting close to Audra... "No. She's too innocent for him," he said. "Bergstrom's way out of her league. He'd eat her alive."

"Let me get this straight." Xavier's voice was ominously soft. "Are you saying you don't trust the other members of the team to do their jobs, Tucker?"

"I'd trust them with my life."

"But not with this woman?"

Put like that, his objections seemed unreasonable. Bergstrom and Middleton were good men, and they'd never given Sam any cause to doubt their competence. But he couldn't imagine either one of them working with Audra.

"I know it wasn't what you wanted, but I made a judgment call," he said. "Given the circumstances, it seemed to be the best option."

For the next several minutes, Xavier steered through the traffic in tight-lipped silence. Finally, he pulled up in the parking lot where Sam had left his car and turned to face him. "The damage is done. You're in now, so we'll just have to play this out and hope Fitzpatrick's men don't recognize you."

"They won't. Like I told you before, they knew me as Tindale the bookkeeper. Those two B-and-E guys aren't out yet, are they?"

"No."

"And Fitzpatrick isn't about to dirty his hands by paying for their bail or their lawyer."

"Not so far."

"Then the risk is minimal. And the McPhersons' policy of only hiring family members works in our favor. Once I'm working for them, I'll have security clearance for the wedding.''

"So you're already part of the company?"

"Not yet. I'm working on it.''

Xavier hesitated, his eyes troubled as he held Sam's gaze. "I don't like it, Tucker. We still don't know enough about this Audra McPherson. I've never liked involving a citizen in an investigation. They're too unpredictable.''

"We can trust her. She's smart, she thinks on her feet and she's highly motivated.''

"Oh?''

"She's counting on that reward money the insurance company's offering so that she can open her own restaurant.'' He twisted to open the door. "I'm on top of the situation, Xavier. I'll keep you posted.''

"Be careful, Sam.''

The quiet tone surprised him. He paused, his hand on the door handle. "I always am, Lieutenant.''

"Don't let this woman distract you from your job. I've seen it happen before. When a cop loses his objectivity, when he gets personally involved in a case, he's a risk to himself and anyone around him.''

"I know that. I have everything under control.''

His gaze intent, Xavier watched him for another minute. Then he nodded once and put the car in gear.

Sam stood on the pavement and watched the unmarked sedan pull away, hoping he could convince himself of what he'd just said as easily as he seemed to have convinced Xavier.

Audra hung up the phone and wiped her palms on her apron. That made five out of six. The only sister-in-law who hadn't yet called was Geraldine, who was seven months pregnant and undoubtedly had more important things on her mind.

The calls had started the minute Sam had brought her back after their dinner last night. She'd heard the phone ringing even before she'd unlocked her door. Her mother had been the first.

She'd been so pleased by the news that she had almost forgiven Audra for not telling her immediately.

Evidently the doting, love-at-first-sight, couldn't-keep-his-hands-off-her act that Sam had put on for Norm and Judy had done the trick. Her own involuntary response hadn't done any harm either. Judy had told everyone about Audra's blushes and flustered, sappy stares. And now the unrepentant matchmakers in her family were overjoyed to think that their relentless campaign to change Audra's opinion of marriage had finally worked.

It was what she wanted, of course. She wanted the deception to succeed, because she wanted that reward money. So why wasn't she pleased?

Frowning, she moved back to the stove and picked up a wooden spoon, mechanically stirring the milk and chocolate mixture that heated in the double boiler. For five years she had been telling her family that she would never marry. She'd tried over and over to explain how she preferred to be independent, and that she didn't intend to fall in love and make herself vulnerable to all that pain again. But obviously, what she had said and how she had lived her life hadn't meant a thing.

People believed what they wanted to believe.

At least Sam understood about her desire to remain alone. She'd seen it in his eyes when she'd told him about Ryan. She'd felt it in the way his fingertips had touched her so gently, sharing sympathy that was supportive, not smothering.

Her hand stilled. She hadn't talked to anyone about Ryan in years. His accident and his eventual death had been subjects that her family scrupulously avoided. Whenever the conversation threatened to go in that direction, the subject was quickly changed.

They meant well. They always meant well. Her family was as protective when it came to her emotions as they were about all the other things, like where she lived and how she made her living. That's why resenting them made her feel so guilty.

She should be thankful for the love they gave her. She should appreciate the fact that she had such a strong, closely-knit family who cared so deeply. It was petty and ungrateful to resent the way they refused to acknowledge her opinions and continued to treat her like a not-too-bright child.

At the knock on her door, she sighed and set down the spoon. Her thoughts had been looping around this same track for more than a day now. But it would all be resolved once Sam's investigation was over and she had the means to finally do what she wanted.

Another knock sounded as she moved the double boiler off the element. That was probably the air conditioner guy—he'd promised to come over sometime this afternoon. Good thing. The heat wave showed no signs of letting up.

She unlocked the door and pulled it open. "Thanks for coming," she said. "I hope you can..." Her words trailed off as she caught sight of the wildly patterned Hawaiian print shirt. She lifted her gaze. "Oh. Hi, Sam."

"Who were you expecting this time?"

"The air conditioner repairman."

"Audra, you really should check to see who it is before you open your door."

"We've had this conversation before."

"And we'll have it again, unless you start being more careful."

"I am not a child. I am a twenty-eight-year-old woman who has lived on her own for several years now, and I'm quite capable of taking care of my—"

"Whoa!" Sam angled his hands into a time-out sign. "I'll call before I come over next time, okay?"

She took a deep breath, then shook her head. "Sorry. Bad timing, that's all."

"You're busy."

"Just trying out a new recipe." She stepped back to let him in. "I'm right in the middle of it, so we can talk while I work."

He closed the door behind him and followed her to the kitchen. "Are your relatives giving you a rough time over our engagement?"

What could she say? That her bad mood was because they had

accepted it too easily? "Not really. Mom's thrilled, but Dad has been kind of reserved about the whole thing. They've invited us to dinner on Wednesday. My father wants to meet you."

"Good. It'll give me a chance to ease into the subject of a job."

She picked up a whisk to beat the egg yolks with the sugar she'd measured earlier. "Don't you think that might be too soon?"

"Trust me, Audra. I've been thinking about what you've told me about your family, and I've decided on the best approach."

"Oh?"

"I won't say I'm broke and desperate for a job, since that wouldn't go over too well with a prospective father-in-law. I'll say I have a good severance package from the computer company, but that I want to work for McPherson Catering for a while to help ease your workload so that we'll have more time together."

"That sounds...reasonable."

"We're so much in love that we can't bear to be parted from each other."

"Okay," she said, lifting the double boiler's top pot off its base. She poured the milk and melted chocolate gradually into the yolks, beating with one hand. "Mom would probably buy that."

"And since your father's so protective, I'll tell him that I'm concerned about you traveling on your own to and from jobs, so I want to come along to make sure you're all right."

Well, he'd certainly picked the right buttons to push when it came to winning over her parents. "That just might work."

"I'm counting on it." He crossed his arms and leaned a hip against the counter as he watched her. "What are you making?"

"Chocolate custard sauce." Transferring the mixture back to the double boiler, she returned it to the stove. "It's one of the fillings I wanted to try with the cream puffs I made this morning."

"It smells delicious."

"Thank you."

"I'm partial to chocolate."

"Isn't everyone?"

He smiled. "Yeah. Cinnamon, too."

It took her off guard, the way her pulse made that quick jump when he smiled at her. After yesterday, she should have been used to it.

Who was she fooling? If she lived to be a hundred, she wouldn't get used to it. Even in a setting as mundane and unromantic as her kitchen, with the humming fan and the bubbling pot providing the only background music, Sam could set her pulse racing with no more than a look.

But this wasn't what either of them wanted. They had both agreed that their relationship was simply a business arrangement. A certain amount of...awareness was bound to occur because of the act they had to put on, but she was mature enough to handle it, right?

She turned her attention back to the sauce. "I have to stir this for another few minutes until it thickens."

"Is this for the retirement party at that office we were in yesterday?"

"No. They only wanted hors d'oeuvres, so Esther and Christopher are handling the food for that."

"Christopher's one of the hotheaded twins, right?"

"Uh-huh. He and Jake are also trained chefs."

"You're pretty good yourself."

"Thanks. I'm testing out some new desserts for a high school reunion we're doing next week. The organizing committee I met with favored everything that was fattening." She stirred around the side of the pot. Thick folds of rich chocolate followed the spoon. "Anyhow, I don't usually do the food preparation for a job here. This kitchen's too small."

"Then where do you work?"

"It depends on the particular job. Sometimes we use the kitchens on site, or if that's not practical, we prepare the bulk of the food at Christopher's. He has a kitchen to die for. Stainless steel gas range, double refrigerator and acres of counter space." She smiled. "I'll be lucky if my restaurant has equipment that good."

"How are you working the Fitzpatrick job?"

"We only started the menu planning yesterday, but it looks as if we'll need to do a lot of the work there because of the number of guests involved and the location of the estate. I'll know more when we have our first meeting."

"Is there any chance of holding the meeting at the Fitzpatrick estate?"

"There's a very good chance. Most of our clients find it's more convenient for us to visit them than the other way around." She stirred the sauce one last time, judged that it was done and took it off the heat. "You'll want to be included in that, I guess."

"Absolutely. So the sooner I can talk to your father and get hired on, the better." He shifted closer, leaning over her shoulder to inhale the fragrant steam that rose from the pot. "What did you say you wanted to do with this stuff?"

Although he didn't touch her, every nerve in her body hummed with awareness. She inhaled sharply. Over the scent of chocolate she caught the clean aroma of his soap and lime aftershave, and a hint of the man underneath. "What do I want to do?"

"With the chocolate."

"Oh. It's for the cream puffs."

"Those little yellow things?"

She glanced at the wire rack where she'd placed the golden pastries an hour ago. "Yes. There's a space inside them that needs to be filled. Once the sauce is cool, I put it into that bag and insert the...tip in the...opening and then... squeeze—" She stopped, aghast at the blush that was creeping into her cheeks. There was nothing suggestive about piping filling into cream puffs. Nothing at all.

His voice dropped as he moved beside her. "Sounds tempting." He reached out to run the tip of his index finger over the wooden spoon she had put down on the counter.

"It's still hot," she cautioned.

"Can't resist," he said, lifting his chocolate-covered finger to his lips. "Do you mind?"

"No, the whole point of making this sauce was to test it, so I..."

She forgot what she was going to say. Actually, she forgot what they had been talking about. She watched, spellbound, as Sam dipped his finger into his mouth and sucked the chocolate sauce off the tip.

This time, the sudden thump of her pulse didn't take her by surprise—her heart rate hadn't entirely returned to normal since Sam had walked into her apartment.

A low sound of pleasure rumbled from his throat as he withdrew his finger. "That tastes even better than it smells."

"I'm glad you like it," she said. She heard the soft, breathless note in her voice but was powerless to stop it. "I, um, used part bitter, part semi-sweet and added a dash of cloves."

"Aren't you going to try any?"

Her gaze strayed to his lips, and the tiny dot of chocolate that was left on the bottom one. She'd felt those lips on hers twice. More than twice, if she counted all the times she'd replayed those brief kisses in her imagination. "No, I'll wait for it to cool, thanks."

"It's good hot."

"I've never tried—"

"Then allow me." He swirled his finger in the sauce that had dripped from the spoon to the counter, then lifted his hand toward her.

It was only an innocent gesture. She'd done this kind of thing with her nieces and nephews countless times when they visited. Heck, they usually fought over the right to lick the bowl clean. There was no reason for her to make a big deal of this by refusing.

Parting her lips, she leaned toward him.

The instant she felt his finger touch her mouth, she knew she'd made a mistake. Hot, thick and sweet, the chocolate burst over her tongue. But the sinfully rich sauce accounted for only a fraction of the sensations that flowed through her. She felt the texture of Sam's skin, the hard edge of his nail and the cool moisture that was left from his own mouth. She sucked lightly, drawing his finger a tiny bit deeper.

Tension sparked in the air between them. At Sam's whispered oath, she raised her gaze to his.

That was her second mistake. Looking at him. His eyes locked with hers, awareness and arousal swirling in the blue depths. There was nothing innocent about what they were doing now. And there was no one else here. They didn't have to put on an act. There was no need for this to go any further.

He pulled his hand away and looked at her for a breathless moment. Then slowly, deliberately, he scooped up more chocolate sauce and returned his finger to her lips.

Holding his gaze, she closed her mouth over his finger, and sucked the chocolate off the tip. A tremor traveled up his arm. A muscle jumped in his cheek. Audra released him and smiled, pleased that she wasn't the only one who was affected by this sensual game. Recklessly, she dipped her own finger into the warm sauce and dabbed more chocolate on his lower lip.

His eyes gleaming in silent challenge, he licked off the sauce with his tongue and smiled. His expression didn't bear any resemblance to a mischievous boy now, it was pure predatory male. He tugged the rounded neckline of her blouse lower, dunked his finger into the pot of chocolate and touched the spot at the top of the cleft between her breasts.

She gasped. "Sam! What are you doing?"

"Testing out the sauce," he murmured, lowering his head.

Audra felt her knees go weak. This was crazy. He wouldn't actually...

Oh, God. He would. He did. His breath feathered across her chest, warming skin that already burned. His lips settled over the place he'd touched, a light caress, as sweetly gentle as the kisses he'd given her the day before. But then he opened his mouth and she felt the stroke of his tongue.

Pleasure shot through her, headier than ten potsful of chocolate custard. She grasped his shoulders, feeling his muscles shift and tense beneath the thin cotton of his shirt as he slipped his arm behind her waist to hold her steady. He pressed closer, turning his head to drag his lips across the upper curve of her breast.

Her nipples hardened with a swiftness that verged on painful. Closing her eyes, she tipped back her head and arched toward him, mindlessly wanting more, afraid he would stop. Afraid he wouldn't.

Sam slipped his hands downward, curling his fingers around her buttocks. Pressing his face to the side of her neck, he tightened his grip and lifted her against him.

She shuddered at the intimate contact. She'd felt his body on hers before. His naked body. On her bed. But she hadn't felt *all* of him until now. Oh, Lord, he really was a big man. Heat gathered between her legs in a response that left her shaking.

"Audra." His voice was rough, as bold and hard as the rest of him. "I—"

Whatever he was going to say was drowned out by the sudden shrill from the phone on the wall.

He muttered a short, crude word and raised his head.

She blinked her eyes open. Sam's face was close, his lips only a breath away. Desire tightened the lines beside his mouth and darkened his eyes. But as she watched, his expression gradually changed. The desire faded. His gaze cleared.

And then he released her so suddenly she staggered.

She grabbed the corner of the table to regain her balance and fought to steady her breathing.

The phone kept ringing, its insistent peals falling like pebbles into the tense pool of silence between them.

Sam rubbed his face, then dragged his fingers through his hair and stepped back. "Sorry about that," he said. "I was out of line."

Her fingers unsteady, she tugged the neckline of her blouse back into place.

"It's one of the hazards of assuming a cover," he continued. "Sometimes you tend to slip into the role even when it isn't necessary."

Tingles still chased over her skin from the dampness he'd left between her breasts. "Slip into the role," she repeated numbly.

"Yeah." He shoved his hands into the pockets of his jeans. "I apologize."

Did he think she'd been *acting?* Had that been all it was to him? A game? Part of the cover they needed to work on?

It had felt real to her. And she might not have a whole lot of experience when it came to this kind of thing, but there'd been nothing fake about that bulge she'd felt pressed against her stomach....

But this was Sam, the macho cop, the man who was perfectly at ease wandering naked around a stranger's bedroom. Engaging in a bit of slap and tickle in a kitchen would mean next to nothing to a man like him. How could she have forgotten, even for an instant? He wasn't interested in her. He was using her as part of his job.

Humiliation surged over her as she turned to reach for the phone.

It was Geraldine, calling to congratulate her on her engagement. That made six out of six. The deception was succeeding even better than they'd hoped.

Oh, Lord. Was it ever.

# Chapter 6

"My parents are expecting us at seven."

"We still have plenty of time," Sam said, pulling off the street into the parking lot of an elementary school. He eased to a stop at the side of the yellow brick building and shut off the engine.

A few children were playing ball on the diamond in the corner of the schoolyard, their faces winking golden as they ran in and out of the slanting sunlight. A set of swings, their pale canvas seats drooping downward, hung motionless in the still evening air. The other side of the schoolyard bordered a small park, where a winding path led past a huge weeping willow and a pair of wooden benches. Sam watched as a white-haired man strolled past, a small terrier tugging at the leash he held while a couple with a baby carriage lingered in the shade of the willow. It was a peaceful scene in a quiet residential neighborhood, as cliché as something out of an old television show.

Audra had probably gone to this school when she'd been a kid. Along with all her brothers. They'd likely played on those swings or that ball diamond while their mother was at home cooking dinner in her ruffled apron and their father was sitting in his

favorite easy chair with his pipe and evening paper. And if that
scene seemed like something out of an old television show too,
it was because watching it on TV had been as close as Sam had
ever come to seeing a normal family.

"My father's a stickler for punctuality."

Propping his forearm on the steering wheel, he turned to face
her. "There's something we need to take care of first."

She stared out the windshield. "All right. What is it?"

He studied her profile, noting the lift of her chin and the tight
set of her mouth. She'd avoided him for the past two days. Ever
since that incident with the chocolate sauce...

Damn, how could he have been so stupid? Xavier had warned
him about letting a woman distract him, about getting personally
involved in a case. And this one was progressing so well—

At least it had been, until he'd let his libido overrule his brain.

He was as bad as Bergstrom. No, he was even worse. He would
have expected Bergstrom to take advantage of the situation, but
Sam wasn't like that. He knew where to draw the line, right?

The frustration he'd felt when he'd come to his senses had been
bad enough, but it was the look on Audra's face that had really
shaken him. Her sweet, spontaneous response had transformed to
shame when he'd told her he'd only been playing a role.

He'd had no choice. It had been the only way out if he'd hoped
to continue working with her.

But it still made him feel like scum.

"Come on," he said, opening his door. "Let's go for a walk."

She hesitated, even after he'd rounded the hood and opened
her door. Then she unbuckled her seat belt and stepped out. They
walked in silence toward the park, following the path where the
grass had been worn down to dusty gray soil. "There's a meeting
scheduled for Friday afternoon at the Fitzpatrick estate," Audra
said, watching her feet. "I'll be going over the menu plans with
Marion Fitzpatrick."

"Good."

"I suppose you still want to talk to my father about a job
tonight."

"That's the whole point of what we're doing."

"Of course," she said crisply. "I know that. I'm not stupid."

He grimaced inwardly, moving aside to let the couple with the baby carriage go by. "Look, Audra, I'm sorry about what happened the other day."

"I'm a big girl, Sam. It didn't mean anything. And if you're worried that I'm going to back out of this, don't be. I have no intention of giving up that reward money." She glanced at her watch, her steps slowing as they reached the shade of the willow. "If that's all you wanted to talk about..."

"No, there's something else." He stopped and reached into the pocket of his slacks, then pulled out a small, velvet-covered box. "Here," he said, holding it out to her. "This is for you."

She drew in her breath, then snapped her gaze to his face. "That looks like a jeweler's box."

"Yeah. It is. I got you a ring."

"But..." She paused, moving her head back and forth in a slow negative. "You didn't have to do that."

"Yes, I did. You need an engagement ring."

"But—"

"Your parents will expect you to have one, won't they?"

"I hadn't really thought about it. I suppose they would."

"Then you might as well take a look at it."

She took the box from his hand hesitantly. "You didn't pay for this, did you?"

"It's a loaner. I worked with the jeweler on a gem-smuggling case last year. He owed me a favor."

"Oh. Well, as long as you didn't have to..." Her words trailed off as she opened the lid of the box. "Oh my."

"If you don't want it, I can exchange it for something better."

"No," she said. "It's beautiful."

Sam felt an unexpected rush of satisfaction at the pleasure he saw on her face. "I'm glad you like it."

Audra ran the tip of her finger over the ring where it nestled in its velvet-lined slot. A delicate design of apple blossoms was etched into the gold, with a diamond sparkling from the center of the largest blossom.

"I had to guess at the size," Sam said. "If it doesn't fit, we'll exchange it tomorrow."

She nodded.

"Here, you'd better try it on." He lifted the ring from the box and offered it to her, waiting until she held out her left hand. But instead of placing it in her palm as she'd obviously expected, he gently grasped her wrist and turned her hand over so he could slide the ring onto her third finger.

It was a perfect fit. And it looked as good on her as he'd imagined when he'd chosen it.

For a moment she stood without moving, her hand still clasped lightly in his, the diamond winking in a slanting ray of sunlight. Her lips softened into a shy smile. "Thank you, Sam."

He wanted to kiss her. That's what a man did when he gave a woman a diamond ring, wasn't it? Not a light brush like the other time in front of her brother, but a real kiss. A lover's kiss. He should dip his head and capture her smile, taste the warmth of her budding passion as her smile turned from shy to sensual. He should murmur intimate secrets against her lips and give her promises...about their future together...and how they might walk here with a child of their own someday, and how their home would be filled with love.... '

Damn, this case was really messing with his head. He couldn't remember getting this confused about a role he was playing before.

He released her hand and stuffed the empty box back into his pocket. "This should help convince your father the engagement is legitimate."

Her smile disappeared. "Yes, of course," she said stiffly. "You're right. It should help convince my father." She checked her watch and turned around. "We'd better go or we'll be late."

Naturally, her mother loved him. She would have loved anyone Audra had brought home, as long as he didn't have running sores or knuckles that dragged on the floor. But her father's reaction had surprised her. It had taken all evening, yet there were definite signs that John McPherson was beginning to approve of his daughter's new fiancé.

Audra grabbed another plate from the stack on the counter and shoved it under the tap. The two men were in the living room now, looking at old photo albums. She could hear them talking together, their deep voices blending with the background sound of the ball game. Her father wasn't an easy man to please. Just ask any of his seven children. Yet Sam had somehow managed to make a favorable impression.

He'd dressed up for the occasion, relinquishing his usual Hawaiian prints and tight jeans in favor of a tailored white shirt and pleated tan trousers. As determined as Audra was not to notice, the neat clothes still managed to add to his appeal. Odd, how clothes could do that, considering the fact that she'd seen him in nothing at all.

It had been fascinating to watch him in action tonight. He'd already figured out what buttons to push with her parents, and although he'd been subtle about it, he'd done exactly what he'd told her he'd do. He'd played on her mother's dreams of a loving, stable marriage for her daughter. He'd played on her father's protectiveness and that old helpless-female-needs-a-big-strong-man attitude. And he'd done it well.

Almost as well as he'd managed to push *her* buttons, right?

Pressing her lips together, she crammed plate after plate into the dishwasher. After she'd told herself not to let him get to her again, she'd been on the verge of making a fool of herself over that ring.

Granted, she never wanted to be really engaged again, but there still was something special about having a man slip a diamond ring over her finger. How could she help feeling something? Although it had been seven years, she vividly remembered when the man had been Ryan.

How different that had been. Ryan had gone through the whole ritual, bringing her a dozen roses, getting down on one knee and swearing his eternal love and devotion. They'd thought it would last forever.

She'd worn that ring proudly. She'd refused to take it off, even after he'd declared that their engagement was over. She'd worn it right up until the time she'd had to sell it back to the jeweler so she could use the money to help pay Ryan's medical bills.

Audra closed the dishwasher and leaned against it. She shouldn't let the ring bother her. Why should one more lie added to all the rest be any worse?

"There you are." Constance bustled through the swinging door with a tray of empty coffee cups. "I told you to leave those dishes for later."

Pasting on a smile, Audra turned around. "I wanted to help, Mom."

"Thanks, dear." She set the tray on the counter and slipped her arm around Audra's shoulders to give her a quick hug. "Oh, I'm so happy for you. Sam is such a nice young man."

"Yes, he is, isn't he?"

"I could tell the moment I saw you two together there was something very special between you. Besides the chemistry, I mean." Her eyes sparkled as she lowered her voice. "I still didn't tell your Dad about...you know, Sam's spending the night at your place."

"Mo-om."

"Come on, sweetie. There isn't much that shocks me. And it all worked out fine in the end, now that you two are getting married." She gave her a squeeze and stepped back. "The way Sam can barely keep his eyes off you is so romantic. He reminds me of your father."

Audra blinked. Sam? And John McPherson? The two men couldn't be more dissimilar. Her father was half a head shorter than Sam, and before his hair had begun to turn gray, it had been strawberry blond like Jake and Christopher's, not thick and black with loose rakish curls that fell temptingly over his forehead. As a young man, her father had been good-looking, but his classic, wholesome features didn't have anywhere near the appeal of Sam's rough-hewn handsomeness.

And apart from the obvious physical differences, there was the matter of their personalities. Her father was calm, conservative and scrupulously honest. He wouldn't be remotely interested in the unpredictable, exciting, dangerous work of an undercover policeman. If he knew what his so-called future son-in-law really did for a living, he'd probably get her brothers to throw Sam out on his ear and lock Audra in her old room.

"Sam mentioned he's been downsized," Constance went on. "That's a shame. There's so much of that happening these days."

"He received a very generous severance package from his former employer," Audra said immediately.

"Oh, yes, he just finished telling us all about it. Now that he has time on his hands, do you think he might lend some of his expertise to Nathan? You know how your brother's been talking about getting all the company bookkeeping on his computer."

"Uh, I'll ask him."

"No hurry. Once he's a member of the family, we'll be able to take advantage of him shamelessly. Speaking of which, would you mind if I asked him to give us a hand with the Fitzpatrick wedding job?"

"What?"

"We're going to be swamped. And he did mention that your work keeps you too busy and he wished he could spend more time with you. If he helped out, you two could work side by side." She sighed. "Just like your dad and me when we started out. We were inseparable."

This was too easy. Way too easy.

But she already knew that Sam had a knack of getting people to do what he wanted.

"That would be nice," she said finally.

"If he's sensitive about being downsized, I wouldn't want to offend him by offering him a job."

"Don't worry about that, Mom. I'm sure Sam would appreciate the offer."

"Wonderful." Her mother patted her hand, then picked up a plate of cookies and backed toward the swinging door. "I'll talk to your father about it tonight."

The guards at the gate had guns. That's why they both wore those jackets, even in this heat. There was no mistaking the lumpy outlines of the holsters under their khaki windbreakers. Audra probably wouldn't have looked for them if Sam hadn't warned her, but now that she knew, she couldn't seem to see anything else.

The taller guard spoke into the microphone of his headset as he walked up to the van. Stopping beside the driver's door, he motioned for Sam to roll down his window. "Name?" he asked. His voice sounded like something from the bottom of a bucket.

"Sam Tucker and Audra McPherson," Sam said, a pleasant smile on his face. "We're with McPherson Catering. Miss Fitzpatrick is expecting us."

The guard tipped his head and spoke into his microphone again. He continued to scrutinize Sam. "Wait here."

A movement at the corner of Audra's vision made her jerk nervously. The second guard had come up to her side of the van and was peering past her into the interior. "What's in there?" he demanded.

She glanced at Sam. His smile still in place, he swiveled out of his seat. "Relax," he whispered as he stooped over to move to the back of the van. "As long as we don't do anything suspicious, they're not going to touch us. This is all routine."

As soon as Sam opened the rear doors, the second guard rounded the van. Propping one foot on the bumper, the guard gave the interior a thorough inspection. Evidently he found nothing suspicious about the empty metal shelves that were fastened to one wall or the loose-leaf binders that rested on the floor. With a grunt, he stepped away and slammed the doors shut.

"Mom told me about this," Audra said, her gaze darting from the guards to the iron gates. There was a square cement building with narrow slits for windows on the other side of the fence. It looked like a bunker. "I just hadn't imagined it would be quite so...fortified."

"This is only the part you see. Fitzpatrick makes sure it's highly visible to discourage trespassers."

She looked at the thick black iron bars that made up the fence. Coils of razor wire looped along the top. "Oh, it looks discouraging, all right," she muttered.

The first guard returned, a clipboard in his hand. "Okay," he said. "You can go through. Drive straight to the end of the lane. Don't stop anywhere."

"No problem," Sam said, nodding cheerfully.

The guard turned away, tapped a combination into a remote control device and the gates slid open. The van had barely made it through before the gates clanged shut.

Audra took a deep breath and wiped her palms on her skirt. "Now what?"

"We go straight to the end of the lane without stopping, just like he said." He kept to the center of the pavement, maintaining his speed at an even twenty. "Would you mind leaning against the door for a while?"

"Why?"

"You're blocking the camera."

"*What?*"

"Calm down and act natural, will you? There's a surveillance camera attached to the birch tree on the right."

"Oh. Why don't you want me to block it?"

"I want you to act natural for the camera in the tree," he said, maintaining his smile as he spoke through his teeth. "It's the camera inside the van that I don't want you to block."

She started to turn her head but Sam's hand shot out to clamp on her thigh. "Audra, for God's sake. Just sit there, okay?"

"When did you put a camera in the van?"

"Last night. It's one of Bergstrom's toys. I fastened it on top of that metal shelving and rigged it so it's focused through the right side of the windshield."

She resisted the urge to turn around and see for herself. Instead, she leaned against the door, shifting her legs so that Sam dropped his hand. "That's why you're driving so slowly, isn't it? You're trying to get video of the grounds."

"That's right."

Guards with guns. A camera in her catering van. Of course. She should have expected it. This was all part of what he did for a living. Until now, her attention had been centered on convincing everyone they were engaged. But as Sam had already reminded her, *this* was the whole point of the charade.

The Fitzpatrick estate oozed wealth. The lane took them past a small pond, a hedge of yew bushes and a lawn that was as smoothly manicured as a putting green. A series of stone-paved terraces led up the side of a low hill where a trio of gardeners bent over orderly beds of colorful flowers. Carved stone benches were placed around a circular fountain where water shimmered from the top of a spouting dolphin.

The house loomed in front of them, its windows appearing to waver in the afternoon heat. Three stories high, with a shorter wing extending from one side, it was built of mellowed red brick and covered with glossy green ivy. It wasn't huge or ostentatious, yet it emanated an impression of money and power. Dirty money and criminal power.

A dark-suited man with a headset and one of those holster-shaped bulges under his jacket directed Sam to drive around the side of the house. "All you need to do is act natural," Sam said, easing the van to a stop behind a low, black limousine. "Remember, it's business as usual for you."

Audra wiped her palms on her skirt again. "Okay."

He shut off the engine and swiveled around to pick up the loose-leaf binders. "I'm hoping to scout out the layout of the house while we're here, but it's not worth jeopardizing the job for it. For now, we'll play it by ear."

"I hate that expression."

He lifted an eyebrow as he handed her one of the binders. "There's no need to be nervous."

"Oh, of course not." She crossed her arms over the binder, holding it to her chest like a shield.

"I'm not going to let anything happen to you, Audra," he said, his voice low. "That's why I want to keep your involvement to an absolute minimum. You've done your part, you got me in. That's all you needed to do."

Another dark-suited man, this one even bigger than the others they'd encountered so far, led them through the rear entrance of the house. They turned left and were ushered down a cool, dim mahogany-paneled hallway to a small sitting room that overlooked the front garden. Audra remained silent while they waited, using the time to review the menus she had typed up that morning.

Ten minutes later, the patio door that led to the garden opened and a petite, red-haired woman stepped in. "I'm sorry," she said, brushing at the dirt that streaked the front of her white shorts. "I hope I haven't kept you waiting long."

Audra glanced up from her notes in surprise. She'd noticed the woman as they'd driven past the garden, and she'd assumed she was one of the gardeners. "Miss Fitzpatrick?" she asked.

"Please, call me Marion." She pulled off her gardening gloves and crossed the room, holding out her hand. "Thanks for coming. You must be Audra. Your mother said you'd be drawing up the menus." She shook hands, her gaze going to Sam.

Audra spoke up quickly. "This is Sam Tucker, my fiancé. He's helping me."

Marion barely paid attention to her explanation of Sam's presence. Instead, she was much more interested in the plans Audra had worked out. Within minutes, they were seated around a low, marble-topped table, deep in a discussion of the quantity of the appetizers and the color scheme of the tablecloths.

Gradually, Audra began to relax. She hadn't known what a criminal's daughter would be like, but it certainly hadn't been this pleasant, self-composed woman. Marion behaved exactly like any other young bride-to-be, excited, a little anxious over details and bubbling with enthusiasm over the approaching wedding.

Bit by bit, the tentative plans that Audra and her mother had worked out were refined and expanded. Scribbling notes furiously, she recorded every new detail while she kept a running total in her head of the supplies they would need. From the sound of things so far, this was going to be the largest wedding the company had done. Not only would they be providing a lavish dinner for over three hundred guests, they would be responsible for the bar and the refreshments during the dancing afterward.

Even without the reward Audra hoped to get out of this, her share of what McPherson Catering was going to make in profit was going to be more money than what she'd normally make in a month.

But Larry Fitzpatrick was a criminal, so that meant the money he would use to pay McPherson Catering would come from the profits from crime. And if Sam and his colleagues succeeded in arresting Fitzpatrick, what would that do to Marion? Did she know what her father was? Did she know where the money to pay for her lavish wedding was coming from?

Probably not. Sam had said that Fitzpatrick kept his daughter and his personal life completely removed from his money-laundering business. Marion probably took their wealth for granted. And although the estate was fortified, so were plenty of other rich people's places. She likely never questioned why they had such tight security—after all, crime was so widespread these days.

"I'd like to have the whole thing in the garden," Marion said, gesturing toward the patio window. "It's always been my favorite place."

"I can see that," Audra said. "It's beautiful."

"I've been trying to talk her out of it."

At the new voice, Audra twisted to look over her shoulder. A plump, middle-aged man moved into the room, a pleasant smile on his face. He crossed to Marion and gave her a quick kiss on the forehead. "How are you managing?"

"Fine, Daddy." She smiled up at him. "I thought you had an appointment."

"I do. I just wanted to say goodbye before I left."

Marion turned back to Audra and Sam. "Have you met my father yet?"

Audra's automatic greeting died in her throat. Her father? *This* was Larry Fitzpatrick, the criminal mastermind? There had to be some mistake. With his red hair and genial expression, he looked more like an overgrown elf.

Sam covered her lack of response, smoothly introducing both of them before steering the conversation back to business.

"My father's trying to talk me out of an outdoor ceremony," Marion said. "He's concerned about the weather."

"I can understand that, Mr. Fitzpatrick," Sam put in, shuffling some binders for Audra in an attempt to look useful. "But this heat wave is bound to break soon. And we could provide tents and awnings, just in case of rain."

"That's a wonderful idea," Marion exclaimed.

Fitzpatrick didn't appear to agree. For an instant his genial expression wavered, and Audra caught a glimpse of cold calculation behind his gaze. But then he patted his daughter's hand and moved to the door. "It could work. Keep everything on the terraces on the east side of the house."

"Thanks, Daddy."

Sam waited until Fitzpatrick's footsteps had faded down the hall before he rose to his feet. "If you show us the exact place you had in mind, Marion, I can estimate the square footage of the tents you'll need."

"All right. Have we covered everything about the menus for now?" she asked Audra.

"Oh, yes. If anything else comes up, I'll call you."

"Terrific," Marion said, leading them to the patio.

The long, black limousine that had been parked around the back of the house drove slowly down the lane toward the gates. Sam watched it until it was out of sight. "After we look at the garden, we'd better tour the kitchen, too," he said. "We'll need to know what kind of facilities you have on site so we can determine a work plan."

Audra nodded. "With the number of guests you're expecting,

we're going to need an area close to the garden where we can work.''

"And we'll want to work as unobtrusively as possible," Sam added. "So it would help if you showed us which areas of the house we should avoid."

"That's easy to do," Marion said, leading them to the patio. "My father keeps his offices in the wing on the other side of the garage. That area of the house is always kept private, but otherwise, my guests will have the run of the place."

Over the next half hour, they accompanied Marion on her impromptu tour of her father's estate. Although Sam kept his posture relaxed and his questions casual, Audra was aware of his intense scrutiny of everything they saw.

She also became aware of her own growing sympathy for Marion Fitzpatrick. Despite what her father was, she seemed to be a genuinely nice person. For her sake, Audra hoped the wedding went off without a hitch. And that Marion was far enough away and had established a life of her own before her father was brought to justice.

Their tour ended in the kitchen. It was an immense, starkly lit room with commercial-size stainless steel appliances and a forest of copper cookware hanging from hooks. It appeared to be capable of feeding an army, and considering the size of the guards, that wasn't too far off. Esther and Christopher would drool when they saw this equipment, Audra thought.

Marion glanced at the clock on the wall and smiled apologetically. "I'm sorry, but I have to run. I'm meeting my fiancé in less than an hour and I really have to change out of my gardening clothes."

"I appreciate the time you've taken to show us around," Audra said, extending her hand. "It's going to be a beautiful wedding."

"Thanks for coming. I'll show you out."

"Please, don't bother," Sam said, placing his hand at the small of Audra's back. "After the tour you gave us, we know our way."

They turned toward the rear entrance as Marion said goodbye

and moved quickly down the hall. The minute she was out of sight around the corner, Sam swiveled and started walking in the opposite direction.

Audra hesitated. "That's not the way out."

"I know. Stay put. If anyone comes, say you're counting pots or something."

Her eyes widened. Of course. He was heading straight for the wing of the house where Marion had told them Fitzpatrick kept his office. She hurried after him. "You said you just wanted to scout the layout," she whispered. "You said that it wasn't worth jeopardizing—"

"I said I'd play it by ear. This is too good an opportunity to miss. The door's open."

He was right. The wide mahogany-paneled door at the end of the hall was ajar. She grabbed his arm. "What if someone sees you?"

"Fitzpatrick's gone, but the more fuss you make, the more chance there is of attracting attention." He pulled away from her and jerked his thumb over his shoulder. "Go back to the kitchen and wait."

"No."

"Audra..."

"I'm not standing around waiting for one of those goons with the lumps to find me. I'm sticking with you."

"I don't have time to argue," he muttered. With a quick check of the hall in both directions, he slipped through the open door.

Audra followed. They were in another hall, but the paneling and light fixtures looked older than those in the rest of the house. She chewed her lip nervously as Sam tried the knob of the first door to his left.

"That's probably his office," he commented when the door didn't budge. He checked the door to his right. It opened easily to a small parlor, with old-fashioned velvet drapes and a brocade-upholstered sofa with two matching wing chairs. Sam gave it a quick perusal from the threshold, then pulled the door shut and moved farther down the hall.

The last room had a set of double doors. Sam opened one and paused to glance over his shoulder before he stepped inside. Audra followed on his heels.

A sudden movement on the opposite wall made her catch her breath, but then she realized it was only their reflections in a mirror. She exhaled shakily and looked around. The room was dominated by a glass-topped table that was at least twenty feet long. High-backed chairs upholstered in black leather lined both sides. Another long mirror stretched across the wall beside them, creating an illusion of multiple rooms.

"Bingo," Sam breathed, turning in a slow circle.

"What?"

"This has to be the conference room." He gestured at the table. "Glass top so no one can hide anything. Mirrors on both walls so no one's taken unawares. I imagine Fitzpatrick uses the chair in front of the window," he continued, walking farther into the room. "With the light at his back he'd have an advantage."

Audra clutched her notebook to her chest. These chairs were for Fitzpatrick's fellow criminals. The "guests" that Sam wanted to observe at the wedding. "What are you doing?" she asked.

"Checking where this window is." Heavy floor-to-ceiling drapes blocked the sunshine. Sam carefully folded one back to look outside. "This is the opposite side of the house from the terrace. That garage shields it from the driveway so it would be completely private."

"Sam, we should hurry. Someone might come."

"That's always a possibility."

"But if we're caught here..."

"We'll think of some excuse," he said, letting the drape fall back into place. He moved to the other wall, pausing to look under the table. "He's made this room as secure as it gets," he muttered. "No way anyone can eavesdrop."

She started nervously as he straightened up and a series of his reflections joined hers. "I think we should leave now."

He ignored her, continuing his slow, thorough study of the room as he made a circuit around the table. He reached the end of the mirror and stopped to peer at the base of the wall. "Vents," he muttered, running his fingertips along the edge of a metal grate. "I wonder where the ducting goes."

"It looks kind of narrow for you, Sam."

He lifted an eyebrow. "Not to crawl through, Audra. Sound carries through ducting."

"What about the room beside this one?"

"That's possible. I'll check the position—" He broke off, glancing toward the door.

Audra looked behind her. She hadn't closed the door completely when she'd followed Sam into the room. She swallowed hard. Was it her imagination, or had she heard a footstep?

With his finger against his lips, Sam cautioned her to silence.

A second later, she caught a trace of movement in the mirror. Someone was moving in the hall outside the room.

Oh, God. With the glass table and all these mirrors, there was no place to hide. No excuse to offer for being here. They could say they'd lost their way, that it was only an innocent mistake, but even if anyone swallowed that, it wouldn't explain why they were lingering in this deserted room after they discovered they were lost. She'd read enough detective novels and seen enough TV cop shows to know that trespassers weren't treated gently by criminal masterminds—

Sam moved quickly. He leapt to Audra's side and tossed her notebook to the floor, then clamped his hands at her hips and lifted her up. She barely had time to draw a breath before he whirled around and sat her on the edge of the table. Without a word he yanked up her skirt, unzipped his pants and came down on top of her.

For a split second shock kept her mind from functioning. Then her brain clicked into gear and she understood what Sam was doing.

*We'll think of some excuse.*

It shouldn't have surprised her. After all, this was Sam. He wasn't a man who let modesty or propriety get in his way. And he sure hadn't hesitated the last two times he'd landed on top of her.

Kicking off her sandals, she wrapped her legs around his waist. Another shock shuddered through her at the intimate position. Her cotton underwear didn't provide much of a barrier...and...oh, Lord, she could feel every ounce of him.

But it was all an act, a role to play. She wasn't going to confuse it with the real thing. No, it meant nothing. To either of them.

The door banged against the wall.

Audra moaned loudly and hooked her ankles together. "Yes," she gasped. "Oh, please."

Sam flattened his palms on the tabletop beside her shoulders and rotated his hips. "Like this?"

The glass was hard and smooth beneath her. The mirror rippled with repeating images of the two of them straining together. She arched her back and tossed her head. "Yes, *yes!*"

He ground his pelvis against her. "You're so hot and tight. You make me crazy."

From the corner of her eye she saw a large figure pause in the doorway. It was the dark-suited man who had guided them to their meeting with Marion. He crossed his arms and simply stood there. Watching.

Sam slipped his hands under her buttocks to lift her more firmly against him. His movement also served to drape the folds of her skirt so that the fabric concealed exactly what they were doing...or not doing. "Oh, baby. Oh, yeah," he murmured, suddenly stiffening.

She writhed and moaned in what she hoped was a good imitation of a woman in the throes of ecstasy. "Ahh," she sighed, finally going limp.

Sam collapsed on top of her, bringing his lips against her ear. "Thanks," he breathed. "I think he bought it."

Heart pounding, Audra glanced back at the mirror. She barely recognized the dishevelled woman who lay on the table. Her hair had fanned out around her shoulders, her skirt was crumpled around her waist and Sam's lean hips were wedged between her naked thighs. She looked shameless...wanton...and sexy.

The jolt of sensation that tingled through her had to be from anxiety. Considering the circumstances, it would be absolutely unthinkable if it were from anything else. They were in the home of a criminal, at the mercy of a hulk with a gun. They were risking Sam's undercover job, her family's catering contract, maybe even their lives...

"Are you folks done now?" came a gravelly voice from the doorway.

Audra summoned up a startled scream and unwrapped her legs from Sam's back. "Oh, my God!" she exclaimed, twitching her skirt down.

Sam swore and jerked upright, keeping his back to the doorway as he fastened his pants. "Hey, man," he muttered. "Do you mind?"

There was no suspicion on the face of the guard, only a leering smile. "Nah," he drawled as he escorted them to their van. "I don't mind at all."

## Chapter 7

"Blue is definitely your color," Judy said, whipping another dress from the rack to hold in front of Audra. "Look how it brings out the color of your eyes."

"I like the red silk," Geraldine said. "It would look sexy as hell with her figure." She glanced around the store, then snagged a chair from beside the wall. Groaning, she grasped the arms and carefully eased herself down. "Might as well flaunt it while you've got it, Audra."

"Oh, pooh," Judy said, rolling her eyes. "This is only your first baby, Geraldine. And carrying them is the easy part. The minute they're born, they start to talk back."

"Easy, she says. I've got more than a month to go and I haven't seen my feet in weeks."

"You'll get your figure back in no time."

"Are you kidding? Did you notice the looks I got when we passed that sports store on the other side of the mall? The clerks probably figured I was trying to shoplift a basketball."

Audra smiled. "You look beautiful, Gerri. Your happiness shines right through—"

"The blubber," Geraldine finished, rubbing the mound on her lap. "Well, that's what I get for marrying a sexy man."

Audra's smile turned into a laugh. "Sorry, Gerri, despite the evidence in front of us, I just can't think of my brother as sexy."

"I should hope not! But speaking of the male species, from what I've heard, you'd better watch yourself around Sam." She wiggled her eyebrows. "I was going to burn my maternity clothes when I'm done with them, but I'll save them for you—" She broke off, her hand going to her mouth. "Oh, my God," she mumbled. "Audra, are you..."

"Am I what?"

"Not that there's anything wrong with it. After all, you two are about to get married anyway and these things do happen."

"You think I'm..." Audra shook her head quickly. "No. I'm not pregnant."

Geraldine wiggled her eyebrows again. "Are you sure?"

"There is absolutely no possibility."

"They're in a hurry because they're in love, that's all," Judy said. "From what I've seen, Sam can't keep his hands off her."

"Mmm, I remember those days." Geraldine sighed. "Jake was so passionate. We tried out every piece of furniture in the house."

*Every* piece of furniture? Audra wondered. Sam had been on top of her in her bed and on the floor, and she knew he wasn't averse to trying out the kitchen. Without warning, the image of herself sprawled beneath Sam on a glass-topped table sprang into her mind. What would it be like if they weren't pretending....

That particular question, along with that particular image, had popped up much too often during the week since the visit to the Fitzpatrick estate. She and Sam had both been equally determined to dismiss the way that visit had ended. Apart from complimenting Audra on her quick thinking and her ability to put on a convincing act, Sam hadn't mentioned it again. He'd been all business. He hadn't so much as touched her.

Of course, that's what she wanted, wasn't it?

Well, wasn't it?

This entire situation was getting more confusing by the day.

She wanted her family to accept the engagement, and then resented it when they did. She wanted Sam to stay away from her, and then was frustrated when he complied.

How could it have meant nothing to him? She'd tried to push it out of her mind, but night after night, it replayed in her dreams. The cool, slick table, the mirrors reflecting their image, Sam's hard body moving between her thighs...

But in her dreams, they didn't have an audience. And neither of them was pretending.

"Audra, are you blushing?" Judy asked.

She glanced up quickly. The three-way mirror in the corner showed two bright spots of color in her cheeks. "It's warm in here, that's all," she said, taking the dress from her sister-in-law and putting it back on the rack. "This outfit is too extravagant. It isn't the kind of thing I usually wear."

"That's the whole point. No offense, Audra, but I've been itching for an excuse for years to get you a change of wardrobe."

"There's nothing wrong with my clothes."

Judy put her arm around her shoulders in a sisterly hug. "Honey, you've been hiding."

"I don't know what you mean."

Judy caught the excess fabric at the waist of Audra's cotton sundress and bunched it in her fist. "You've got a dynamite figure under there, but you don't want anyone to notice."

"Loose clothes are more comfortable."

"Then why don't you wear your hair loose?"

"It would fall into the food when I'm cooking."

"Judy's right," Geraldine said. "You've been hiding the fact that you're an attractive woman because you've been so determined not to attract a man."

"That's ridiculous."

"I'm not criticizing you, Audra. Heaven knows, considering what you went through with Ryan, it's perfectly understandable that you'd be cautious about letting yourself get close to any man again. Your clothes and hair were just your way of putting out a message that said, 'hands off.'"

There was enough truth in what she said to make Audra uncomfortable. She eased the bunched fabric from Judy's hand and brushed out the wrinkles. "I never thought of it that way. I wasn't aware that my appearance was that bad."

"If you started wearing coveralls and army boots, it wouldn't make any difference how I feel about you," Judy said softly. "Don't you see? It's not your appearance that concerns me, it's the reason behind it."

Geraldine nodded. "We're your sisters. We want to see you happy."

"I haven't been unhappy."

"Oh, Audra, you've been burying your heart," Judy said. "You've been hiding it away the same way you've been hiding your looks. Now that you've found Sam, you don't have to be afraid to let it show."

"But—"

"It's not just her pregnancy that's making Geraldine glow. It's love." Her smile turned wistful. "Go ahead and enjoy those feelings, Audra. I can't think of anyone who deserves a second chance more."

"Oh, no," Geraldine said, reaching into her sleeve for a tissue, her eyes brimming.

Audra bent down beside Geraldine's chair, immediately concerned. "What's wrong?"

"It's Judy's fault. She should know better."

"What?"

"She means I got mushy," Judy explained.

"Don't mind me." Geraldine waved her hand. "It's just hormones. I cry at everything these days. Pictures on baby-food jars. Long-distance commercials. Country songs. I've become a complete marshmallow."

Judy dug into her purse for a fresh tissue and handed it to Geraldine. "It's downright embarrassing. I can't take her anywhere."

"Maybe you'd feel better at home," Audra began. "With all

the work I have to do, we could postpone this shopping trip 'til some other time.''

''Oh, no you don't.'' Geraldine blew her nose. ''You're not getting out of it this easily. We're on a mission.''

''Mission?''

''We're not leaving here until you buy a dress that's going to knock Sam Tucker's socks off.''

''But—''

''I know, I know,'' Judy said. ''You've probably already gotten him out of his socks, if those looks he's been giving you are any indication.''

Oh, yes. She'd seen him when much, much more than his feet had been bare. Somehow it didn't seem fair that he had made such an indelible impression on her when she didn't appear to affect him at all. He probably hadn't been losing any sleep imagining *her* in that room with the mirrors.

Geraldine gave a watery laugh. ''You're blushing again, Audra. Whatever are you thinking about?''

''Save it for later,'' Judy declared, snatching the blue dress from the rack, along with half a dozen others. She gave them to Audra, turned her around and gave her a gentle shove toward the fitting rooms. ''After this place, we have an appointment at the hairdresser's.''

Sam kept his gaze fixed on the road, his hands gripping the wheel so hard his knuckles were white.

He didn't want to take Audra to the barbecue at her parents' house. He didn't want to make pleasant conversation with her father and her mother and pretend he was about to become part of their big happy family. He didn't know how he was going to get through another evening of playing the devoted fiancé when what he really wanted was to turn the car around, take her back to his apartment and make her naked.

She shifted, crossing her legs, and the sound of her skin sliding together made him grind his teeth. She wasn't wearing any stockings again. Was it a concession to the heat, or was she trying to drive him crazy?

Her legs had been bare last week. Which was why that impromptu charade in Fitzpatrick's conference room had looked so convincing. The way her naked skin had flashed as she'd wrapped those long legs around his hips...the heat of her thighs...the breathless moans as she'd arched to meet his rhythm...

Faking sex had been the only option he could think of at the time. It had worked like a charm, too. But it was a good thing they'd finished so quickly. Another thirty seconds and they wouldn't have been faking.

It should have been laughable. He'd been clumsy and awkward, with all the finesse of a grunting teenager on a drunken dare. There'd been nothing seductive about the way he'd pounced on Audra with no warning. And the things he'd said. *Oh, baby. Oh, yeah. You're so hot and tight....* He grimaced. Geez, real smooth, Tucker. She probably thought he was an idiot.

He'd kept busy for a week, hoping that by concentrating on his job his preoccupation with Audra would start to fade. He'd drawn up a detailed floor plan of the Fitzpatrick house, listed all his observations about the security system and his plans for the day of the wedding and given everything to Xavier, along with the videotape of the grounds.

Despite Xavier's continuing reservations about Sam's involvement in this case, he was pleased with the progress so far. And why shouldn't he be? Sam's cover was firmly established, he was exactly where he wanted to be and had already gathered invaluable information. Rumors were rampant about the heavy hitters who were making arrangements to be in Chicago for the weekend of the Fitzpatrick wedding. Even the chronically logical Xavier was admitting to a gut feeling that something big was in the works. Now more than ever it was essential that Sam stay on the inside.

So he couldn't take Audra home and show her how he really made love, no matter how much he enjoyed the sound of her skin sliding together....

"Did Nathan call you?" Audra asked.

"What?"

"My brother. Mom said he was going to ask for your help setting up the financial program on his computer."

One at a time, he pulled his hands off the wheel and wiped his palms on his pants. "We did that yesterday."

"Oh. How did it go?"

"No problem. He learns fast, so he was working on his own by the time we finished."

"So you didn't have to fake your expertise?"

"I have plenty of expertise. There's a hell of a difference between faking it and doing it for real."

She shifted to face him, her eyebrows lifting. "I didn't mean to offend you."

It wasn't his computer expertise he'd been thinking about. "I got interested in computers after seeing the way Lieutenant Jones uses them. Xavier's the real expert."

"From what you've told me, he sounds like a demanding man to work for."

"He is. We don't always see eye to eye, but he's a good cop. We go back a long way."

"What made you decide to go into police work, Sam?"

As it had so many times before with her, the truth was there on the tip of his tongue, waiting to be spoken. He eased to a stop at a red light and turned to look at her, giving her part of the answer. "I met Xavier when I was a teenager. He..." Sam paused, considering the word to use. "He encouraged me to consider law enforcement as a career."

She tilted her head, and a lock of hair slid over her bare shoulder. It seemed brighter somehow, with golden highlights shining from each pale curl. It wasn't twisted into her usual braid or knot today. Instead, it flowed in sensuous abandon, reminding him of how it had looked spread out on her pillow....

"What did you do to your hair?" he asked.

She started, her hand going to her head. "I, um, had it trimmed this afternoon. Judy and Geraldine kind of talked me into it."

"It looks good."

"Thanks. It feels strange."

He lifted his hand, sliding his fingers through the lock that draped her shoulder. "It feels good."

"Thanks," she repeated. She moistened her lips. "The hairdresser gave me a conditioning treatment while I was there."

His fingers brushed her shoulder and his gaze dropped to the dress she was wearing. It was blue. She often wore blue, but he'd never seen her in this shade before. It was the color of the evening sky just before the stars came out, the same color as her eyes. He ran his thumb across a narrow strap where it rested against her collarbone. The fabric was more supple than the crisp cotton she usually wore. It draped gracefully over the swell of her breasts, dipping just far enough to reveal the shadow of her cleavage. He vividly remembered the taste of that spot. He remembered how he'd pressed his lips there and stroked his tongue over her skin…

"Sam?"

His gaze lowered farther. The soft fabric fitted snugly to her waist and hips, making his palms tingle with the urge to run his hands along those curves. The dress ended well above her knees, revealing the long, slim legs that had felt like heaven locked around him—

"Sam, the light's green."

Damn, he thought, whipping his gaze back to the road. Maybe she really was trying to drive him crazy.

Ten minutes later, Sam pulled up at the curb half a block away from the McPherson house. The quiet, tree-shaded street was lined with cars tonight. He offered his hand to Audra as he opened her door. "Looks like someone's having a party," he said, trying his best to keep his gaze off her legs.

She glanced around at the parked cars. "You're right. I wonder who…" She broke off, her forehead furrowing. "That looks like Christopher's station wagon. Mom didn't say that he was going to be here tonight."

He tucked her hand into the crook of his arm as they started down the sidewalk. "Maybe he just dropped by."

"There's Geraldine's black Jeep," she said. "And Nathan's pickup. I hope nothing's wrong."

"Someone would have phoned you, wouldn't they?"

"Yes, you're probably right, but if nothing's wrong, why would everyone be here..." Her steps slowed. "Oh, no."

"What is it?"

"I should have known. That's why they took me shopping today."

"Who?"

"Judy and Geraldine. God, I'm so gullible. Now I know why they made me promise to wear this dress tonight." She stopped in front of her parents' place and looked back toward Sam's car. "It's not too late. Maybe we could leave before anyone sees us."

He moved in front of her before she could retreat. "Audra, would you mind explaining what you're talking about?"

"I hope I'm mistaken, but I suspect that you're about to meet the rest of my family."

"What's wrong with that? Don't you think I can convince them we're engaged?"

She gave him a look. "Believe me, Sam, I have no doubt about your acting skills."

"Then what's the problem?"

"It's just that I'd hoped everyone would be too busy to do this." She gestured toward the house. The scent of burning charcoal floated over the backyard fence, along with the sound of laughter and clinking glasses. "I should have known we wouldn't get away that easily. They're throwing us an engagement party."

"But that's good, isn't it?"

She hesitated, glancing back at his car. "Well..."

"Auntie Audra, Auntie Audra!" A child with strawberry-blond pigtails burst through the McPhersons' front door. She ran across the lawn toward them, ribbons from her ruffled dress trailing behind her. "Come and see the balloons," she said, grabbing Audra's hand. "I did the pink ones."

The door banged open again and a baby in a striped cap and overalls toddled after the girl. "Au-ba!" he screeched. "Au-ba!"

"J.B. popped one when he threw it on the barbecue," the girl went on, tugging Audra forward. "He wouldn't stop crying until Uncle Nathan hung him upside down. Are you the hunk?" she asked, turning a pair of wide blue eyes up to Sam. "Auntie Judy said—"

"Sam," Audra said, muffling the girl's words by pressing her to her stomach in a quick hug, "this is my niece, Barbara Mc-Pherson. She's Christopher's oldest."

"Au-ba!" The baby collided with Sam's leg and took a death grip on his trousers. "Au-ba."

"And that's J.B.," she added. "His youngest."

A short, worried-looking woman raced out of the house. "Barbara, have you seen..." She paused, her face breaking into a relieved smile. "Oh, hi, Audra."

"I've got him, Esther." Audra released her niece and bent down to detach the baby from Sam's leg. "I see you're up to your old tricks, J.B.," she said, lifting the baby into her arms. "Shame on you, running away from your mother again."

The baby chortled and slapped his pudgy fists against Audra's cheeks. "Au-ba."

Sam felt a tug on his hand. He glanced down to see the pig-tailed girl staring up at him. "You're Sam-I-am," she said. "Sam-I-am."

"What?"

She launched into a nonsensical rhyme about eating preferences, then grinned, revealing a missing front tooth.

"It's Dr. Seuss," Audra explained. *"Green Eggs and Ham."* Her eyes widened and she jumped to the edge of the sidewalk. "Look out!"

Wheels rumbled hollowly. Sam barely had time to snatch Audra's niece out of the way before two freckle-faced boys raced past on their in-line skates.

"Wayne! Peter!" A tall, slim, bespectacled man was striding down the front walk. "You boys get back here this instant!"

The girl wriggled out of Sam's grip and skipped back across the lawn. "Uncle Gordon, I did the pink balloons. J.B. broke one.

Grandma!'' She changed directions as Constance McPherson stepped out of the house. ''Did you see my tooth?''

Constance admired the gap in her granddaughter's smile as she tied the trailing ribbons at the back of her dress into a neat bow. Straightening up, she waved at Sam and Audra. ''Well, don't just stand there. The circus is in full swing.''

Sam glanced at Audra. ''The circus?''

''What we affectionately call a gathering of McPhersons, but don't let that mislead you.''

He dodged to the side as a soccer ball went whizzing past his head. ''Oh?''

''It's not as orderly or dignified as a circus.'' She propped the baby on her hip and gave Sam a rueful smile. ''Welcome to the family.''


Sam leaned against the oak tree beside the garage and scanned the crowd. Well, the party had been good for one thing anyway. With all these people around, he'd had plenty to distract him from his unacceptable thoughts of Audra. He caught a glimpse of blue and shifted to get a better look. She was sitting on the edge of a picnic table, a baby bouncing on her knee while she laughed at something her sister-in-law, Geraldine the pregnant one, was saying.

Although she'd been reluctant about staying when she'd first realized what was going on, it hadn't taken long before she was right in the middle of things. He couldn't remember seeing her looking so relaxed before. In spite of the chaos around her, she was obviously right at home surrounded by her family.

And what a family. He'd met the rest of her brothers, along with their wives and kids, uncles and aunts and a grandmother. He'd lost count half an hour after arriving, but there had to be over three dozen people named McPherson in this yard. The only ones who weren't here were Norm and Judy. Sam knew that Norm hadn't gotten past his initial distrust of him—he hoped their absence wasn't an indication of trouble to come.

''Want a beer?''

Sam turned his head as a stocky young man with a blond pony-tail moved under the tree and offered him a glistening can. "Sure. Thanks, Nathan."

"I've finished entering the books from the last five years," Nathan said, popping the top on his own can and taking a sip. "I thought I'd set up some links to the calendar program."

"Sounds like a good idea."

"Yeah. Mom wants to be able to access my files from her laptop. Thanks again for helping me get set up."

"No problem."

"She mentioned you'll be helping Audra with the wedding that's coming up next week."

"Uh-huh."

"That's shaping up to be one of the biggest jobs we've done, so we can use every extra pair of hands we can get. It was lucky for us that the other wedding we'd had booked for that date can-celled when we got the Fitzpatrick contract."

Luck? Somehow Sam doubted that. "I've already been in touch with the equipment rental firm you use," he said. "They'll supply the awnings and furniture, but the client wants us to set it up ourselves."

"That's more work for us, but more money, too. I don't know if Norm talked to you about your salary—"

"I'm just helping out the family," he said. "The money isn't important."

"So you're doing all right financially?"

Sam opened his beer and lifted the can for a long swallow, watching Nathan over the rim. During the course of the evening, he'd had a variation of this conversation with each of the other four McPherson brothers who were here. "Yes. I had a good severance package from my last job, and it shouldn't take me long to find another."

Nathan nodded toward the group of children around Audra. "She's always been great with kids."

"She seems to enjoy them, all right."

"Funny thing with kids. You get really protective about them, you know?"

"So I've heard."

"Well, the thing is, I've always thought of Audra as my baby sister. She's only two years younger than me, but I guess because she's a woman, I feel I should look out for her. Women tend to get carried away by their emotions."

"I understand that, Nathan."

"She went through a bad time a few years ago, and I'd hate to see her hurt again." He gave Sam a long, level stare. "You seem like a decent guy, Sam, but even though you're marrying my sister, I'll still be looking out for her. I hope you'll treat her right."

He'd had four variations on this topic, too. Five, if he counted the subtle interrogation he'd had from Audra's father the last time he'd been here. The female McPhersons seemed to have accepted the engagement, but the men were trying to be more cautious.

That's what a family was supposed to do, though. They cared about each other, they celebrated the good times and gave support during the bad. And they protected everyone who belonged to them. "You have my word," he said, holding Nathan's gaze. "I'll take good care of her."

Nathan lifted his beer in a silent toast, then moved away. Sam watched him thoughtfully for a moment before returning his gaze to Audra.

She'd told him she would never marry. She'd been insistent about that all along, but now that he'd seen her with her family, he wondered whether it was true. As Nathan had said, she was good with kids. She had a natural warmth, and if it hadn't been for her fiancé's accident, she probably would have been bouncing her own baby on her knee right now.

Was she still in love with Ryan? Was that why she was so determined not to let another man take his place? She was adamant about being independent, and she was determined to open up a business of her own...but she would never be truly alone as long as she had her family behind her.

Sam, on the other hand, was completely alone. He liked it that way. And he didn't belong here.

He'd known that from the start. Even before he'd brought Audra into this case with him, he'd known they were worlds apart. The warmth and love that glowed from this gathering were meant for her, not him. The fraud he was pulling off went much deeper than the case. These people were all so upstanding, and had such solid roots and good character, they made him feel dirty just because they were so clean.

The baby on Audra's lap grabbed a handful of her hair. She laughed, untangling her curls before she pressed a kiss to the tiny fingers and handed the baby to one of her sisters-in-law. Slipping off the table, she looked around until she spotted Sam, then wove her way toward him. "Well, have you had enough yet?" she asked.

"I'm ready to leave whenever you are." Automatically, he put his arm around her waist, splaying his fingers over the curve of her hip as they started toward the house.

"You made a real hit with Barbara."

"Who?"

"My niece with the missing tooth."

"Oh, right. The Dr. Seuss fan."

"It's hard to tell the players without a program," she said. "What were you and Nathan talking about just now? It looked serious."

"Man stuff."

She dug her elbow into his ribs. "Don't you dare start that. I've had to put up with that attitude from my brothers all my life, and I'm not about to tolerate it in...my..." She stopped, her face flushed as she looked up at him.

"In the man you're going to marry?" he finished for her. He saw the denial in her eyes and spoke quickly before anyone else could notice. "Nathan was just doing his brotherly duty, making sure I'll treat you right."

"He *what?*"

Smiling, Sam stroked her cheek, his fingers brushing the same curls that the baby had been playing with. "What were you and Geraldine laughing about a few minutes ago?"

Her lips twitched. "Woman stuff."

"Care to elaborate?"

"Not on your life. There are some things that—" She broke off, her forehead creasing. "I wonder what's going on."

Sam became aware of a commotion near the house. Constance was talking to two of Audra's brothers, her expression grim. John moved through the crowd toward her, listened for a moment, then immediately took her into his arms.

"Something's wrong," Audra said, pulling away from Sam.

He caught her hand and moved with her toward her parents. A hush was quickly spreading over the yard.

For a second, Sam thought that someone had discovered who he was, that they were about to declare him a fraud and throw him out. But that thought was dismissed as quickly as it had come up. No one was looking at him. Their attention was focused on Audra's mother.

"I just got a call from Norm," Constance said, her voice unsteady in the silence. "He and Judy didn't come over tonight because they'd been waiting for Jimmy to get home. They'd had an argument with him, so they'd thought he was just taking time to cool off but—" Her chin quivered. Pressing her hand to her mouth, she looked at her husband.

"Jimmy left a note," John said. "He's run away."

"Dear Lord, he's only fifteen." Constance leaned against John, blinking back her tears. "Norm's worried sick."

"He'll be all right, Mom." Jake stepped up, placing his hand on his mother's shoulder. "He hasn't been gone that long."

She shook her head. "Jimmy left this morning. It's been more than twelve hours. They thought he was with one of his friends, but when it got dark they called everyone and no one knows where he is. When I think about all the things that could happen to him..."

"We'll find him," Christopher said, moving to stand beside his twin.

The silence was swallowed by a growing hum of questions and desperate reassurances. One of the babies began to cry. Constance wiped her eyes and looked around until her gaze found Audra. "I'm sorry to ruin your party like this—"

"Oh Mom, don't worry about that," she said immediately.

"But we wanted this to be so special for you. For both of you," she added, looking at Sam. "Oh, God. I don't know what to do. Jimmy will never forgive us if we call the police. But where do we start looking?"

He shouldn't interfere, Sam thought as he watched Audra's mother fight her tears. As far as everyone here knew, he was only an out-of-work computer programmer. His main concern was that they accept his engagement to Audra, that was all. He wasn't really part of this family. Their problems were their own business, and as long as it didn't put a crimp in his plans to work the Fitzpatrick wedding, he should let them handle this trouble themselves.

Audra tightened her grip on Sam's hand and looked up at him. Her eyes were filled with worry, her lips pressed into a thin line, as if she were holding back the plea she wanted to make.

It would be stupid to risk blowing the cover he'd gone to such lengths to establish. The kid was probably just sulking. He'd turn up eventually. No kid in his right mind would want to run away when he had such a solid, loving family behind him.

The memory took him unprepared. The cold, greasy alley behind a warehouse, the moldy mattress he'd dragged into a secluded corner, the long nights when he'd been too frightened to go out and too hungry to stay where he was...

Sam had been less than twelve the first time he'd run away. It had taken almost a week for his mother to notice he'd gone. He'd returned on his own that time—he hadn't been quick enough to steal, and he hadn't been desperate enough to accept the offers from those well-dressed men who cruised the neighborhood in cars with tinted glass.

The second time he'd left, he'd been more prepared. He'd been a year older, and he'd thought he'd been wiser, but after a month his money ran out and he learned the hard way about poaching on gang turf.

Jimmy wouldn't know what was out there. He was an innocent. He'd be easy prey for the lowlifes who lived on the street...

Sam clenched his jaw, took a deep breath and stepped forward. "Maybe I can help."

# Chapter 8

Holding a needlepoint pillow to her chest, Audra tucked her legs underneath her and curled into a corner of her couch. Rain pattered against the window, glimmering in the glow of the street-light on the corner. The living room was filled with shadows, the lamp on the end table unable to hold back the gloom entirely. Over the sound of the rain she could hear Sam's voice, deep and firm, as he talked on the phone with yet another of his colleagues at the police department. Although he spoke quietly, her senses were raw enough for her to hear every word. Hospital. Morgue.

It had been more than two days since Norm's call had put an end to her engagement party. Almost three days had passed since anyone had seen her nephew. He had to be all right, didn't he?

Judy was barely hanging on. The change in her had been ter-rible to see. Her ready smiles, her quick, flippant manner, all her warmth was buried beneath a suffocating layer of worry. With Jimmy's younger sister Jennifer staying close by her side, Judy hadn't budged from her vigil beside the phone each time Audra had been over there.

But if Judy was in a bad way, Norm was worse. His eyes were

puffy from lack of sleep, his jaw bristled with unshaven gray whiskers and his hands shook from all the coffee he'd been drinking. He hadn't said much about the argument that had precipitated Jimmy's decision to leave, but it was plain to see that Norm blamed himself.

There it was, the flip side of love, that terrible vulnerability you opened yourself up to when you opened your heart. The blame, the guilt, the questions that could never be answered, the doubts that would always haunt you.

Would things have been different if you'd listened more closely? Or if you hadn't lost your temper? Or if you'd known what he was planning, if you'd picked up on the signals, if you'd found the note earlier...

She closed her eyes, burying her face in the pillow. She knew what Norm was going through. She'd been there herself with Ryan.

Sam hung up the phone. A minute later, Audra felt a gentle touch on her hair.

"It's late," he said. "I'll make the rest of the calls from my place so you can get some sleep,"

Rubbing her forehead, she looked up. "No, I'm fine. What did you find out?"

"Nothing so far. It looks as if Jimmy doesn't want to be found. But I've put the word out, and there are a lot of people looking for him."

"Thanks." She caught his hand. "I really appreciate all that you're doing."

For a second he started to smile at her, but then he stepped away and shoved his hands into his pockets. "I made a few phone calls. It's no big deal."

"Yes it is. I know you didn't want to get involved."

He lifted his shoulders. "As your fiancé it would be expected of me."

Why didn't he want to admit he was doing something nice? From the moment he'd offered his help to her family, he'd not only channelled their collective energy into an organized search, he'd given them hope.

Audra's brothers had been ready to jump into their cars and start randomly cruising the streets, but Sam had convinced them to make a plan first. So they'd cleared the children and the left-over food off the picnic table and drawn up lists of Jimmy's friends and places where he might go. They'd rounded up all the recent pictures of Jimmy, details about the clothes he was wearing, his habits and mannerisms. Esther and Christopher photocopied posters, Geraldine and Jake took care of the phone and Nathan kept track of all the information they gathered.

Throughout it all, Sam was there, steady as a rock. As far as anyone else knew, Norm was the one who brought the police into the search for Jimmy, but Audra knew that behind the scenes Sam was making full use of his connections. For someone who kept maintaining that he was only playing a role, he was already becoming an important part of the family.

On the other hand, the sooner Jimmy was found, the sooner the family and their catering business would get back to normal.

Was that why he was going out of his way to help them? To ensure that the Fitzpatrick job would go smoothly?

*That's the whole point of what we're doing.* He'd said that to her before, just before he'd given her the engagement ring.

She turned the ring around on her finger, rubbing her thumb over the pattern of apple blossoms. It would be foolish to think there might be anything more between her and Sam than the Fitzpatrick case. Her feelings were confused enough already.

Sam sat on the arm of the couch, reaching for a brownie from the plate she'd left on the coffee table. "I can't understand why the kid would want to run away in the first place."

"He and his father haven't been getting along well lately."

There was a brief silence while Sam turned his attention to eating the brownie. When he finished, he crossed his arms and looked at Audra. "Does Norm ever get rough with him?"

"What do you..." Her eyes widened. "No, of course not."

"Don't look so offended. It's one of the first things I'd check into if I was the one assigned to his case."

She shook her head fiercely. "Norm has never raised his hand to either of his children. No one in my family would."

"That's what I figured, from what I saw of the way the kids were treated at that party the other night, but you can never know for sure."

"He might be strict, and he can be an opinionated pain sometimes, but Judy and their children are the center of my brother's life. He'd never hurt them. If anything, he goes too far the other way."

"What do you mean?"

"It probably comes from being the oldest. He's always tended to be overprotective. Jimmy doesn't want to be treated like a child anymore."

"Some kids mature early."

"Jimmy might be big for his age, and he might think he's fifteen going on twenty, but inside he's still just a boy." She curled more tightly into the corner of the couch. "He must be so scared by now."

Sam slid off the arm of the couch to sit beside her. "Why weren't he and his father getting along?"

"It's an old argument. Jimmy has always wanted to become an artist. Norm and Judy thought it was just one of those childhood fancies, and that he'd grow out of it, but lately he's been letting his schoolwork slide so he can spend all his time with his painting. The more Norm got after him, the more rebellious Jimmy got."

"From the artwork I saw on the side of Norm's van, the kid's good."

"Yes, he is. He did those two paintings beside the window."

Sam studied them for a few minutes, then pursed his lips in a low whistle. "He *is* good."

"The problem is that Norm has always hoped that his son would join the family business." She sighed. "I can understand how that would frustrate Jimmy. His parents mean well, but he doesn't want to have his life controlled by everyone else's good intentions. He loves them, but he wants his independence.''

"Sounds a bit like you.''

"In a way, I suppose we both find the family overbearing at times. That's probably why I have such a soft spot for Jimmy.''

He stretched his arm along the back of the couch and brushed his fingertips across her shoulder. "Somehow I can't picture you as a rebellious teenager.''

She tilted her head to meet his gaze. "Oh, my rebellion was delayed a decade. When I was younger, I did everything that was expected of me. I never argued. My life was all mapped out for me and I never thought twice when I went straight from the protection of my parents to my fiancé.''

"You couldn't have been much more than twenty when you got engaged.''

"Ryan and I met the day I started kindergarten and were going steady by the time we were in high school.'' She turned Sam's ring around on her finger. "He proposed on my twenty-first birthday.''

"Your family must have liked him.''

"They adored him. He was in and out of the house so much when we were younger, they treated him like one of my brothers. They weren't surprised in the least when we told them we were going to get married. I had always assumed we would end up together.''

"It sounds as if you were suited to each other.''

"We were. We'd made so many plans. A bunch of kids, the house with the tire swing in the yard and a dog in front of the fireplace. But then he had his accident...'' She paused. "I had to change my plans.''

He cupped her shoulder, his fingers warm and reassuring. "I'm sorry, Audra.''

"He didn't want me to stay with him. I told you that, didn't I?''

"Yes, you did.''

"At first I thought it was because he wanted to be noble, that he loved me too much to have me see him in that wheelchair."

"That's understandable. No man would want to be pitied."

"I didn't pity him. I loved him. But he hated having me take care of him because it turned around his entire perception of who I was. He was like my father, always assuming that it was his duty to be the one to take care of me. I hadn't realized just how helpless he considered me to be."

"You're far from helpless, Audra. I have a lot of respect for your competence."

She sighed, leaning her cheek against his knuckles. It was so easy to talk to Sam. He was so direct and matter-of-fact, he listened willingly to things her family was still careful to tiptoe around. "Sometimes I wonder whether things would have turned out differently if I hadn't stayed."

"Why?"

"Maybe someone else would have noticed the warning signs. I was so busy trying to pay the bills and arrange his nursing care that I didn't see them. I honestly didn't realize what was happening."

The couch dipped as he shifted closer. "Audra, what are you talking about?"

"At first we argued all the time. He didn't want to be dependent, but I couldn't imagine simply deserting him when he needed me. I believed I knew what was best for him. Love meant forever, so I stuck by him and didn't let myself see how it was killing him inside." She tried to swallow past the lump in her throat. This was the point where she usually stopped talking. For five years she'd kept this inside because no one wanted to hear the rest.

Sam tugged aside the pillow she'd been clutching and covered her hand with his. "Go on."

She felt the prick of tears behind her eyes. It wasn't from pain—that had grown dull long ago. It was from Sam's offer of sympathy. She inhaled unsteadily. "Before Ryan's accident, he'd always taken pride in his athletic abilities. He'd thrived on competition, on being the best. So he never adjusted to life without the use of his legs.''

''It would be hard for anyone.''

''I tried to get him into therapy, but he wouldn't go. I tried to get counsellors and psychologists out to the house, but he refused to talk to them and only got more agitated. His doctor finally put him on tranquilizers, to ease him through the transition, he said, and for a while it seemed to work. Ryan's moods settled down and his outlook improved.''

He squeezed her fingers, an invitation, a silent gesture of support.

''Ryan hadn't been taking his tranquilizers, he'd been hoarding them,'' she continued. ''He was always very meticulous. He found out how much he'd need for a lethal dose, then waited until he'd accumulated four times that amount. He chose a time when I was at work and no one was due to visit. He filled the bathtub to the rim, pulled himself into it and swallowed his pills. He slipped beneath the surface of the water as soon as he lost consciousness, so he drowned before the pills could actually kill him.''

Sam swore under his breath, a short, rough expletive, yet his touch was achingly gentle as he reached out and lifted her onto his lap. His warmth surrounded her as he cradled her head against his shoulder. ''I had no idea. I'd assumed he died because of his injuries.''

''His mother swears it was an accidental overdose, but there's no doubt in my mind it was suicide. I found his note before I found him. And I've always wondered whether I could have saved him if I'd come home earlier. Or whether he wouldn't have done it at all if I hadn't stayed with him in the first place.''

''It wasn't your fault, Audra.''

''But I hadn't realized how much he hated being dependent on me, or how stifling our love was to him.''

''It wasn't your fault,'' he repeated firmly. ''It was Ryan's decision, not yours.''

She pressed her face to his collar, taking comfort in the solid strength of his embrace. "I went for counselling after the funeral, and I realize how complex suicide is. In my head, I know I'm not to blame, but in my heart I still have doubts."

"That's understandable. It's never easy to come to terms with a tragedy like that. Death is hard enough to accept, but when the death is by choice, it's many times worse."

"My family still won't accept it. They're like Ryan's mother, they insist his death was accidental. They're stuck in denial and just can't handle the truth. So they keep pushing me to try again, as if marriage is some kind of horse that threw me and I'm supposed to climb back up on it for my own good."

"They care about you. I saw that at the party."

"And I care about them, but I'll never get married," she said. "I know how destructive love can be, and the lengths Ryan was driven to because he couldn't endure being dependent."

"That's why you want to be on your own, isn't it? It's because of the consequences of Ryan's dependence, not yours."

God, he understood, she thought. He really understood. Within the space of the few weeks they'd known each other, he'd grasped what her family never could. It wasn't only her own pain that made her vow never to commit to a man again, it was Ryan's pain. Deep down, she was afraid of ending up as vulnerable and desperate to escape as he'd been.

Sam moved his hand over her back in slow, soothing circles, then caught her chin and angled her face toward his. "It must be hell for you to pretend you're engaged to me. When I came up with the idea, I didn't know what I was asking."

There was such honest sympathy in his gaze, she felt the knot of old guilt inside her start to loosen. "It's okay, Sam. You couldn't possibly have known."

"If there's anything I can do to make it easier..."

"You just have," she whispered.

He stroked her hair back from her face, tucking it behind her ears. Silence stretched out between them as he continued to hold her gaze. Then as if it were the most natural thing in the world, he leaned toward her and settled his lips over hers.

# Yours FREE...
## when you reply today

This delicate book locket is a necklace with a difference... The hinged book is decorated with a romantic floral motive and opens to reveal two oval frames for your most cherished photographs. Respond today and it's yours free.

---

# Yes! Please send me my two FREE books and a welcome gift

**PLACE FREE GIFT SEAL HERE**

**Yes!** I have placed my free gift seal in the space provided above. Please send me my two free books along with my welcome gift. I understand I am under no obligation to purchase any books, as explained on the back and opposite page. I am over 18 years of age.

S9JI

Surname (Mrs/Ms/Miss/Mr) _____ Initials_____

Address _____

_____

_____

_____ Postcode _____

## HOW THE READER SERVICE WORKS

Accepting the free books places you under no obligation to buy anything. You may keep the books and gift and return the despatch note marked "cancel". If we don't hear from you, about a month later we will send you 4 brand new books and invoice you for only £2.70* each. That's the complete price – there is no extra charge for postage and packing. You may cancel at any time, otherwise every month we'll send you 4 more books, which you may either purchase or return – the choice is yours.

*Terms and prices subject to change without notice.

The Reader Service™
FREEPOST CN81
CROYDON
CR9 3WZ

The kiss was sweet, his mouth soft and giving. Audra sighed and relaxed in his arms, her hands sliding up his chest until she could feel the steady beat of his heart beneath her palm. Compared to the situations they'd already been in, this kiss could almost be called chaste.

Yet somehow it was more intimate than anything they'd done before.

Too soon, he lifted his head. But he didn't pull away. Instead, he cupped her cheeks in his palms and came back for more.

It was only a kiss, she reassured herself. Not love, not commitment or any of those things she was afraid of, just a kiss. Somewhere in the back of her mind, Audra knew there were reasons she shouldn't do even this much with Sam. Yet it felt too good, too…right to stop. Parting her lips on a sigh, she melted against him.

Sam deepened the kiss slowly, accepting her invitation with a gentle increase in pressure. The tip of his tongue played over her lower lip in a smooth caress, back and forth, almost in, hovering on the edge until he made a low sound of pleasure and eased inside.

She felt his heartbeat accelerate at the same time she felt her own pulse speed up. The comfortable glow that suffused her body warmed to awareness. He slid one hand into her hair, holding her more firmly as he angled his head to press closer. His other hand dropped to her shoulder, coaxing her forward until she slipped her arms around his neck and leaned with him as he reclined against the corner of the couch.

How different this was from that time in her kitchen, when playfulness had led so swiftly to passion. Or that time in the conference room, when he'd been so fast, charging ahead with no preliminaries, giving her no time to think. She'd had no idea that he could be so…tender. So caring. As if they had all the time in the world, as if all his attention, all his energy, were focused on the urge to give her…what? Comfort? Pleasure?

She didn't want to think about what he was giving her any more than she wanted to think about why they shouldn't be doing this. It still felt right. So right, she made no protest when his hand smoothed down her side and closed gently over her breast. The soft moan that rose in her throat surprised her almost as much as the certainty of her response. She arched her back in a wordless request, smiling against Sam's lips when he moved his hand to the middle of her blouse and one by one, unfastened the buttons.

A tremor went through her at the first touch of his fingers on her bare skin. He traced the edge of lace, skimming his thumb over the slope of her breast while his palm rubbed across the center. She felt herself swell into his hand, every nerve tingling. When he pulled her blouse from her skirt and slid his other hand up her back to unfasten her bra, reason and logic shut down completely. All she could do was feel.

He took her breasts with the same focused tenderness he put into his kiss. As his tongue teased and savored her lips, his fingers explored her shape and texture, lifting, rubbing, squeezing in sweet persuasion. She pressed against him, her breath catching on a wave of delight.

"Sam," she whispered. She didn't say anything more. Just his name. But he took it as another invitation. He moved his lips to her ear, grazing his teeth over the lobe in a caress that made her tremble. Shifting her beside him on the cushions, he slid his hand beneath her skirt.

The touch of his fingers on her thigh was electric. Slow heat unfurled inside her. Wants she'd never before suspected, desires she'd never dreamed of, blossomed in delicate pulses of sensation. She threaded her fingers into Sam's hair and pulled his face back to hers. This time she kissed him. She didn't care that she might be awkward or that her experience was no match for his. All she could think about was getting closer.

The eagerness of Audra's response jolted Sam back to full awareness. Her lips sealed over his, her tongue swept into his mouth and the pleasant haze he'd been lost in transformed to urgency. No, it was more than urgency. It was raw need. His blood pounded and his body tightened so insistently his hands shook. His hands. Inside her blouse. Under her skirt.

What the hell was he thinking? He was doing it again, letting his libido overrule his reason. She was merely a means to an end. A civilian. A respectable woman.

He was getting in deeper all the time. He knew he shouldn't have involved himself in her family's problems. And he sure as hell shouldn't have listened as she'd opened up her past to him. The physical thing that he felt for her was hard enough to handle, but now he had let her get close to him in an entirely different way.

There was no excuse this time, none at all. He couldn't claim he was only playing a role. He couldn't pretend there was anything fake about the emotions she'd revealed to him. There was no one else to put on a performance for.

This wasn't part of the plan.

All those thoughts whirled through his brain, demanding his attention, but they faded to insignificance at the impulse to finish what he and Audra had started here. What if he eased the blouse off her shoulders and leaned down to close his lips over that hardened nipple, and moved his hand farther up her thigh and used his thumb and his fingers to make her moan for him, and brought her delicate hand to the front of his jeans and showed her—

Fighting to keep hold of the last shreds of his control, he lifted his head.

Audra's cheeks were flushed, her lips moist. From beneath half-closed lids, her gaze gleamed with arousal. He'd fantasized about her like this. For weeks he'd wondered what it would be like to really hold her, to taste her and touch her as if he had the right...

But he didn't have the right, did he? And he never would.

Gritting his teeth, Sam withdrew his hands from beneath her clothing. "Listen, Audra..."

The flush on her cheeks deepened. She touched her tongue to her swollen lower lip, her gaze steadying on his. A mixture of regret and embarrassment flashed across her face as she pushed away from him and dropped her arms to her sides. "Don't say it."

"What?"

"Don't say you were only pretending, that this was only part of your role."

"I wasn't. I can't deny I'm attracted to you, Audra. You're a desirable woman and I'm a normal man, but this was a mistake."

She tugged the front of her blouse closed, her hands unsteady. "A mistake," she repeated.

"I shouldn't have kissed you. It's late, we're both tired and you were upset. I took advantage—"

"No. You didn't take advantage of me, Sam. I...kissed you, too."

He rubbed his face roughly. She wasn't making this easy. "I apologize. It won't happen again."

She dipped her head without replying and started to refasten her buttons. Her hair swung forward, hiding her expression.

"With the Fitzpatrick wedding coming up in less than a week, we can't let ourselves get confused about the reason for our association—"

"Yes, you've made that abundantly clear. Several times. We definitely don't want to get confused."

He heard the thread of hurt in her voice, and he wanted nothing more than to reach out and take her back into his arms. Pushing himself to his feet abruptly, he walked to the other side of the room. "We can't get involved as long as we're working together. Distractions can be dangerous."

"Distractions," she repeated, her fingers fumbling. She'd misaligned the buttons.

He itched to help her with those buttons. He shoved his hands safely into the back pockets of his jeans. "I didn't mean for things to go so far."

"It was no big deal, Sam. After all, it was just a kiss. I'm twenty-eight years old. It's not as if I haven't done that before."

*Just* a kiss? If she could get his blood pumping with only a kiss, what would it be like if they did more?

The thought was there, in the back of his mind. What if they didn't stop next time? What real harm would it do? Maybe it would be better to relieve the tension between them so they could concentrate on the job—

But this was Audra, the woman who baked bread and bounced babies on her knee. She wasn't the kind of woman who would go for a quick, meaningless tumble on the sofa.

Or would she?

No. He couldn't start thinking that way. He still had another week to get through. He knew what his priorities were here, right?

She raised her head, shaking her hair back from her face as she met his gaze. With her blouse misbuttoned and her cheeks still flushed, she was a tempting mixture of innocence and sensuality. He wavered, taking a step toward her. "Audra, I..."

The telephone on the table beside the lamp shrilled suddenly, drowning out whatever he was going to say.

It was a timely interruption. It was just what he needed to yank him back to reality.

But the hell of it was, Sam didn't know whether or not he was grateful for it.

Smoothing her skirt down awkwardly, Audra reached for the phone. "Hello?" She paused, her hand tightening on the receiver. "Jimmy? My God, *Jimmy!* Where are you?"

It was two in the morning when Sam turned his car into the alley. The rain that had started at sunset had tapered off to a steady drizzle, saturating the muggy air. Puddles gleamed in his headlights, rippling along the pavement between the dark brick walls.

The car nosed over a speed bump and the headlights grazed a neat cement curb. They were behind an upscale mall in an affluent neighborhood, and this alley was cleaner than a lot of streets. There was no trash piled in the corners or graffiti scrawled on the bricks. The flat steel doors that were set into the wall were labeled with neat signs and reinforced with the kind of hardware that would discourage all but the most determined thief.

"He said he'd be watching for us," Audra said, gripping the dashboard as she leaned closer to the windshield. "I wish he hadn't made me promise not to call Norm. He'd want to know Jimmy was all right.''

"The kid obviously didn't want to talk to his father. He trusts you."

She drew her lower lip between her teeth as her brow furrowed. "Poor Jimmy. He sounded so scared."

Sam controlled the urge to snort. Scared? The kid had put Audra and her entire family through hell for the past three days and all the time he'd been perfectly safe, sketching and painting to his heart's content, living comfortably in the back room of an artist's supplies store.

From what Audra had learned on the phone, one of Jimmy's friends had lied—big surprise—when she'd been asked whether she knew where Jimmy was. In the name of friendship and misplaced loyalty, she'd covered for him for days, hiding him in her mother's store. The only reason he'd decided to leave now was because Pamela Stanuck, the store owner, was due back from a buying trip in the morning.

"I'm so relieved that he's all right," Audra said.

"Yeah. He was lucky. A lot of things can happen to a kid on his own."

She rubbed her palms over her arms. "That's what's been driving Judy crazy."

"There it is." Sam braked to a stop beside a rain-soaked sign. "'Pamela's Palette,'" he read. "This is the place."

"Oh, I hope he hasn't changed his mind."

"Probably not. Why else would he have called you?"

"What if he didn't want to wait? What if he's run off again?"

"He wouldn't get far." He nodded toward the end of the alley. "I had Bergstrom put the place under surveillance the minute you got off the phone."

"You *what?* But I promised Jimmy I wouldn't tell anyone else."

"This isn't a game, Audra. We're only humoring the kid so he won't lose face and try running again. Just because he doesn't seem to have come to any harm doesn't mean his luck will hold the next time."

"You're right," she said. "I guess his welfare is more important than his trust. What's one more lie added to all the rest?"

He touched his fingertips to the back of her hand. "You didn't break your word. I was the one who brought in backup."

Her gaze lowered. "Sorry. I didn't mean to sound ungrateful. We all owe you our thanks for what you're doing."

"Let's get the kid home safe before you start thanking me."

The back door of the shop inched open a crack as soon as they stepped from the car. Sam took a firm hold on Audra's elbow to keep her from rushing forward, but as soon as she called Jimmy's name, the door swung wide.

Sam immediately recognized the gangling height and sullen posture of the teenager who stood in the doorway. As Audra fussed over her nephew, Sam checked out the place where the kid had been hiding. Jimmy had had a comfortable setup here, thanks to his friend. But he made no argument about leaving. Stuffing his artwork into a cardboard tube, he hitched his backpack over his shoulder and accompanied his aunt outside.

It all went smoothly until the three of them were in the car and Sam turned onto the street. It seemed Jimmy didn't want to go home after all. He wanted to go to Audra's place.

She twisted around to stare at her nephew. "You can't possibly mean that," she said. "Your parents have been worried sick. I'm not going to hide you at my apartment and let them continue to—"

"You promised you wouldn't tell anyone." Jimmy scowled as Sam met his gaze in the rearview mirror. "I don't know why you had to bring *him* along."

"I was there when you called," Sam said, scowling back at him. "Did you expect your aunt to wander around a dark alley in the middle of the night by herself?"

Jimmy glanced away. "Okay, but I don't want you to tell anyone else. I'm not going home. If you won't let me stay with you, I'll just live on the street."

Audra pressed her lips together and inhaled slowly through her nose, obviously striving for patience. "Jimmy, I understand that you're having a difficult time at home with your father..."

Sam drummed his fingers on the steering wheel as he listened to her try to reason with the boy. The kid wasn't dumb—he'd rather have another comfortable hideout than try to get by on his own. And he was doing a good job of playing on Audra's sympathy, trying to put her in the middle between him and his father. He'd already succeeded to some degree, by choosing to contact her instead of his parents.

There was no way Sam could let Audra get involved any deeper in Jimmy's problems. If she agreed to Jimmy's request and let him stay with her, it would mean she and Sam would have to act engaged for twenty-four hours a day—he doubted whether his self-control would last that long. Besides that, having the kid around would interfere with the preparations for the Fitzpatrick job. And it would probably cause a rift between Audra and Norm, who happened to be the brother who was one of the people in charge of the hiring. That was something they couldn't afford with only one week to go before the wedding.

And for what? So some pampered, sheltered, *loved* child could play rebel? Jimmy had no idea how grateful he should be for the home and family he had. If he knew how rough the streets could be for other less fortunate kids...

Palming the wheel in a circle, Sam suddenly changed direction.

"Where are you going?" Audra asked. "This isn't the way to Norm's place."

"Hey, this isn't the way to Aunt Audra's either," Jimmy said, leaning forward. "What's going on?"

"We're taking a detour," Sam said.

Forty minutes later, he slowed the car to a crawl as he steered under the shelter of an overpass. An orange cat streaked across the road and disappeared into the shadows beside the support pillars. An abandoned truck, its wheels missing, every one of its windows smashed in, leaned nose-downward at the edge of a ditch. Sam pulled up beside a rusty dumpster and twisted in his seat to look at Jimmy.

"See that pile of boxes beside the dumpster?" he asked.

"Yeah. So?"

"How would you like to live there?"

"Oh, right. Sure. That's just a pile of garbage."

"Watch," Sam said, turning around.

For the next ten minutes, the only sound in the car was the low whir of the fan and the rhythmic thump of the wipers. Then Audra drew in her breath sharply. "There's someone in that truck," she whispered.

All three of them were silent as they watched a thin man with a ragged beard slip out of the truck cab and disappear into the rain. A few minutes later, a flap on the cardboard box that was farthest from the dumpster moved and a pale face peered out warily. The orange cat that had run across the road earlier stalked into the box and the flap closed.

It had been a calculated guess, Sam thought. A few months ago he'd met an informant at this spot and had noticed that some derelicts had been using the dumpster for shelter, so he'd suspected it might still be in use. Somehow it didn't make him pleased to be right.

"These people don't have a home to go to, Jimmy," Sam said, putting the car back into gear. "They don't have the opportunities that you're so eager to turn your back on."

"What is this? Some kind of lesson?"

"Something like that," Sam murmured.

The next stop was a youth shelter that Sam and Xavier had helped to set up four years ago. It was locked up for the night, but the nun at the door recognized Sam and let him in. When he explained what he wanted, she nodded in understanding and gave the three of them a tour of the facility. She related the grim backgrounds of some of the teenagers she'd taken in, her soft voice brutally frank as she spoke about the fate of children who end up on the street. By the time they returned to the car, Jimmy's expression had lost some of its sullenness.

Sam saved the hospital for last. He was in luck. There'd been a gang shooting.

# Chapter 9

Smoke billowed out of the oven in a choking black cloud. Wiping her tears on her forearm, Audra grabbed the pot holders and reached for the pans. The mounds of charred dough looked more like coal than dinner rolls. Coughing, she dropped the pans in the sink and went to open the window.

So much for her contribution to Esther and Christopher's anniversary party. It seemed as if she couldn't concentrate on anything lately. She'd forgotten to set the timer. She'd forgotten to check the temperature setting of the oven. She was a complete mess. She was in love with Sam Tucker.

Bracing her hands on the windowsill, she gulped deep lungfuls of fresh air. No, she couldn't be in love. Definitely not love. She knew better than that. What she felt for Sam was gratitude for letting her unburden herself about Ryan and for helping her nephew. Anyone would be grateful.

He'd used exactly the right approach with Jimmy. There were already enough people willing to protect the boy from reality. Showing him the alternatives to the comfortable, loving home he had was precisely what he needed to shock some sense into him.

By the time they'd finished at the hospital, Jimmy was more than ready to work things out with his father.

Of course, now Sam was a hero to her entire family. Ever since they'd reunited Norm and Judy with their son, Sam's role in his return had begun to take on the status of a legend. Whenever she talked to anyone these days it was Sam this and Sam that and, "When are you two coming to dinner?" or, "When are you two going to set a wedding date?"

If his reason for getting involved with Jimmy had been to gain the acceptance of her family, then he'd succeeded beyond his expectations.

Then again, Sam was an expert at knowing the right buttons to push.

Turning around, she sat on the edge of the windowsill and put her head in her hands. Was that all he was doing? Pushing more buttons for the sake of his case? She'd been through this before in her mind, and she still didn't know what the answer was.

Yet whatever Sam's motives were, it didn't change what he'd done. His actions spoke for themselves. He was a sensitive, compassionate, intelligent man, and she definitely was starting to like him. Who wouldn't? According to Norm, he was a hell of a guy.

So it wasn't necessarily love. It was…an infatuation, that's all. He was her fantasy man, the naked, good-looking hunk who would make any normal woman, well, burn her buns.

Incredibly, she felt the desire to laugh. After all these years, it had finally happened. Audra McPherson, who wasn't in the habit of entertaining men—naked or otherwise—in her bedroom, was on the verge of panic simply because she had fallen victim to the most basic of human urges.

"It isn't love," she murmured. "It's lust."

Okay. Now what?

Her shoulders shook as she released the laughter that had been building. The irony of the situation was too much to bear. Most of her family, her mother included, believed that she and Sam were already sleeping together. And she'd seen from the start that Sam didn't have any hang-ups about his sexuality. Like everyone else, he probably assumed that she wasn't completely innocent either. After all, how could any modern woman reach her age without having sex?

How? Well, for starters, there were an old-fashioned father and six overprotective older brothers. Then there was an engagement to the boy who had been her best friend and a foolish, romantic notion of waiting until her wedding night to make the transition from friend to lover. And then there was that accident that took away much more than Ryan's ability to walk....

So, here she was. A virgin at twenty-eight. In lust with the sexiest man she'd ever imagined. And she had no idea what to do about it.

*You've been hiding the fact that you're an attractive woman because you've been so determined not to attract a man.*

That's what Geraldine had said. And it was true that Audra hadn't wanted to attract anyone. It was so much easier to go on the way she was, pouring her energy into her work, letting her ambition for her business fill her life. Until now, she hadn't been tempted to do otherwise.

She lifted her head, combing her hair back with her fingers. She'd left it loose today. As a matter of fact, she hadn't worn a braid or a bun since Sam had complimented her on her new hair-style. She liked the way he sometimes stroked a lock back from her cheek, and the way he'd lift his hand to toy with her curls when he put his arm around her shoulders.

And she liked the way he looked at her when she wore that dress Judy and Geraldine had talked her into buying. His eyes darkened, those masculine lines beside his mouth would deepen and his whole expression intensified somehow, as if his thoughts were filled with nothing but her. So she'd gradually been changing her wardrobe, using belts to cinch the waist of her loose dresses, leaving the top few buttons of her blouses undone, wearing heels, using perfume...

*I can't deny I'm attracted to you, Audra. You're a desirable woman.*

Her stomach did a pleasant little lurch as she remembered his voice, so deep and strong, as he'd said those words. He was attracted to her. Sensitive, intelligent Sam, who lived next door, who was loved by her family, who oozed sex appeal without even trying, found her desirable.

And this was a problem?

Of course it was a problem. They had to work together. She didn't want anything to interfere with Sam's investigation because she wanted that reward money. On top of that, she didn't want to commit herself to any man again, no matter who he was. She didn't want to love anyone....

But she wasn't in love. And neither of them wanted commitment. Their relationship was only temporary.

And when she'd returned his kiss, he'd pushed her away.

Muttering under her breath, she stood up and went to the sink to run cold water over the smoldering buns. Was she so inept that she made him lose interest? Was she misreading his signals again? And how far would she have let him go if he *hadn't* lost interest?

She didn't know the answers to those questions. Part of her wasn't entirely sure she wanted to know.

Besides, as soon as the Fitzpatrick wedding was over, her problems would be over, too.

Sam wiped his forehead with the back of his hand and scowled through the windshield. "When are you going to install air-conditioning in this rust heap, Berg?"

"You have no appreciation of beauty, Sam. She happens to be a classic." Piers Bergstrom ran his hand across the wheel of the old Mercury affectionately. "I found her in a garage in Waukegan last month. She's been around awhile, but she's still got plenty left to give."

"Whatever you say."

"They don't make them like this anymore. Her beauty is a lot more than skin-deep, too. One peek under her hood and I was in love." He gunned the engine, sending gravel spewing out from the rear tires as they climbed another hill. "Listen to that. Eight cylinders, four hundred and forty-one cubic inches. Man, can she cook.''

''And guzzle gas like a pig.''

''Whatever baby wants, baby gets,'' Bergstrom said, his dimples flashing. He had a smile that could charm a cat, as he was well aware. Tall, blond and tanned, he was the image of the all-American boy next door...unless you looked carefully enough to see the calculating glint in his eyes. ''She's so responsive. Just like a woman when you stroke her right.''

Sam slouched against the back of the seat and watched the countryside roll by. After the past week, he wasn't in the mood for Bergstrom's usual patter about his cars and his women. The man was a good cop, but his locker-room mentality could grate on the nerves. ''Any more news on who's coming to town?''

Bergstrom switched gears easily. ''Last I heard, Hasenstein, Packard, Gallo and Dryden are definites. Green and Falco look possible.''

''Emilio Falco? There's been bad blood between him and Fitzpatrick for years.''

''I don't think he was invited to the wedding just to toast the bride.''

''Fitzpatrick's ambitious. Could be he's gathering everyone to consolidate his position. Maybe even redraw the lines of power.''

''Ah, you've been talking to our friend Xavier.''

''Not since Tuesday. Why?''

''He's thinking the same thing. This fishing expedition of yours might pay off bigger than we expected. All you need to do is get yourself into the right place at the right time.'' He eased his foot off the accelerator as they approached a curve in the road, then turned into a narrow weed-choked lane. ''Sorry, baby,'' he murmured as the car thudded over a bump. The lane narrowed even further as it led through a stand of trees and emerged on the crest of the hill. Bergstrom coasted to a stop in the shade of an oak, then pulled a pair of binoculars from under his seat and handed them to Sam. ''Take a look.''

Sam aimed the binoculars at the redbrick, ivy-draped house in the distance. Pushing the focus wheel with his index finger, he grunted approvingly as he scanned the Fitzpatrick estate. "I see what you mean, Berg. It's a good vantage point."

"It better be, after the scratches I put in the paint job to find it."

"What paint job?"

"Don't listen to him, baby," he murmured to the car. "I love you anyway."

"The ceremony's supposed to take place on the terrace with the fountain." Sam moved the binoculars a few degrees to the left. "We'll be setting up the chairs and awnings tomorrow morning."

"How big are the awnings? Will they impede the view?"

"From this angle, not substantially. Now that I know where you'll be, I'll make sure of it."

"Okay. There's no rain in the forecast, so as long as everyone stays outside where the band's going to set up, I should get some interesting pictures of who's talking to whom. I'll position myself behind that knoll. Xavier's putting people near the estate entrance and on the west side of the house, but the garage blocks the view of that wing of the house where you figure they'll hold the meeting."

"Yeah, I was afraid of that."

"We'll be monitoring what we can."

"Just make sure none of Fitzpatrick's guards spot the glint from your toys."

Bergstrom laughed. "Toys, eh? State-of-the-art photographic technology and he calls it toys. What's wrong, Tucker? Coming down with a case of—" he paused and lowered his voice "—equipment envy?"

Sam lowered the binoculars and wiped the rubber collars from the eyepieces on his shirt as he glanced at the man beside him. Bergstrom kept his muscular body honed with as much dedication as he devoted to the upkeep of his cars. And if even half his stories were true, there was nothing wrong with any of his equipment. "It's not what you've got, it's how you use it that counts," he said. "Some of us don't need to rely on technology to enhance our performance."

"Oh, yeah? Next time you can be the one to cozy up to a telephoto lens and I'll take the woman, how's that? By the way, how is she?"

"Who?"

Bergstrom sketched a generous shape in the air with his hands. "Your intended. The blushing bride."

"Miss McPherson has been very cooperative."

"The quiet ones really go for cops. Something about danger and guns always excites them. You show her yours yet?"

"Knock it off, Berg. It's strictly business."

"Uh-huh," he drawled. "Sure."

Sam ground his teeth. It *was* strictly business between him and Audra. And if he kept telling himself that often enough, maybe his brain would get the message to his body.

Bergstrom twisted around to reach for a black nylon backpack that was on the back seat. He searched through it for a minute, then pulled a small plastic bag from an outside pocket. "And speaking of equipment, here's your transmitter."

"Forget it. If Fitzpatrick beefs up his security tomorrow, that would blow my cover. I already told Xavier I don't want to wear a wire."

"You might humor him this time. He's still complaining about you being in there solo."

Sam took the bag Bergstrom handed him and looked inside. "Why? You know that's the way I usually work."

"And you know how Xavier likes to prepare for the worst-case scenario. He wants us to be able to move in fast. If something goes down, you're going to need backup."

Sam shook his head, handing the bag back to Bergstrom. "I'll carry a cell phone. Between that and the surveillance you're putting in place, it should be enough."

"Hey, fine by me. I just thought you might consider using one of my toys this time, seeing as how you're always so concerned about protecting civilians. So far the McPherson woman's the only one who knows, right? Sure would be a shame if her family got caught between some of the big boys—''

''What else have you heard?'' Sam demanded.

''I've already filled you in.''

He gestured toward the transmitter. ''If that's more than Xavier's belt and suspenders paranoia, I need to know.''

''It's not.''

''Because if there's going to be trouble, I don't intend to play around with the safety of civilians. I'll tell John McPherson to cancel the job, and the hell with gathering evidence—''

''Whoa there. We're not expecting problems. Let the McPhersons do their job and you do yours and everyone will be happy.'' Taking the binoculars from Sam, Bergstrom stored them carefully back in their case and tucked it under the seat. ''Relax. It'll all be over by tomorrow night.''

''Yeah.'' Sam watched the estate disappear behind the trees as Bergstrom eased the car back toward the road. One way or another, it would all be over. The undercover job, the engagement, his association with Audra...

He should be pleased it was all working out the way he'd intended. He didn't know where the regret came from. As long as they got what they needed to put Fitzpatrick away, that's all that mattered. Right?

The guards at the gate were the same as the last time, except that their khaki windbreakers had been replaced by sober black suits. The suits, and the white carnations on their lapels, were obviously the security staff's idea of appropriate clothing for a wedding. There was still a telltale bulge under their left arms, though. For a crazy instant Audra wondered whether they'd polished their guns for the occasion.

''Drive straight to the end of the lane. Don't stop anywhere.''

Audra was unable to suppress her shudder as she heard the steel gate clang shut behind her. This was it. The real thing. All she had to do was get through this day and she could start scouting for locations for the restaurant of her dreams. As long as Sam was successful. As long as the evidence he was after was deemed worthwhile enough to earn that reward. As long as she was able to keep her nerves under control—

"Oh, my goodness. This place is like something out of a magazine." In the passenger seat, Esther leaned forward, her face lit up in a smile of pure pleasure. "Look at those flowers, Audra."

"Marion Fitzpatrick is quite an avid gardener. That's why she wanted the wedding outside."

"I can understand that. Oh, the roses are stunning."

"Yes, they certainly are," she answered, doing her best not to glance at the camera in the birch tree that Sam had pointed out the last time they'd been here. They rounded the bend in the driveway and she caught a glimpse of blue and white stripes.

"Great. It looks as if they've managed to get everything set up," Esther said. "I was worried about that, since the Fitzpatricks didn't give us much time to work with."

Audra slowed as they started up the hill. The terrace with the fountain was covered with neat rows of white chairs that were shaded by a scalloped nylon awning. She spotted Nathan and Jimmy moving tables on the patio at the side of the house, and Judy balancing on a stepladder to tack a string of lights along the edge of the French doors, but there was no sign of Sam.

He had arrived two hours ago to help with the setup. It had been a surprise to her when he'd told her they wouldn't be arriving together—like the rest of her family, she'd begun to think of them in terms of a couple.

Where was he? Had he decided to try snooping around again? What if he got caught? What if...

Her heart gave a sudden thump as she finally saw Sam. He was standing outside the rear entrance of the house, and he was toe-to-toe with a dark-suited guard. Pulling up behind Norm's van, Audra yanked on the parking brake and opened her door.

"Where are you going?" Esther asked. "We have to get these canapés into the kitchen—"

"I'll be right back," Audra said over her shoulder as she hurried toward Sam.

She heard the tail end of what seemed to be a discussion about ice buckets just before the guard shrugged his beefy shoulders and turned away.

Sam glanced past her for an instant, then caught her gaze and broke into a broad smile. "Sweetheart, I was wondering when you'd get here."

Audra came to a stop in front of him. "What was all that about?" she asked. "Is everything okay?"

"No problem," he said, catching her by the waist. Without hesitation, he lifted her off her feet and planted a solid kiss on her mouth.

Speechless, she could do nothing but cling to him, his kiss filling her senses. Even like this, when she knew it was only for show, with half her family looking on, the feel of his lips on hers sent tingles racing along her nerves.

She liked how he made her feel. She hated how helpless she was to prevent it. God, she was a mess.

"You're doing a good job, Sam."

"I'm glad I could help, Mr. McPherson," Sam said, taking the tray of glasses from Audra's father. He was getting to be an expert at balancing a tray on one hand. He was also getting to be pretty good at setting up furniture and serving dinner.

He was doing a good job, all right. But it wasn't the one he'd come here to do. Gritting his teeth while he put on a polite smile, he wove his way through the crowd of wedding guests.

The limos had started arriving mid-afternoon. Sam had been too busy in the kitchen to see them all, so he hoped Bergstrom had managed to get some good shots of the occupants. From what he'd heard, the ceremony had gone off right on schedule without any complications—he'd been too busy to see much of that either.

At least he'd been able to take careful note of the seating arrangements during dinner. In his caterer's standard clothing of white shirt and black pants, Sam was virtually invisible to the people he served. No one bothered to stop talking as he hovered at their shoulder with the plates, but so far he hadn't overheard anything worthwhile.

After everything he'd done in order to have this opportunity, it was frustrating to see that his time was running out. The dinner had long since finished. The bride and groom had left half an hour ago. Although people were still dancing to the music from the band on the terrace, the crowd was starting to thin.

He paused to unobtrusively scan the gathering, searching for Fitzpatrick's red hair. The man had been everywhere during the course of the evening, shaking hands and slapping backs, playing the jovial host to the hilt. To look at him, it was difficult to imagine he could be anything more than a successful businessman celebrating his daughter's wedding. And apart from the individuals that Bergstrom had warned him about, the rest of the people here seemed to be totally legit, which they probably were. After all, that was the way Fitzpatrick liked to distance himself from the dirty end of his business.

When Sam didn't spot Fitzpatrick, he worked his way to the other side of the crowd, searching more carefully. Now it wasn't only Fitzpatrick who had disappeared, it was Packard, Dryden and Falco.

"I'll take one of those."

Sam kept the tray steady as a large, white-bearded man exchanged his empty champagne flute for the only remaining full one. This had to be Hasenstein. Sam had only seen him in out-of-focus surveillance photos, but there was no mistaking that hooked nose. "Of course, sir," Sam said politely.

The man took a quick sip and moved away. Sam waited until he was almost out of sight, then hoisted the tray and followed. Instead of remaining with the other guests on the patio, Hasenstein slipped through a door and disappeared into the house.

Sam's gut tightened. This had to be it. The players must be gathering for the meeting he'd figured would happen. He entered the house and moved toward the corridor that led to the wing with Fitzpatrick's office.

He hadn't really expected it to be as easy as the last time he'd been here. Not only was the door at the end of the hall closed, there was a dark-suited man lounging against the wall on one side of it. Frowning, Sam shifted direction and headed for the kitchen.

Two of Audra's nephews were stacking the dinner plates back into their cartons while Norm and Judy maneuvered a large stainless steel coffeemaker onto a wheeled cart. Audra stood at one of the counters, a pencil between her teeth and a clipboard in one hand as she counted flatware.

Setting down his tray of empty glasses, Sam stopped beside her. "I need you to do something for me," he said.

She removed the pencil and made a note on her clipboard before she looked up. "What?"

"Can you fix up a plate of food? I want to take it into the meeting."

She turned to face him. "The meeting?"

He tipped his head toward the hallway.

"You mean in the room with that...table? It's really happening?"

"Looks like it. I need an excuse to get down there."

She glanced around quickly. "How about coffee?"

"Audra, I don't have time to—"

"Coffee," she repeated, moving toward Norm and Judy. She grabbed the handle at the end of the cart. "Here, Sam and I'll do that."

Judy smiled tiredly and blew her bangs off her forehead. "Thanks, Audra."

Sam helped her wheel the cart into the hall. "Okay. I'll take it from here."

She didn't loosen her grip on the handle. "I'll come with you. I might be able to help."

"Audra, I appreciate the concern, but if you really want to help, then leave me alone to do my job."

"We usually do the coffee in pairs, so this is doing your job. You can push the cart and I'll pour— Oh, God. That guard. He's the one who...you know."

Sam recognized him at the same time the man caught sight of

them. It was the guard who had found them the last time. With a leering smile, he escorted them to the conference room, then took the cart himself and pushed it inside. They had only a momentary glimpse of the half-dozen men seated around the glass table before the door was firmly closed.

Scowling, Sam stepped back. The dim corridor was deserted for the moment, but that wouldn't last long. Moving quickly, he strode to the door of the next room.

Audra was right on his heels. "What are you doing?"

"Plan B," he muttered. He twisted the doorknob and pushed lightly, letting the door swing open slowly. In the light from the hall, the same curving sofa and high-backed chairs he'd seen before loomed from the shadows, but otherwise, the room appeared to be empty. "If I told you to go back to the kitchen without me—"

"I wouldn't go," she said immediately.

"That's what I figured." Grasping Audra's wrist, he tugged her inside with him and closed the door.

"Sam—"

Covering her mouth with his hand, he brought his lips close to her ear. "Remember those vents I found when I was checking out that mirrored room?"

She nodded.

"If they connect to a central system, there should be corresponding vents somewhere on the left wall of this room."

She pulled his hand down and twisted to the side. "But that guard's going to wonder where we went."

"He'll figure we went back to the kitchen. And if he does decide to check and can't find us, he'll figure we're off somewhere doing what we did last time."

"What... Oh. But people don't really..."

"Have sex at the drop of a hat?"

"Well, no. I mean, we're working. We wouldn't..."

"It's what he believes that counts. Wait here and don't move, okay?"

Sam closed his eyes, giving himself a minute to let his vision adjust to the darkness, then started forward carefully. With the sliver of light that seeped under the door to the hall and the square of starlight that shone through the window, there was barely enough illumination to see his hand in front of his face. Stretching out his arm, he touched the wall with his fingertips. If he remembered correctly, the closest vent was about six feet from the corner of that conference room, just at the edge of the long mirror. Methodically, moving a few inches at a time, he ran his palm along the wall.

Two minutes later, his fingers touched a metal grill. He held his breath and squatted down, tilting his head to listen.

A muffled voice reached him from beyond the wall. It was disappointingly garbled, too faint to distinguish more than a few words.

The floor behind him creaked just as a hand settled lightly on his back. Annoyance warred with pleasure as he recognized Audra's touch. He should have known she wouldn't stay where he'd told her. Twisting carefully, he reached behind him to grasp her hand. Tracing his way up to her face, he pressed his finger to her lips. She nodded in understanding, her soft breathing the only sound she made.

Sam shifted his position to press his ear against the vent. He recognized Fitzpatrick's voice now, but he was speaking too quietly for Sam to catch all the words. Frustrated, he moved another inch to the right when there was a brief silence, followed by the scrape of chairs and the sound of the conference room door opening.

Acting on instinct, Sam swiftly straightened up and made a grab for Audra. Latching onto her arm, he pulled her across the room toward the window. One glance at the old-fashioned hand crank was enough to make him realize he wouldn't have time to open it. Turning around, he wedged himself into the window frame and pulled Audra against him. Stretching his arm past her, he caught the edge of the velvet drapes and yanked them closed.

Seconds later, the door to the corridor opened. "We can talk privately in here while the rest of them have their coffee, Ben."

''I don't think the others are going to support this idea, Larry.'' There was the click of a switch and the sound of the door closing. Light flowed around the edges of the drapes. ''Specifically, if Emilio doesn't agree, you're going to lose Green for sure. Possibly Dryden.''

''Don't worry about Emilio Falco. I'll deal with him.''

''He didn't sound too pleased with your offer.''

''Then I'll make him one he can't refuse.'' Low laughter followed the comment. Heavy footsteps came closer, then furniture creaked as the two men sat down. ''If he's out of the picture, do you think you can bring the others onside?''

''Depends what's in it for me.''

''Let me explain it to you, and I'm sure you'll see my plan is to our mutual benefit.''

Sam forced himself to keep his breathing slow and steady. The edge of the windowsill was digging into his left hip, his shoulder pressed hard against the glass, his legs were braced apart with the tips of his shoes precariously close to the lower edge of the drapes, but he couldn't risk moving so much as an inch.

Audra had landed off-balance when he'd pulled her against him. She'd done her best to steady herself, flattening her palms on the window frame on either side of him and straddling his thigh. If it wasn't for the hand he kept clamped to the back of her waist, she'd end up sliding backward. But there wasn't enough space for her to straighten up without setting the drapes into motion. He tapped his fingers on her hip in a silent warning.

To her credit, she didn't make a sound, although he could feel her body trembling. Her hair tickled his chin as she turned her head to press her cheek into his shirt. Their position was forcing most of her weight onto his right leg, but he didn't dare move. Ignoring the strain on his muscles, he concentrated on the conversation that was taking place less than a yard away.

Right place at the right time, Bergstrom had said. And damn, this was it. Hearing what had been said around the table next door would have been useful, but *this?* Larry Fitzpatrick and Ben Hasenstein in a private meeting. Xavier might actually smile.

Sam listened with growing satisfaction, memorizing every name and date as Fitzpatrick laid out in explicit detail how he wanted to expand his money-laundering venture over the next three years. Fitzpatrick explained the progress he had already made toward setting up a pipeline that crossed the border to Canada, where the banks had no limit on their cash transactions. From there the funds would be filtered through the books of offshore corporations and then returned to the country through the sale of shares in his various business holdings. The big difference would be the matter of the amount. He wanted a thirty percent increase in the investments made by his associates.

If this plan ever got off the ground, it was going to lead to an escalation of criminal activity from here to the East coast. But armed with this information, for once the police would be one step ahead. And when Fitzpatrick's main source of income was cut off, the rest of his businesses would fall like dominoes. They were going to get him. Once Sam related what he'd heard—

A sudden tremor went through Audra's body. She moved her head, rubbing her nose against Sam's collar. Seconds later, she held her breath and stiffened, obviously trying to suppress a sneeze.

Moving as smoothly as he could, ready to stop at the first rustle of clothing, Sam lifted his hand to the back of her head and pushed her face into his chest. She shuddered, her arms tensing in her effort to keep herself still. Then her breath rushed out, her shoulders jerked and the top of her head cracked Sam hard in the chin.

He grimaced, his fingers threading into her hair. Luckily there was no break in the conversation on the other side of the drapes. They might have been able to put on a convincing excuse for that guard, but he doubted whether someone as shrewd as Fitzpatrick would buy the sex-crazed lovers bit.

As soon as the thought entered Sam's head, the image sprang vividly to his mind. Despite their situation, he became conscious of the position of their entwined bodies. She jerked with another silent sneeze, and he felt the full curves of her breasts jiggle against him. Her feet slipped, and the warmth between her legs rubbed across the top of his thigh. He moved his hand back to her waist in an attempt to hold her steady. And somehow he managed not to groan when his fingers encountered bare skin where her blouse had pulled out of her pants.

With her arms raised and her palms flattened against the window frame for balance, she couldn't move. She was stuck like this. Silent. Motionless. So if he slipped his hand under her blouse and ran his fingertips up the side of her breast, she'd have to stay motionless. He could touch her however he pleased. And if he tensed his leg and lifted his heel to rub his thigh back and forth...

The swiftness of his reaction stunned him. It probably had something to do with tension-produced adrenaline, but he could do nothing to stop the sudden, intense rush of blood to his groin. He clenched his jaw as he felt himself swell and harden against her hip.

She shuddered. Only this time Sam didn't think it was from a sneeze. The way she was plastered against him, she couldn't have missed the change in his body. Her breath was hot and rapid on the base of his throat, her chest rising and falling in short, tantalizing strokes. Frustration mixed with pleasure as he felt the unmistakable pressure of her stiffening nipples.

This was crazy. Worse than crazy, it was stupid and dangerous. Nothing but adrenaline, a reaction to tension. But he couldn't move away. He had to stay as motionless as she did, so he couldn't do anything about their bodies' demands—

Damn, when had the conversation stopped? Sam strained to listen. There was the clink of glass on glass and the gurgle of liquid being poured. Fitzpatrick and Hasenstein briefly toasted their future venture, then walked across the room. There was the click of a light switch and the door to the corridor opened and closed.

Audra stirred and lifted her head but Sam tightened his grip on her in warning. They waited. Finally, after a full minute of silence, Sam turned his head to bring his mouth next to Audra's ear. "I think they're gone," he breathed. "But we'll wait another few minutes to be sure."

She nodded...and the rim of her ear brushed his lips.

It was too much to resist. Parting his lips, he closed his teeth gently over her earlobe.

Her body quivered, her legs tensing around his thigh. Sam shifted his position gradually, sliding his hand down from her waist, lifting his other hand and splaying his fingers over her buttocks. Leaning more of his weight back against the window, he slowly drew her upward.

She sighed shakily. "Sam..."

"Shh," he whispered, brushing his mouth along her jaw. "Don't make a sound."

One at a time, she pulled her palms from the window frame and slipped her arms around his neck. Although he couldn't see more than a dim outline of her face in the starlight that filtered through the glass, he was certain he could feel her smile.

He traced her lips with the tip of his tongue, savoring the taste of her, letting the memories of the kisses they'd shared build the desire for more.

But there wouldn't be any more. The wedding was over. He had the information he needed. Once they left here, there would be no reason for them to see each other again.

Well, hell. What did he have to lose? If this was going to be their last kiss, he'd make it one to remember.

# Chapter 10

Audra tunneled her fingers into Sam's hair and held on as the world tilted around her. He had never kissed her like this before. He wasn't being gentle. He wasn't being generous or playful or patient, either. No, this time he used his tongue and his teeth without any tender wooing, taking what he wanted as his lips crushed hers in total possession.

The darkness, the need for silence, the threat of being discovered...all those things heightened Audra's perception to a pitch she'd never imagined was possible. Her pulse pounded, her skin tingled with sensitivity. She couldn't see Sam's face, but she felt him. Everywhere.

He tightened his hands on her bottom as he flexed his leg, rocking her forward on the hardened muscle of his thigh. The friction of their clothing against her flesh was delicious. Electrifying. Without changing their position, with no more than the subtlest of movements, he was making her crazy. Her breasts ached. Quick, damp heat pooled between her legs. He rocked her again.

She would have moaned, but she couldn't make a sound.

Maybe it was the risk involved in where they were and what they were doing that intensified this sense of urgency. Whatever the cause, the sudden strength of her response left no room for inhibitions. Melting against him shamelessly, she opened her mouth and met his tongue in a recklessness that matched his.

She could feel his breath on her cheek, hot and fast as he brought his hand forward. Spreading his fingers over her thigh, he pressed his thumb boldly, knowingly, to the apex of her legs.

No one had touched her like this before. She'd read about it, heard about it, but she'd never experienced these sensations herself. The awareness that had been simmering for the past week, since she'd felt his hands on her body, since she'd faced the desire she had for him, flared to passion. There was a tightening, a pressure unfolding deep inside, a restless need for something that was almost within her grasp...

"No!"

The voice was muffled. It wasn't Sam's. His mouth was still sealed to hers as he rubbed his thumb in a slow circle, making her tremble.

"You're going too far, Fitzpatrick. I won't stand for it. You're working for me, not the other way around."

Someone was shouting in the corridor. Audra squeezed her thighs around Sam's leg, trying to hold on to the wonderful, hazy feeling for just another minute, oh please, maybe another second and she might...

Sam lifted his head suddenly, his hand going still.

Heart pounding, Audra bit down on her lip to keep from crying out in protest. Every nerve was quivering, straining toward a goal that was inexorably receding. The wonderful, hazy feeling faded like fog on the wind.

There was a sudden thump against the far wall, as if someone had knocked over a chair in the next room. Reality finally intruded and her mind began to function. Oh, God. What was wrong with her? What had they done? What had they been thinking?

She pressed her face to the front of Sam's shirt, waiting for the inevitable wave of embarrassment. But it didn't come. No, not this time. As tawdry and mindless as this embrace might have been, as inappropriate as the timing was, she'd wanted it. She wasn't ashamed—she'd already come to terms with the fact that she wanted Sam.

Moving his hands to her waist, he slowly eased her to her feet and straightened up. "We've got to get out of here," he whispered. "Now."

She leaned her forehead against his chest until her breathing steadied, then stepped back. The curtain swayed as she reached to push it aside, but Sam caught her arm to stop her.

"Not that way." He jerked his head toward the window. "Let's just hope the alarm system was turned off for the party," he muttered under his breath as he reached for the lock.

"Tell your hired muscle to get out of my way." The demand sounded as if the speaker were right outside the door. "I came here in good faith. You can't—"

"Please, Mr. Falco. Let's go back and discuss this calmly."

Sam grasped the brass handle and gave it a yank. There was a grating creak as the seldom-used mechanism cranked the window open, but no alarm bells or sirens. He spared less than a second to peer outside, then stepped back and guided Audra in front of him. "After you," he said.

It was a six-foot drop to the ground with only a bed of dahlias to cushion the fall. Audra didn't dare hesitate. She jumped, then rolled to the side as Sam landed beside her. Keeping to the shadows, they made their way along the side of the house.

Music from the band on the front patio grew louder, sounding reassuringly ordinary. Audra followed Sam past a long, low garage to the courtyard outside the entrance that led to the kitchen. Her van was still parked where she'd left it behind Norm's. With a sob of relief, she leaned against the side of the hood and stopped to catch her breath.

As hard as it was to believe, not more than twenty minutes could have elapsed since she'd taken that coffee cart from Judy.

"Are you okay?" Sam asked.

She nodded. Her pulse was still racing with a mixture of exhaustion and exhilaration. Her emotions were a tangled mess. Would he always have this effect on her?

"You didn't hurt yourself when you jumped?"

"No, I'm fine," she said.

His hand settled lightly on her shoulder. "You did great back there, Audra."

She snapped her gaze upward. Light from the lamps that lined the driveway illuminated one side of his face. Now that she could see him, he somehow looked more distant. "I did?"

"With those details I heard, we'll be able to shut down Fitzpatrick's operation for good. And I'll make sure Xavier greases the wheels for your claim."

She combed her hair back with her fingers. He was talking about what they heard, not what they did afterward. "What?"

"The fifty thousand."

The reward money. The reason she'd done all this. Her ticket to independence from her family. "Great. Thanks."

He pushed his hands into his pockets, turning his face away from the light. "I appreciate the cooperation you've given me, Audra. I know it wasn't easy for you to play along with our engagement. I'll break the news to your family myself if you want."

The news. He meant the truth about their relationship. Oh, God. Everything was happening so fast. She knew it would end, but she hadn't thought it would be over this quickly.

But what more was left? The wedding was over. He had the information he'd set out to get, and she was going to get her money....

*That's the whole point of what we're doing.*

She curled her fingers into her palms. No. There *was* more between them than this job. It might not have started out that way, but after tonight, they couldn't deny it. She might be naive about some aspects of relationships between the sexes, but she knew what she felt.

She wanted more than the money. She wanted Sam.

"It might be best to wait until we're off the property," he said.

"I could go over to your parents' place first thing tomorrow right after I make my report to Xavier. Unless you want to tell them tonight."

"No, I—"

"Fine. We'd better get back to the kitchen before they start asking where we went."

"Sam, wait!" She caught his arm before he could step away.

His muscles bunched beneath his sleeve as he finally met her gaze. "What?"

Now that she had his full attention, she didn't know what to say. This didn't seem the right time or place for telling him how she felt. But once they drove through those iron gates in the catering van, this really would be over. If she didn't do it now, would she ever get the chance again?

Would she ever have the nerve?

"Maybe we could..." She paused, trying to find the right words. *I'm infatuated with you. I love the way you make me feel. I don't want what's going on between us to end.* "You said we shouldn't get involved as long as we're working together."

"That's right. I was totally out of line when I touched you tonight. I'm lucky I didn't get us killed."

"It was..." *Wild, crazy, wonderful.* "It wasn't the best timing, but now that this job is over, and we're no longer working together—"

"There's no reason to maintain my cover," he finished.

"Yes, but that doesn't mean we can't see each other again."

He pulled his arm from her grasp and rubbed his face with his hands, then raked his fingers through his hair with a short, violent motion. "You don't know what you're saying."

"Yes, I do. I don't want a commitment, and neither do you. But there's nothing stopping us from, well..."

"Finishing what we started?"

"Well, yes."

He muttered an oath and paced the length of the van, then spun around and came back to stand in front of her. "It wouldn't work."

"Wouldn't work?" she repeated. "I can't believe you'd stand there and deny that you enjoyed…what we did."

"I'm not denying I enjoyed it. Hell, I've enjoyed every one of our encounters. You probably felt for yourself how much. It's a natural physical reaction when two people are rubbing against each other like we were. It would have happened to anyone."

The embarrassment she should have felt five minutes ago slowly started to stir. "I know it's a natural reaction."

"We got caught up in the stimulation of the job. What you're feeling is the adrenaline that's still pumping through your system, that's all. Once that wears off, you'll see how pointless it would be to prolong our association."

"Our association," she said numbly.

"We're from different worlds. You don't know me."

"But I do know you, Sam. It's more than just a physical reaction. Over the past few weeks, we managed to get along pretty well. And the way you've been there for me and my family—"

"It was an act," he said. His voice was as hard and distant as his expression. "Don't fool yourself, Audra. I acted the way your fiancé would be expected to act. That's all."

It was exactly what she'd told herself. Several times. And refused to believe. "You didn't fake everything," she murmured.

"Like I said, you don't know me. I don't belong with a woman like you," he said. "I thought we got that straight right at the start."

They had. But she was the one who wanted to change the rules. She looked away.

"Audra, I'm sorry."

"It's okay."

He stepped back. "I never meant to hurt you."

"Forget I brought it up." She took a few deep breaths, then pushed away from the van and brushed past him.

"Audra."

Along with the embarrassment came a belated flush of humiliation. Where was her pride? She was practically throwing herself at him and he wanted no part of her. Did she have to be hit over the head to figure it out? How much clearer could he be? "Please," she said, squaring her shoulders in a last-ditch attempt at dignity. "I've made a fool of myself enough for tonight. Don't make it worse with your pity."

"I don't pity you."

She closed her eyes. Nothing but an act. Nothing but adrenaline. It would wear off. God, she was pathetic. "Just go away, Sam. Please. Leave me alo—"

Her words cut off on a startled gasp. Glass exploded behind her as the window of her van shattered. Something slammed into her side, forcing the air from her lungs. Stunned, she staggered backward and spun around.

Sam lunged forward, closing his arms around her as he tackled her to the ground.

Hot liquid ran over her ribs. Blood. She must be bleeding. What on earth had happened to the window to make it break like that?

He twisted his torso before they hit, taking their weight on his back. "Keep your head down," he said, rolling her beneath him.

"What..." She tried to inhale. She couldn't seem to get her breath. "What's going on?"

"Someone's shooting."

"But why?" She shuddered. Over the music from the band she didn't hear any shots. Guns should make noise, shouldn't they?

"That argument we heard must have escalated," Sam said, stretching over her to shield her with his body as he peered beneath the van. "I can't tell where the shot came from."

She lifted her head to look past Sam's shoulders. At the corner of the garage she could see two men. One of them was pointing a long, silver handgun at the other. Oh, God. She parted her lips to warn Sam, to tell him to look behind him, but her voice wouldn't come. She tried to swallow, but somehow that took more strength than she had.

Like a slow-motion horror movie, the scene unfolded in front of her eyes. The gun jerked. One man crumpled. And the other simply slipped the gun under his jacket and turned away. His red hair gleamed under the lights from the driveway for a split second before he disappeared into the shadows.

Something important just happened, Audra realized dimly, but for the life of her she couldn't make out what it was. She dropped her head back to the pavement. She panted, wincing at the sharp pain that stabbed across her middle. Her side was on fire. But that didn't make sense because the rest of her was so cold.

Sam's face was grim as he crouched beside her and extended his hand. "Come on. I'm getting you somewhere safe and then I'm calling for backup—" His breath hissed out, his gaze riveted to his hand. It was glistening with blood. "What the... You're hit!"

"It's probably just some glass," she said. Or thought she said. Her eyelids felt so heavy.

"Goddamn it, Audra! This wasn't supposed to happen."

No. None of this was supposed to happen, she thought groggily. But that's what she got for falling in love.


Sam crushed the paper cup in his fist and hurled it at the wall of the waiting room. What the hell were they doing in there? He should have gone in with her. He shouldn't have let the doctors take her away. She was his responsibility. Everything was his responsibility. His fault. Goddamn.

"She'll be fine, son. Audra's a fighter."

Sam clenched his fists at his sides as John McPherson stopped in front of him and squeezed his shoulder. Couldn't they see that he didn't deserve their sympathy? He'd involved her in this. He'd failed to protect her. And now it was his fault she had a bullet in her lung.

"She has to be all right." Dabbing her eyes with a sodden tissue, Constance stepped into her husband's embrace. John pulled her close, pressing his cheek against the side of her head.

They'd stood like that before, Sam remembered. In their backyard, when they'd heard the news about Jimmy's disappearance, John had held his wife the same way. They were both tense with worry, but they drew strength from each other. That's what people who loved each other did. And now their worry was for Audra.

God, she'd looked so pale. He should have noticed the blood sooner. It was all over his hand, all over her white blouse, darkening her pants, puddling on the pavement...

Closing his eyes, he turned away and rubbed his face hard, but the image wouldn't fade. He'd probably take it to his grave. It wasn't the first time he'd seen someone shot. He'd seen far worse, and he'd likely see far more. But this was the first time, the only time, it had been someone he...cared about.

The admission was a hard one. Yes, he cared about Audra. She mattered to him. A lot. He liked being around her. He liked her wry humor, her generous warmth and her air of innocence. Sure, they were all wrong for each other, but that didn't stop him from caring.

He should have been the one to take the bullet, not her. She hadn't wanted to be involved in this case in the first place, but he'd assured her there wouldn't be any danger. Xavier had wanted him to wear a wire, but he'd been too arrogant to take his advice, so sure he could handle the job his way.

Yet he hadn't kept his mind on the job, had he? He'd let himself get distracted. He should have gotten Audra out of there sooner, as soon as Fitzpatrick and Hasenstein had left them alone. But no, he'd only been thinking of himself, of his own need to kiss her one last time. And then when he'd known there was trouble brewing, instead of wrapping up and getting out, he'd stayed in the open with her and left her vulnerable—

"I know she'll pull through."

He dropped his hands from his face. Judy reached out to lay her hand on his arm, her eyes brimming with tears. "God wouldn't be so cruel to take her now, just when she's finally found some happiness. We have to have faith."

"They should have told us something," Sam muttered. "What's taking them so long?"

"You're wearing yourself out. You should rest, or get something to eat. We'll let you know—"

"I'm not leaving her," he said.

Judy blinked. A tear slipped from the corner of her eye. "Of course, you wouldn't leave her. You love her."

Another load of guilt got dumped on the growing pile. None of Audra's relatives knew the engagement was a farce. It had been the furthest thing from Sam's mind when he'd put in the call to the paramedics. And then when they'd reached the hospital, he hadn't seen any need to reveal the truth. Hell, that's how he'd managed to stay with Audra as long as he had, by claiming to be her fiancé.

Later, when she was out of danger, he'd have to tell her family. And if she didn't make it...

Sam wrenched his mind away from that possibility. He couldn't conceive of never seeing her again, or hearing her voice or feeling her touch.

But when she'd asked to see him again, he'd said no. She'd offered him what he'd feared the most—wanted the most—and he'd rejected her. So she'd told him to go away. She'd told him to leave her alone.

Guilt—it had to be guilt—tore through him like a physical pain. Pulling away from Judy, he shoved his hands into his pockets and strode down the hall.

The elevator doors slid open as he passed. "Tucker?"

Sam glanced over his shoulder. Xavier Jones stepped from the elevator and walked toward him. Sam swallowed a curse. He didn't want to deal with this now. For the first time since he'd joined the force, he didn't care about his job. And he didn't give a damn about his case. It all seemed so meaningless when Audra was lying on a table under the knife of a stranger—

"How is Miss McPherson?" Xavier asked, getting right to the point.

Sam shrugged stiffly. "They have her in surgery."

"How did it look when they brought her in?"

"Bad. She lost a lot of blood."

Xavier fell into step beside Sam as he walked. "Has she said anything?"

"She hasn't regained consciousness."

"Let me know when she does. We need to question her."

"I don't think she could have seen anything. I didn't hear the shots. The music was loud, but not that loud, so the gun must have had a silencer. The whole thing doesn't make sense."

"Falco's dead. Single shot to the heart. Judging from where we found the body, you two were in the line of fire."

"Falco? We overheard an argument between him and Fitzpatrick earlier, but we didn't see anything."

"Neither did Bergstrom. His view was blocked by the garage. It's possible that it could have been a stray bullet that hit Miss McPherson, but it's also possible she's a witness. Either way, it was a botched hit. It's not Fitzpatrick's usual style to let his men leave loose ends like that. I'm betting that if you hadn't called us in when you had, the body wouldn't have been found at all."

Sam stopped in front of the window at the end of the hall and gazed blankly at the night sky. All he saw was Audra's face, her eyes closed, her lips drawn back in a grimace of pain. Another image flowed over the first, Audra as he remembered her seconds before she'd been shot, when she'd firmed her jaw and lifted her chin with a different kind of pain.

He'd said he hadn't meant to hurt her. The lies were really stacking up, weren't they?

"Sam, are you listening?"

Breathing hard through his nose, Sam tried to focus his thoughts. "I want Audra to have protection. Station someone outside her room, round the clock."

"You said you two hadn't seen anything."

"I don't want to take any more chances."

"It's probable that her shooting was accidental rather than deliberate. Considering the way you were out in the open, if someone was trying to kill you, you both would have been dead. Unless I know she's a witness, I can't justify—"

"Then I'll stay. It'll be on my own time."

"No, I want you downtown. I need your report."

"To hell with the report, Lieutenant."

Impatience flashed behind Xavier's impassive policeman's expression. He grabbed Sam's elbow and gave him a hard shake. "Settle down, Detective. This is no time to indulge your emotions. One man's dead and a civilian's injured. I need to know what happened tonight."

Violence simmered just beneath the surface. Sam wanted to smash something to vent his rage. He was angry at the situation, at the endless cycle of crime he'd devoted fruitless years to fighting. At fate. Most of all, he was angry at himself.

"I want you downtown," Xavier repeated. "We have to move fast if we want to put the information you obtained on Fitzpatrick to use, so I need the details—"

"Not now, Lieutenant," he said through his teeth. A woman in surgical greens was headed for the waiting room. Sam yanked his arm from Xavier's grasp and strode toward her.


She was floating. Wafting weightless in a cotton batting world. It was so warm and cozy, drifting here among the shapeless, colorless puffs of nothing. She didn't want to leave. But there was a glow. A pinprick of red piercing her comfortable dream. It grew slowly. Pain. It was pain that tugged on her, pulling her back to consciousness.

She struggled to open her eyes. The lids were so heavy. Why were they so heavy? Why was she so weak? Where was she? What was that beeping noise?

Gathering her strength, Audra managed to open her eyes a tiny slit.

She was lying on a bed with metal rails. Tubes in her arms. Cool air flowing into her nose. Pain as if a truck were parked on her chest.

She looked down. No, there was nothing but a white blanket and a fold of blue. A nightgown. Not her nightgown. Not her bed. But Sam was here.

He was sitting in a chair next to the bed, his arms crossed on the blanket beside her hip, his head pillowed on his arms. His hair had fallen over his forehead, his eyes were closed. Dark stubble shadowed his cheeks and deepened the lines beside his mouth. Poor Sam. He looked so tired.

She thought she'd seen him there before, when she'd drifted in and out from her cotton batting dream. Or had she? Her mind was as difficult to focus as her eyes.

Sam jerked awake. He lifted his head and rubbed his eyes. His face moved into a smile when he met her gaze. "Audra," he breathed. "Hi."

She parted her lips, but the only sound she could make was a moan.

"It hurts, sweetheart," he murmured. "I know. I'm sorry. God, I'm so sorry." He stroked her hand, his fingers gentle. "I'll get the nurse to give you something. Hang on."

She wanted to hang on, but she could barely move her hand. He clasped it between his, his touch pushing the red pinprick of pain back into the haze. Sighing, she let her eyes drift shut. It would be okay. Sam was here. She loved him.

It was mid-afternoon when Audra woke up the next time. The pain that had muddled her brain had receded to a rumbling throb. She squinted at the light that flooded the room.

"I think she's waking up."

It was her mother's voice. Audra blinked and slowly opened her eyes. "Mom?" It was a croak instead of a word. She tried to swallow.

"Yes, I'm here. So's your dad." Constance moved toward the head of the bed, into her range of vision. Her cheeks were wet, but she was smiling as she leaned over to press a kiss to Audra's forehead. "How are you feeling?"

"Don't know."

"Here, the doctor said you'd be thirsty." Her father was on the other side of the bed, holding a blue plastic tumbler. He guided the straw between her lips as she lifted her head and fought to swallow. Cool water trickled down her throat, easing the dryness. "Thatta girl," he murmured.

Exhausted, she dropped her head back on the pillow. "Where am I?"

"You're in the hospital, Audra," her mother answered, stroking her cheek with the back of her hand. "You're going to be fine."

Snippets of memory flitted past. She'd been at the wedding. She'd been talking to Sam. There'd been pain. She frowned, trying to piece the memories together. "Sam was here."

"Yes, he was here all night. He wouldn't leave your side until the doctor promised you were out of danger. We finally talked him into going home to change clothes."

"He looked so tired. What happened?"

Her mother hesitated, pressing her lips together. Audra turned her head toward her father. "Dad?"

"You...you had an accident."

"What kind of accident? Was I driving? Is Sam okay?"

"Yes, he's fine, baby. Don't worry."

The memories crowded her mind, jostling for position. The wedding. Jumping from a window while glass shattered. No, the glass was from her van. Sam lying on top of her. Blood. Pain. "What happened?" she demanded, looking from one parent to another. "What aren't you telling me?"

"Please, don't get upset," her mother murmured. "You need to rest."

Glass flying. Sam pulling her down, shielding her with his body. Something...wrong. Blood. Heat. Cold. "Oh, God."

Her father placed a calming hand on her shoulder. "I'm not sure how it happened, but someone was killed at the Fitzpatrick estate last night. Evidently, you were hit by accident."

"What do you mean, I was hit? The glass couldn't have..." She drew in her breath too quickly and pain stabbed down her side. "*I* was shot?"

"But you're going to be fine," Constance said immediately. "They were able to take the bullet out and you'll be as good as new in no time."

Audra lifted her hand, trailing an intravenous tube as she cautiously touched her fingers to her side. There was an ominously thick padding under her gown. She remembered the impact that had spun her around, the searing agony in her back and her side, the blood that had flowed over her ribs... "I was shot," she repeated numbly. "I can't believe this. I was shot."

"Let me tell Sam you're awake," her father said, patting her shoulder. "I promised I'd call him."

"Sam." More memories stirred. A kiss behind a velvet curtain. Wonderful, crazy feelings. Her heart pounding. Adrenaline. A conversation beside her van. Sam telling her it was over. Sam saying it was just an act....

The events of the night before, everything that had taken place before the blur of pain, finally clicked into place. Whatever drugs they'd given her hadn't dulled her brain sufficiently. Before she could slam the door shut on her thoughts, every word, every feeling of that final conversation with Sam came back to her in a merciless rush.

The job was over. Their *association* was over. There was no need to deceive anyone, especially herself.

Oh, God. She'd been shot. But before she'd been shot, she'd been dumped. Rejected. No, it hadn't been as dignified as a rejection. It was a dismissal. A denial.

She couldn't face him again. Not now. Not ever. "No," she said.

"What?"

"I don't want to see him."

"But honey, he loves you," her mother said. "He was so worried."

*That's what she got for falling in love.*

The thought popped up from nowhere. No. It was wrong. It was all an act. "He lied. He doesn't love me," she said, closing her eyes. "Tell him to go away."

"Oh, Audra. Sam's already seen you. He won't be bothered by those needles."

They were deliberately misunderstanding her. Did they think

she cared what she looked like? "Where's the ring?" she asked, flexing her left hand.

"Your ring? It's right here beside you. I'll put it back on your finger."

"No." She inhaled slowly, steeling herself against the pain in her side. And the pain in her heart. "Give it back to him. We're not engaged."

# *Chapter 11*

Sam raked his fingers through his hair impatiently as the elevator whined its way upward. He'd been gone almost two hours. He'd left the number of his cell phone with the nurses and with Audra's father, and had called to check on her twice while he'd been down at the station with Xavier, but no one was telling him anything.

The minute Sam stepped from the elevator, he knew something was wrong. Judy and Constance were standing near the nurses' station, their heads together as they spoke in subdued tones. Judy looked up briefly as he passed, her gaze brimming with a mixture of sadness and sympathy before she quickly averted her gaze. His stomach twisting, Sam lengthened his stride as he headed down the hall. He never should have left her, even for a minute. But the twins had said they wouldn't let anyone in who wasn't hospital staff or family. And there still wasn't any indication that the shooting had been deliberate....

Before he could reach Audra's room, the door opened and John McPherson stepped out, followed by Jake and Christopher, their faces wearing identical scowls.

"What happened?" Sam asked. "Is she all right? What's going on?"

John glanced at his sons before he answered. "Audra woke up an hour ago, but she's sleeping now."

"Has the doctor seen her?"

"Yes, she has. She says so far there don't seem to be any complications."

"Thank God."

"Audra's still weak. She needs rest."

"I won't wake her up," Sam said, stepping toward the door. "I'll just sit with her."

As one, Jake and Christopher moved to block his path. "Sorry, but you can't go in there," Jake said.

"Look, I appreciate you keeping an eye on her while I was gone, but—"

"Audra doesn't want to see you."

"What?"

Christopher set his jaw and glared at Sam. "She specifically asked us to keep you away."

He looked at the closed door. "Did she say why?"

"Yes," Jake said, eying him warily. "She did."

Sam glanced from one twin to the other, a sick feeling rising in his throat. There was a coolness in their gazes, a distance that hadn't been there two hours ago.

It didn't take a genius to figure out what had changed.

"Maybe we'd better go and sit down, Sam," John said. "There are some things I'd like to discuss with you."

"Yeah," Christopher said. "There are a few things I'd like to say too, *Detective* Tucker."

Oh hell, Sam thought as the three men escorted him to the cafeteria. They settled at a corner table, the atmosphere thick with building tension and the smell of frying food.

Sam had been through this kind of thing before, when an undercover job was over and it was necessary to reveal the truth to the people concerned. It hadn't bothered him in the past—the independence and the challenge of undercover work had always made up for the occasional awkward situation. Only this time it was different. He'd gone too far. He'd done what Xavier had warned him against and had gotten personally involved.

The McPhersons had welcomed him into their homes. They'd entrusted him with their affection. They'd believed all his lies. And now Audra lay in a hospital bed with a bullet hole in her lung. This time he wasn't sure he could excuse his betrayal of innocent people by claiming he was only doing his job.

Reaching into the pocket of his jeans, Sam pulled out the folder with his badge, flipped it open and tossed it onto the middle of the table. Then he proceeded to tell them everything, from his plan to infiltrate the wedding to the dispute among Fitzpatrick's guests that had led to Falco's murder. When he was done, he crossed his arms and sat back in his chair, prepared for whatever names they wanted to call him.

For a full two minutes, no one spoke. John stirred sugar into his coffee with controlled, deliberate movements while Jake and Christopher regarded Sam in stony silence.

Over the years, Sam had seen a variety of reactions at this stage, from incredulity to anger. Yet the McPhersons' quiet condemnation cut him deeper than he would have imagined.

Of course, he'd always known that he was an impostor, that he hadn't deserved the acceptance of a solid, respectable family like this.

Picking up his badge, Sam cleared his throat. "I apologize for the deception. If you have any further questions, I'll give you the name of my supervisor."

"You knew this man Fitzpatrick was a dangerous criminal," Christopher said. "Yet you didn't see fit to warn us."

"It was a calculated risk. We hadn't expected any violence at his daughter's wedding."

"Well, you were wrong, weren't you?"

"Yes. I made an error in judgment."

"And Audra's the one who's paying for it."

He nodded, making no attempt to defend himself. He deserved their scorn for the pain she was going through.

"You said Audra was shot by accident when that man was killed?" Jake asked.

"I believe so. Ballistics confirmed that the bullets came from the same gun."

"How do you know it was an accident? How can you be sure she wasn't deliberately shot?"

"I'll know more when I can question Audra."

Christopher stabbed his finger at Sam. "You've done enough. I'm not letting you go near her, you bastard."

"Then another officer will have to take her statement."

"Fine. As long as it isn't you."

"The sooner she talks to someone, the better," Sam persisted. "I've been trying to get her protection—"

"My brothers and I can take care of her. Do you have any suspects?"

"We're working on it."

"Did you put Fitzpatrick in jail?"

"Not yet, but we've learned enough to build a case."

"So the criminal is free and an innocent woman's in the hospital." A muscle in Christopher's jaw jumped as his glare sharpened. "Tell me, *Detective*. Do you consider this undercover operation a success?"

The guilt just kept piling up, but they couldn't be any harder on him than he was on himself. "I can't tell you how much I regret—"

"You're an incompetent idiot!" Jake said, slapping his palm on the table.

Sam clenched his jaw against the urge to defend himself. He deserved everything they threw at him.

"And the fact that you chose to involve Audra only proves your lack of judgment. Audra, of all people, mixed up in an undercover investigation," Jake went on, his voice rising. "She's a complete innocent. She wouldn't know how to cope!"

"She's had a sheltered life," Christopher put in. "We've always done our best to take care of her."

"She's helpless when it comes to dealing with problems. This whole fiasco is going to—"

"Now you wait a minute," Sam said, bracing his hands on his knees and leaning forward. "You can say what you want about me, but I won't let you criticize Audra. She's an exceptionally intelligent and resourceful person."

"You get our baby sister shot and *you* have the nerve to lecture *us?*"

"Yes, I do. Because she thinks too highly of all of you to do it herself. Protecting her is one thing, but don't underestimate her capabilities. Don't mistake inexperience for incompetence. She's not some helpless little girl to be coddled as if she has no mind of her own."

"I never said—"

"She's a mature woman. She deserves your respect. And when it comes to dealing with problems, she's found the strength to handle a tragedy that the rest of you haven't begun to accept."

"You've known her for what? A month? Six weeks?"

"Long enough to know her better than you think."

"What's that supposed to mean?" Jake said, rising from his chair. "Just how far did you take this fake engagement? If you've laid a hand on her—"

"Boys, that's enough," John cut in, his voice hard. Until now he'd watched the exchange between Sam and his sons in silence. "This is a difficult situation, but I think we'd all better calm down before we say something we regret."

Jake wavered, his face flushing with anger. Then without another word, he shoved back his chair and walked away. A tense minute later, Christopher stood up and followed.

Sam rubbed his jaw. It might have been easier if they'd simply taken a swing at him. "Mr. McPherson, I regret the way this turned out, but I want to assure you that I have the highest respect for your daughter."

John picked up a paper napkin and took his time mopping up the coffee that had spilled from his cup when Jake had hit the table. "You mean my exceptionally intelligent, resourceful, mature and capable daughter."

"Yes."

Crossing his arms, John leaned back and regarded Sam unblinkingly. Unlike his sons, he kept his thoughts hidden behind his expression. "No one likes to be lied to."

"I understand that."

"You and Audra fooled us all, you know. You were very convincing."

"Audra wasn't comfortable about deceiving her family. It was my responsibility entirely."

"It was quite a performance, the way you pretended to be so worried while she was in surgery, and the way you insisted on spending the night by her side. You certainly behaved like a man with strong feelings."

"Your sons are right. It was my fault she was put in danger."

John continued to study him, his face unreadable. "When she woke up this afternoon, her first concern was your welfare."

That jarred him. "What?"

"She was probably confused from the drugs. I have to congratulate you. You're both excellent actors." He pushed himself to his feet and took a step away, then stopped to reach into the pocket of his shirt. "Here," he said, tossing something to the center of the table. "I believe this is yours."

Sam saw the gleam of gold. He waited until he was alone before he extended his arm and picked up the ring. He traced the pattern of apple blossoms, his fingertip brushing over the diamond the same way he'd seen Audra touch it a hundred times.

It was only a symbol of something that didn't exist. But if everything else was fake, why did *this* seem so real?

Curling his fingers over the circle of gold, he brought his fist to his mouth and closed his eyes.

The flowers were everywhere. On the windowsill, on the floor and on the table along the wall, they bloomed in a dazzling array of color. There were delicate, lacy-edged pink carnations from

Norm and Judy, a lush purple African violet from Esther's greenhouse and sprigs of orange gladioli and blue morning glories from Audra's parents. Cheery get-well cards, some glossy and a foot high, some hand-drawn with crayon on colored paper, were taped to the bathroom door. Plastic containers and foil-wrapped plates of food smuggled in by Jake and Christopher covered the tray table beside the bed and a stack of mystery novels teetered beside the telephone.

A rented television, suspended from the ceiling in one corner, flickered silently, but Audra wasn't watching. Leaning back against the raised head of her bed, she focused on the single red rose she held in her hand. It was from Sam.

According to the nurses, he'd been at the hospital every day. He'd taken up a post at the end of the corridor where he kept track of the people who entered her room. She'd already told the police that she didn't remember anything about the shooting, but he was stubbornly hanging around anyway, making sure she had no unauthorized visitors.

At least he seemed to have accepted the fact that she didn't want to see him. She didn't *have* to see him. There was nothing between them anymore, so he didn't need to pretend otherwise. After what he'd said to her, he had a lot of nerve sending her flowers. What did she need with more flowers? This place was getting too ripe with them.

Now that her mind was clearer, she'd figured out why he'd kept a vigil by her bed after she'd come out of surgery. He'd been concerned about her welfare, that was all. If she had died, he would have had all kinds of inconvenient extra paperwork to fill out.

He was probably feeling a healthy dose of guilt, too. After all, he'd assured her there wouldn't be any danger when she'd agreed to help him. Maybe he was concerned she'd bring a lawsuit against the police department. Maybe that's why he was still hanging around.

And of course, he undoubtedly felt sorry for her. Poor, pathetic sex-starved old maid, mistaking his acting and her adrenaline for something more genuine. Lucky for her he'd set her straight so promptly, before she could make an even bigger fool of herself. She hadn't needed to be hit over the head for it to sink in after all—being shot was sufficient.

Narrowing her eyes, she ripped a petal off the rose and dropped it to the floor. It was a darn good thing she hadn't fallen in love, right? Having to recover from a hole in her lung was painful enough without having to worry about a hole in her heart.

Her brothers didn't have any trouble accepting the news that she wasn't engaged. They avoided the subject completely, never speaking Sam's name, glossing over the whole Fitzpatrick wedding job, going right back into full protectiveness mode. Except for Norm, but he'd been getting mellower ever since he and Jimmy had started to work out their problems. Surprisingly enough, he and her father had wanted to discuss her plans for her restaurant. Not that they approved of her ambition to strike out on her own. But at least they were listening. That was progress.

"Good morning," Geraldine chirped, pushing open the door. "How are you feeling, Audra?"

She tore another petal off the rose and flicked it over the side of the bed. "Just peachy, thanks."

"Can I get you anything?"

"Thanks, but Christopher already dropped off some breakfast."

"I saw Sam in the hall. He's looking terrible," Geraldine said, hooking a chair with her foot to drag it closer to the bed. She took hold of the side rail and eased herself down. "I really think you should talk to him, even if it's only for a few minutes."

"We have nothing more to say."

"Oh, Audra. It wouldn't hurt to unbend a bit. He looks like his puppy's died, he lost his best friend and he hasn't slept in a week."

Concern stirred, but she tamped it down and mangled another petal. "Gerri, how many times do I have to tell you? Sam doesn't love me. I don't love him. The engagement was a lie. It's over."

Geraldine shook her head. "I don't care what Jake and the

boys say. Sam's a nice guy. You could do a lot worse. And you both had that special glow when you were together. It was clear to me there was a lot more than a professional relationship going on between you.''

''Those are your hormones talking.'' She looked pointedly at her sister-in-law's bulging stomach. ''When are you planning on having that baby, anyway?''

She groaned. ''Please. Last night I saw a documentary on elephants. Did you know their gestation period is twenty-two *months?* I'm thinking of checking myself into a zoo.''

''Are you feeling okay? When was the last time you saw your doctor?''

''Two days ago, and I'm fine. But you're changing the subject. We were talking about Sam.''

Audra reached for the remote control and turned up the sound on the television.

''I saw for myself what a wreck he was while you were in surgery,'' Geraldine continued, ignoring the drone of the talk show that was on the screen. ''The man's devoted to you.''

''It was Sam's cover. It was all part of his job so he could get into that wedding. He wants Fitzpatrick and I want the reward. That's it. That's all. End of discussion,'' she said wearily. She'd told the same story so many times, it was coming by rote.

''So? Lots of couples have an interesting story about the way they met. Think of how much fun it'll be to tell your grandchildren someday.''

Sighing, Audra flopped her head back against the pillow. Geraldine wasn't the only one who thought this way. Her mother and Judy had said pretty well the same thing yesterday.

In her mother's case, it wasn't that surprising. She was willing to overlook what she called Sam and Audra's rocky beginning in the hopes that her daughter would eventually settle down into marital bliss—she was such a romantic, she wouldn't believe that the stars she'd thought she'd seen in their eyes were merely proximity and adrenaline. And Judy's stubborn defense of Sam was understandable too. She was still grateful to him for his help with Jimmy, no matter what his motives were.

"You're in denial," Audra said. "Judy, Mom, Esther, the whole bunch of you. You just won't accept the fact that you've been duped."

"Audra, I've seen him. No one's that good an actor."

"You'd be surprised. Sam's a real expert at taking on a role."

"Maybe you'll feel differently once you're home and things get back to normal."

"Normal," she muttered. "I can't wait."

"Speaking of waiting, I can't either." Geraldine said, grasping the side rail to lever herself to her feet. "The kid's decided to take up tap dancing on my bladder. Don't go away," she added, heading for the bathroom. "We haven't finished this conversation."

Audra flicked the channel on the television impatiently. It would be good to get home, all right. Then she wouldn't be such a sitting duck for more well-meaning relatives who wanted to run her life.

As soon as she got out of here, she was going to start scouting out locations for her restaurant. Her claim on the reward wouldn't be honored until Fitzpatrick was actually convicted, but with the information she'd helped Sam obtain, it was only a matter of time now. That's what that policeman had said when he'd taken her statement. What was his name? Berger or Bergman?

Bergstrom, she remembered. He'd been wonderfully friendly and polite all through their interview. A nice young man, as her mother would have said. Well-built, blond and blue-eyed, he'd been blessed with the kind of bone structure a camera would love. When he'd smiled, he'd even managed to bring a blush to the cheeks of Monique, the sadistic nurse with the needles.

Well, he'd been handsome enough, in a classic, symmetrical way. Many women adored that kind of neatly tailored, toothpaste-ad-smile look. Yet even if Audra hadn't been flat on her back trailing tubes and bandages and feeling like something a cat wouldn't deign to drag in, she wouldn't have given Bergstrom a second glance. Maybe if his hair had been darker, with a stubborn wave that kept flopping over his forehead, or if he'd worn one of those loose, defiantly irreverent Hawaiian print shirts, or if he had a dimple in his chin and a crooked smile and square jaw and keen blue eyes...and hands that could be gentle or knowing...and shoulders that were broad and solid...and lips that felt like heaven...

Grinding her teeth, she crushed the rose in her fist, then dropped the remains of the flower to the floor and reached for a book. Time to get back to normal. Her involvement with Sam and his investigation was over. From now on, if she wanted excitement, she could find it at the library.

The painting on the book cover showed a skeletal hand clutching the dusty stock of an old revolver. The blurb on the back of the book promised it would be filled with plenty of surprise twists and unexpected betrayals. Just what she needed to get her mind off all those things she didn't want to think about.

She ran a fingertip along the cover, focusing on the fancy engraving the artist had seen fit to add to the gun's barrel. She used to rub her ring that way. She'd liked the feel of those delicately etched leaves and apple blossoms—

Making a disgusted noise, she flipped open the book. She didn't get past the first line before she felt compelled to look at the cover once more. It wasn't the engraving that was niggling at her, it was the gun itself. It seemed wrong somehow. It was too thick, and the barrel wasn't shiny enough or long enough. Yet it was a large revolver, and the barrel couldn't very well be any longer unless it was a rifle. On the other hand, a pistol would appear longer if it had one of those cylinders at the end for a silencer....

Her hand shook, and the painting wavered in front of her eyes. A silencer. Why was she thinking about that? And who cared how shiny the gun might be?

But it had glinted in the shadows. She remembered. Two men standing. One man crumpling to the ground. Hard to make sense of it through the pain...

It wasn't a book cover she was seeing. It was a memory.

Oh, God. The man that Bergstrom had kept asking her about...she *had* seen him. She'd seen him shot. Murdered.

The collection of get-well cards that was taped to the door flapped suddenly as Geraldine emerged from the bathroom. "Twenty-two months," she was muttering. "Can you imagine? No wonder elephants are so gray and wrinkled. I'm never going to look at one the same agai— Oh, my God! What's wrong, Audra?"

The book tumbled to the floor as Audra raised her hand to her forehead. Her skin was slick with a cold sweat.

"You're white as a sheet," Geraldine exclaimed. "Hang on, I'm getting the nurse." Bypassing the call button that dangled from the side of the bed, she yanked open the door to the corridor and called for help.

Audra's head spun. She'd honestly thought she hadn't seen anything. Her memory must have been blocked. Maybe it was from the pain, or the drugs they'd given her for it. Maybe it was from her own unwillingness to examine that evening in any more detail. But now there was no stopping it. The images were tumbling over each other in a frenzied rush to be seen.

Brisk footsteps sounded from outside. A nurse appeared, bustling to her side. Cool fingers touched her arm, then pressed over the pulse in her wrist.

"I'm okay," Audra said, her voice unsteady. "Really."

More footsteps pounded up the hall, these ones heavier than the nurse's. Seconds later, Sam burst into the room. "What happened? What's going on?"

"Sir, I'd like you to wait outside," the nurse said.

"Like hell I will." He strode to the other side of the bed without hesitation, his tall frame rigid with tension. "What's wrong?"

Audra's eyes widened when she saw him. His hair stood in ragged furrows, as if he'd been raking it with his fingers. Dark shadows smudged the skin beneath his eyes and the hollows in his cheeks looked downright gaunt. His crumpled shirt and jeans looked as if he'd been sleeping in them.

Geraldine was right. He was a wreck.

"Please, sir. I can't allow—"

"It's okay, he's family," Geraldine said, returning to stand at the foot of the bed. "Is she having a relapse?"

"I'm all right," Audra managed to say. "Just dizzy."

The nurse slipped a blood pressure cuff around her arm while she pressed the disc of a stethoscope inside her elbow. She went on to check her temperature, then ordered Sam to turn his back before she rolled Audra to her side and pulled her gown aside to inspect the dressing over her wound. "No sign of infection and your vitals are fine," she said, moving to pick up the chart at the end of the bed. "You're not due for more medication for another two hours. If you'd like me to get you something for the break-through pain—"

"I don't want any more painkillers. My sister-in-law shouldn't have called you."

"No problem. You probably just overexerted yourself." She hung up the chart and moved briskly to the door. "Don't stay too long," she said, fixing Sam and Geraldine with a stern look. "Your sister needs rest more than she needs visitors."

As soon as she was gone, Geraldine heaved herself around to the other side of the bed and squeezed Audra's hand. "I'm sorry. I didn't mean to tire you out. You were sounding so much like your old self earlier, I guess I forgot you still have a long way to go." She smiled ruefully. "Hormones again. I tend to over-react."

"It's okay."

"I'd better go," she said, turning toward the door. "See you later, Sam."

Audra moved her head to look at Sam. "You don't have to stay, either."

He stepped closer, then bent down to pick up her book and set it on the table beside the telephone. He looked down again, his face drawn. Without a word, he stooped over, gathered the shred-ded rose and dropped it into the wastebasket.

Her heart did a painful thump. She hadn't wanted to see him

again, she reminded herself. But she didn't want to hurt him. Or have him suffer.

*I've missed you.*

No. She couldn't miss something she'd never really had. She couldn't miss a lie, a role.

"What happened?" he asked. "I don't care what that nurse said, I can see something's wrong."

"I was remembering that night," she said. "After the wedding."

The lines bracketing his mouth deepened. It didn't seem possible, but his expression turned even grimmer. "You have no idea how sorry I am, Audra. I've been hoping you'd give me a chance to apologize for my behavior and the ham-handed way I—"

"No, that's not what I meant. I don't want to talk about...our personal relationship."

"I am sorry, Audra."

"It's over now. I..." She cleared her throat. "It's about something else. I remember seeing a gun."

"What?"

"After I was shot. After you pulled me down."

"You saw a gun? Where?"

"Behind you." As she spoke, the memory strengthened, as if seeing Sam again had released something she'd been doing her best to keep bottled up inside. "You were lying on top of me, but I lifted my head to look past your shoulder. There were two men at the corner of the garage."

"Audra," he said, gripping the rail of the bed to lean closer. "What else did you see?"

*The gun jerking. One man falling. Red hair in the light from the driveway...*

"I saw him put the gun under his jacket and turn away. The end was thick. It must have been a silencer—" Bile rose in her throat. She felt her palms grow damp as the full impact of what she was remembering finally registered.

"Take it easy," Sam said, touching her hand. "It's over. No one's going to hurt you now."

"Sam, I saw a murder. Right there, in front of my eyes, a man died."

His fingers were warm and soothing as he stroked her skin. "Focus on the man left standing. What do you see?"

"I was scared he was going to shoot us too, but he didn't. He didn't see us. He put the gun away and walked into the shadows beside the garage."

"Was he short? Tall? Do you remember what he was wearing?"

"He had a light gray suit. You remember, don't you?"

"I didn't see—"

"You saw him all evening. It was Fitzpatrick."

"Are you sure? It was dark, and you were lying on the ground."

"Of course, I'm sure. It was Fitzpatrick."

Sam's hand tightened over hers. For a moment, he simply stood there watching her. Then a slow, glorious smile spread across his face. "We've got him," he murmured.

Oh, God. All it took was one of those endearingly boyish, lopsided smiles and all the old confusion came right back. She didn't want to send him away anymore. She wanted to pull him into her arms and hold him until that haunted look faded from his eyes. She wanted to apologize for mangling that flower he'd given her and for making him miserable and for...

What was wrong with her? Hadn't she learned *anything*?

Sam marveled at the strength that lay beneath Audra's delicate features. Despite the trauma she'd suffered, despite the way he'd mishandled the personal side of their relationship, she was going to give them exactly what they needed to put Fitzpatrick away for good.

Murder. It was more than he could have dared hope for. They didn't have to wait around to reel the man in for money laundering and tax evasion. With Audra's eyewitness testimony, they'd be able to get him for murder.

With Audra's eyewitness testimony...

Gradually Sam's smile faded into uneasiness. She had just confirmed Xavier's theory that her own shooting had been accidental. Fitzpatrick hadn't seen her watching him. So he'd had no reason to deliberately want to harm her.

Until now.

Protectiveness, and a renewed burst of the ever-present guilt, surged over him as he looked at the way Audra lay propped up in the hospital bed. She was still too pale. Her prognosis was good, but she had a long recovery in front of her. And even after the wound healed, she would always carry the scar from that bullet.

His gaze dropped to their joined hands. He'd let his emotions interfere with his duty before, and this was the result. For Audra's sake, he wasn't going to screw this up again. He had to concentrate on his job. He had to ignore the way he wanted to climb on that bed with her and cradle her in his arms and promise her he'd never let anyone or anything hurt her again...

"When are you scheduled to be discharged?" he asked finally.

"Tomorrow or the day after."

"I'll be there."

"It's not necessary. My family's already set up a round-robin schedule of monitoring visits."

"I'll be there," he repeated. "I won't leave you."

Her fingers trembled beneath his. "Sam, I don't need your guilt or your pity. What happened to me was an accident. I don't want you to feel obligated to keep up this...whatever it is you're doing."

"What I want to do is move into your place. Or you can move in with me, whichever you're more comfortable with."

"You..." She hesitated. "You want to move in with me?"

He glanced around the room, noting the cards and flowers that packed every available surface. "I'll explain the situation to your family for you. Your brothers will probably object, but I'm sure Xavier will back me up on this."

"Xavier?"

"We'll try to keep this under wraps as long as possible, but we have to be prepared in case Fitzpatrick decides to try something—''

"Sam, what are you talking about?"

He returned his gaze to hers. "You're an eyewitness. Your testimony is going to be crucial to convicting Fitzpatrick, so we can't afford to take any chances with your safety. I want to stay with you to ensure your protection."

For a moment she stared at him, her eyes stark and vulnerable in her too-pale face. Then she tugged her hand from his and looked away. "No."

"But you need—"

"No. I definitely don't need someone else who wants to run my life for my own good."

"Audra, for God's sake, I'm only trying to do my job."

"Of course. Why else would you do anything?"

# Chapter 12

Audra glanced out the front window of the restaurant and felt her heart thud with the combination of pleasure and pain that was becoming all too familiar. Through the drizzle that darkened the street, she could clearly see the flash of yellow, blue and green from Sam's shirt. He was standing under the awning of a fruit market, his hands in his pockets, his ankles crossed, his gaze fixed on the restaurant door.

He had become her shadow, and it was tearing her apart. Every time she turned around, there he was, the stubborn, macho cop who refused to listen to reason or admit he was overreacting. In the weeks since she'd left the hospital, there hadn't been so much as a hint of a threat from Fitzpatrick. Yet Sam had appointed himself her bodyguard, and nothing she could say seemed to have any effect on his decision.

It wasn't as if he actually *wanted* to spend all this time with her. His feelings weren't in the least confused. She was certain that his pulse didn't jump and his stomach didn't do that ticklish little lurch each time he saw her. No, she wasn't going to delude herself into thinking there was anything personal here. He was just doing his job.

Of course, Audra had refused to go along with his initial plan of sharing an apartment, but she was unable to stop him from turning up wherever she went. And for that, he had help. Her mother and sisters-in-law were only too happy to make it easier for him by telling him Audra's plans as soon as she made them—hopeless romantics that they were, they found the whole body-guard idea appealing.

Naturally, her brothers still didn't like to see Sam anywhere near her—they bristled and postured like alpha males defending their territory. But their protests had lost steam when Xavier had confirmed the potential risk faced by any witness to a major crime. It seemed like a remote possibility that Fitzpatrick might try to coerce her into not testifying, and so far there was no evidence to back it up, but that was enough for the McPherson males. Not only did they want her to stay away from work, they wanted her to drop her plans for a business of her own.

Men. They were all alike. They might pay lip service to women's rights and the equality of the sexes but scratch the sur-face and there was the protective, possessive attitude of a cave-man. Maybe she'd have more hope of getting through to them if she tried grunting instead of arguing.

"The exhaust fans were replaced three months ago."

"Excuse me?"

"The fans. They're top-of-the-line, state-of-the-art equipment as you'll see."

Audra gave herself a mental shake to get her thoughts back on track as she followed the restaurant owner through the swinging doors into the kitchen. This was the third place she'd checked out this morning. She should have stopped at two, since she could feel her energy flagging, but she was determined to narrow down the locations by the end of the week. "Why were they replaced, Mr. Worsley?" she asked.

"Oh, routine maintenance. Nothing to worry about." The man

smiled widely and ushered her toward the walk-in freezer. "Now, let me show you the storage capacity..."

"I see the area behind the fans has been replastered," she said, stopping as she viewed the wall from a different angle.

"Ah, yes. We had some minor repairs."

She looked at the notes she'd made on her clipboard, then tapped her pen against the page. "Was all the wiring replaced after the fire, or was it only the fans?"

"Who told you about—" He coughed. "What makes you think we had a fire?"

"It's a matter of record."

"Oh, it was nothing, really. Just some overheated grease."

"Ignited by a short in some faulty wiring. You were ordered to have it upgraded."

"The preliminary work has all been taken care of," he said, his tone dismissing the issue as unimportant. "Did I mention the custom-made tablecloths would be included..."

Suppressing a sigh, Audra drew a diagonal line across the page and tucked her clipboard and pen into her purse. She should have known there was a catch. The location was great, but the work that would be needed to bring the wiring up to standard would put this place beyond her budget. "Thanks for taking the time to see me, Mr. Worsley," she said, extending her hand.

"Oh, it was my pleasure, Ms. McPherson. I hope to hear from you soon." He leaned toward her with the air of someone imparting a confidence. "I think I should tell you that there are several other people who have expressed an interest in my place, so you might not want to wait too long."

The only other person who'd be interested would be the Fire Marshall, she thought, heading for the door. She paused on the threshold to open her umbrella, then started along the sidewalk.

Ten seconds later, Sam fell into step beside her. "Hi."

The sound of his voice sent a pleasant vibration down her spine. As it always did. And along with the pleasure came an echo of pain and humiliation. As it always did. Frowning, she focused on her feet and concentrated on avoiding the puddles.

"I'm meeting Judy in the coffee shop on the corner. From there, I'm going straight home, so you can go off duty now."

"Judy left twenty minutes ago. She asked me to pass along her apologies."

"What? How would you know?"

"She called me on my cell phone. Said she had forgotten about a dentist's appointment and asked me to make sure you got home."

"It figures," she muttered. She should have known this would happen when Judy had insisted they drive downtown together. This was the third "accidental" encounter with Sam Judy had engineered in four days. Resigned, she lifted the umbrella so he could share it. "Where are you parked?"

"In the lot just past the lights. Thanks," he said, stepping closer. "How are you doing? Are you okay to walk that far?"

She wasn't going to let his concerned tone deceive her. It was from guilt, not affection. She'd figured that out in the hospital. "I'm fine."

"No luck, huh?"

"What do you mean?"

"With those places you visited. You look discouraged."

She shook her head. "Someone had already beat me to the first one. The second one is a bad location and the last place is a fire hazard."

"Doesn't surprise me. I recognized Worsley through the window. He owns two apartment buildings on the south side that are a lot worse."

"He tried to downplay the problems."

"Yeah, but he couldn't put anything over on you."

His confidence in her was a welcome change from the attitude of her brothers. Then again, Sam had always respected her business sense, even if he was a stubborn, macho, caveman cop.

"Have you thought about developing a site instead of buying into a preexisting business?" he asked.

"That's my next choice. It's going to be more of a hassle, since I'll have to deal with the zoning regulations and take care of the necessary permits, and without an established clientele it would take longer to get the business up and running.''

''The initial investment would be lower.''

''That's true. And it would be more of a risk, but I'd be doing it my way.''

''You should have your money within a few months. The D.A. doesn't want to waste any time getting Fitzpatrick to trial.''

''And once I testify, this will all be over.''

He hesitated. ''Yes.''

She'd thought it would be over with the Fitzpatrick wedding. She'd thought the same thing when she'd been shot. It seemed as if they were always setting a time limit on their relationship and then extending it for one reason or another.

But this wasn't any kind of relationship, was it? Guilt, obligation and duty, that's all she meant to Sam.

His arm brushed her shoulder as they waited for the light to change, and despite Audra's fatigue, every one of her nerves instantly came to attention. She tightened her grip on the umbrella, striving to ignore the pulse jumps and stomach lurches that followed the contact, but it was no use. She was acutely conscious of how close they were standing, isolated together as they sheltered from the rain. He smelled so clean, and the muscle beneath his sleeve felt so taut....

How much longer would this awareness keep up? It didn't matter how often or how vehemently she tried to prevent it, she still felt drawn to him. Maybe it was because of her inexperience, maybe that's why she couldn't dismiss those kisses and the intimate things they had done. Now that the physical longings that had lain dormant for years had finally been awakened, they couldn't be switched off.

It was all so frustrating. She'd been getting along fine before she'd met Sam. She'd known what she'd wanted, and it hadn't included having her life turned upside down by a man. How was she supposed to get over her feelings for him when he was there each time she turned around? It hurt to see him. And it felt good to see him. The constant tug-of-war couldn't go on.

So why did she let it? She was taking charge of all the other aspects of her life. Why should she put up with this? Was it because she still hoped they could build a relationship? Was she willing to endure the misery simply to have the chance to be around him?

The light changed. People streamed past, but Audra stayed where she was.

Sam touched her elbow. "Audra?"

The sensation of his fingers on her skin sent pleasure through her body...and misery through her heart. She jerked away. "This isn't working," she said.

"What's wrong?"

"This bodyguard arrangement you've decided on. It isn't working."

"It's only until you testify."

"No. I've had enough." She turned around and started back the way she'd come.

Sam splashed after her. "Audra, wait!"

She lowered her head and kept walking. "I'm relieving you of your duty, Detective Tucker. I'll find my own way home."

"I can't let you do that."

"Of course you can. I'm sure you'd rather be off tracking serious bad guys than baby-sitting me. Get Xavier to assign someone else."

"He won't."

"Then I'll call him and insist—"

"He won't assign someone else because he didn't assign me."

"What?"

"I'm on my own time."

She stumbled to a halt and spun to face him. "You're *what?*"

He lifted his shoulders in a stiff shrug. "I had a few weeks coming to me. The department doesn't have any say in how I choose to spend them."

For an instant, the hope was there, the stubborn, ridiculous dream that she did mean more to him than duty, that maybe he had other reasons for staying with her....

Oh God, she was pathetic. How many times was she going to replay his rejection of her? Pressing her lips together to keep herself from saying anything more, she stepped to the edge of the street and scanned the traffic for a cab.

The black car seemed to come out of nowhere. One second it was part of the slow-moving stream, the next it was veering directly toward her.

Reflexively, she jumped back, but her shoes slipped on the wet pavement. Her heel caught the rim of a sewer grate, wrenching her foot sideways. She flailed her arms to catch her balance.

The car accelerated, its wheels throwing up fins of water as it sliced through the puddles. Audra's first thought was that her good suit was going to get sprayed if she didn't get out of range. It was a silk suit, part of her new slimmed-down wardrobe. Great. It would have to be dry-cleaned before she met with the realtor tomorrow.

She twisted her foot, trying to work the heel loose from the grate, all the time expecting the driver to steer back to his lane or at least be courteous enough to slow down.

Her heel broke off. Hopping backward, she got to the curb.

The fender of the car struck a newspaper box, sending it spiraling over the hood as the right wheels mounted the curb.

It all happened so fast. Just as Audra realized that the driver wasn't making any effort to avoid her, she felt Sam's arms wrap around her waist. He hauled her back against his chest, snatching her out of the way. A split second later, her umbrella was yanked from her hand, caught under the wheels as the car roared past.

There wasn't enough time to draw a breath for a scream. She dug her nails into Sam's arm, her entire body shaking as she focused on the heap of torn fabric and twisted metal ribs, all that was left of her umbrella.

"Are you okay?" Sam's voice was tight with strain. He didn't loosen his grip.

She tried to nod. "Did you see him? My God, did you see what he did, Sam?"

"Yeah." He kept one arm anchored solidly at her waist as he turned her away from the street. "Let's go."

"No, we have to report that driver. He must be drunk or something." She twisted to look over her shoulder, but the black car had disappeared into the traffic. "Look what he did to my umbrella."

"Can you walk?"

"And my suit. This rain is going to ruin..." Her words trailed off. Slowly, she raised her gaze to Sam's face. "He could have killed me."

"That was the general idea."

"Oh...my...God. Sam, he could have killed me," she repeated, stunned at how quickly everything had become so...real. Her teeth began to chatter. It wasn't from the rain.

He propelled her forward. "That's it. We're going."

"Where? What are you planning to do?"

"What I should have done in the first place."

Sam's shoulders bunched as he swung the axe. The blade whispered through the air, striking the block of wood dead center. The wood split and fell apart, thudding to the growing pile of kindling while the axe blade sank deep into the chopping block.

Releasing the handle, Sam took a step back. His hands were shaking with the urge to hit somebody. No, not just somebody. Fitzpatrick. This was more than a case to him now. It had been more than a case for a long, long time. Now it was personal. The man had crossed the line. The bullet had been an accident. The car wasn't.

A drop of moisture trickled along the side of his jaw. He didn't know whether it was from his wet hair or from the cold sweat on his forehead. It had been so close, so damn close. If he'd let Audra send him away, if he hadn't seen the blur of black out of the corner of his eye, if he hadn't grabbed her in time—

No, he couldn't consider that. She was all right. She was here. With him. And he wasn't going to let her go.

No matter what she said.

He wiped his face on his forearm, then leaned over to pick up the firewood and headed for the shed door.

The bare framework of an old barn, its weathered boards stripped away and sold to trendy decorators, stood silhouetted against the heavy sky. In the neighbor's field, hay dipped and swayed under swirling gusts of wind. It was only late afternoon, but the daylight had already been swallowed by the thick layer of clouds. Sam ducked his head against the rain and strode across the yard to the house.

Middleton had inherited this place from one of his grandparents a few years ago. Sam and Bergstrom had used it last fall, when they'd been keeping a witness under wraps before a drug smuggling trial. For privacy the house was ideal, set back from the road, miles from the nearest town, separated from the closest neighbors by hayfields and an apple orchard. At the moment it was vacant, so Middleton had no objection if Sam used the place as a safe house for Audra.

Too bad Audra didn't feel the same way.

Boards creaked as Sam climbed the wooden steps to the porch. He hooked the screen door open with his toe, then freed one hand to twist the inside knob.

Silence greeted him. It wasn't empty. He could feel the tension in the air like the charged calm before a storm.

He pushed the door shut and turned the dead bolt, then toed off his wet shoes and carried the wood to the living room. The fireplace was huge, built of rounded stones that had been painstakingly fitted together, probably by whatever pioneer Middleton ancestor had built the original house. It was meant for warmth, not decoration. Sam hoped that the chimney was still clear enough to draft the fire. He wanted to chase the dampness from the air. He wanted to do something, anything, that would keep his mind from returning to that moment when the car had flashed past—

"I'd like to leave now."

The wood clattered to the hearth. Sam raked his wet hair off his forehead and turned around to face the room. "No."

Audra pushed away from the front window and walked toward

him. Her feet were bare. Her pale green skirt was still damp, hanging limply to her knees. She'd discarded her soaked jacket on the trip here, but the dash from the car to the house had left wet patches on her white blouse. A shiver rippled over her shoulders as she held out her hand. "Give me your car keys."

"This is the safest place for you, Audra. Now that Fitzpatrick has shown his hand, he has nothing to lose by trying again."

"It might have been an accident. I didn't see who was driving."

"You don't believe that car *accidentally* climbed the curb and tried to run you down, do you?"

"Okay, even if it was deliberate, you're overreacting."

"Audra..."

"This isn't the dark ages. You have no right to keep me here against my will. If I had known what you intended, I never would have let you bring me here in the first place."

She was right, and that's why Sam hadn't explained anything until they'd arrived. "You have to keep out of sight."

"Until the trial? That's weeks away. I have other plans. I have obligations. I can't stay here that long."

"Disappearing is the best way to ensure your safety."

"But not the only way. I'll be more careful next time I go out, okay? There's no reason for me to stay—"

"If Fitzpatrick wants to take you out, do you think he'll care who else is in the line of fire? He didn't care who got hurt when he killed Falco."

"Yes, but—"

"There were other pedestrians on the sidewalk today. What if the car had hit one of them? What if you'd met Judy after all and she'd been in the way?"

She wavered, then dropped her hand. "That's not playing fair, Sam."

"I'm not playing." He noticed another shiver travel over her body. The moisture on her blouse had turned the fabric practically transparent, and he had a glimpse of a lacy bra before she crossed her arms and stepped back.

Turning around, he knelt in front of the fireplace and stacked the kindling on the grate. "There's a blanket on the sofa if you're cold. I think there are some towels in the closet at the top of the stairs."

"Thank you, I'm fine."

He tore up a few pages of newspaper, crumpled them and stuffed them under the kindling. The scrape of the match was loud in the quiet room. Sam watched the flame take hold and tried to think like a cop. "The place should warm up in a few minutes, but in the meantime, it would be a good idea to get out of your wet clothes and put on something dry."

"I am not wearing a towel, Sam."

His jaw tightened as he stared at the strengthening fire. Despite himself, he could all too easily imagine Audra in a towel. Or Audra in that short, gauzy nightgown she'd worn the night he'd crawled through her window. Or Audra on the couch with her blouse unbuttoned and her bra pushed aside and her lips swollen from his kiss...

"We can check the upstairs bedroom," he said, his voice rough. "Middleton might have left something you can use."

"How big is he?"

"One of his shirts would be a good tent."

"Does he have a wife or a girlfriend who might have left something here?"

"No, definitely not."

"Wonderful," she muttered.

"Audra, I apologize for the lack of preparations, but I did what I thought was best at the time."

"You could have stopped long enough to let me pack a bag."

Yes, he could have, but then she might have refused to come with him, and if this was the only way he could have her to himself—

No. He was protecting her, that was all. Doing his job. No one was going to get to Audra. He was going to keep her safe until the trial, and then...

And then, afterward, he'd finally have to let her go.

The fire crackled as the kindling ignited. Sam swore under his breath as he threw some thicker pieces onto the flames and moved the spark guard into place.

Who was he fooling? Certainly not himself. He'd known this wasn't merely a matter of doing his job ever since he'd defied Xavier and taken his vacation time. He didn't want to let her go. "I'll phone one of your sisters-in-law and ask her to get some of your things together. I'll have Bergstrom pick them up."

"What about the appointments I've made?"

"They can be canceled."

"But—"

"Audra, it's for your own good."

The minute he'd said the words, he knew he'd made a mistake. Straightening up, he turned to face her.

Her cheeks, until now pale from cold and fatigue, were flushed with anger. Her damp hair, tipped with gold from the firelight, curled in a wild halo to her shoulders. With her fists propped on her hips and her shoulders thrown back, her wet blouse was pulled tight across her breasts, straining the buttons.

"For my own good," she repeated through her teeth. "Why does every man in my life think that he knows what's best for me?"

"You need protection."

"You've done things your way from the moment we met. I've had enough, Sam. Do you hear me? I refuse to put up with any more."

"We'll be able to work something out, Audra."

"I didn't agree to you staying in my apartment, and you expect me to live with you here? Look at this place," she said, sweeping her arm to encompass the room. "It's tiny. We'll be tripping over each other every time we turn around."

"It's not that small."

"What are we going to eat? Where will I sleep? What on earth do you expect me to do with my time? How can I keep seeing you every day when... No," she said, spinning around and striding across the floor. "I'll stay out of sight, but I'm doing it on my terms. If you won't drive me, then I'll walk."

"It's raining."

"I'm already wet."

"Your shoe's broken."

"I'll hitch."

He sprang after her, slapping his hand against the front door before she could grasp the knob. "No."

"Get out of my way, Sam."

"I can't let you go."

"Then you go."

"What?"

"If you think it's so vital to your stupid case that I stay here, then get someone else to do your baby-sitting for you. I already told you, I've relieved you of your duty. I don't need you deciding what's best for me. I already have plenty of brothers for that."

He could feel her temper rolling off her in waves of heat. His own self-control, already strained, stretched dangerously thin. "I'm not one of your brothers," he said through gritted teeth.

"Really? Could have fooled me." She lifted her chin and glared up at him. "You're sounding just like them. I'm not a child, I'm a woman."

"I'm well aware of that."

"Could have fooled me on that one, too. Oh, excuse me. Sometimes, when the adrenaline or the circumstances are right, you do realize I'm a woman. But then you forget about it for my own good."

"I never forget. Not for one second have I forgotten how your body felt stretched out beneath mine that first night. Or the way your legs felt around my waist. Or how you trembled when I touched you in the dark."

She started, her mouth dropping open. But then she lifted her finger and stabbed it into his chest. "That was a natural reaction, remember? That's what you told me. It didn't mean anything. You shouldn't mistake it for anything special."

He heard the pain beneath her words and felt his heart turn

over. "I never meant to hurt you, Audra. I respect you too much to take advantage—"

"Take advantage? Oh, spare me the pity. It might have taken me a while to catch on. I might not be as experienced as you are when it comes to sex, but I know when I'm not wanted."

"Not wanted? *Not wanted?* Is that what you think?"

Her gaze shone with moisture. "I can't take any more, Sam. I feel as if I'm being pulled apart. You might be able to turn it on and off without any problem, but I guess I'm not that way. That's why we can't stay here together. Get someone else. Or I'll leave."

"What do you want, Audra? An apology? You've got it. I know I've screwed everything up from the start."

"I don't need your guilt any more than your pity."

"I don't pity you. And it's not guilt that makes me want to keep you safe."

She squeezed her eyes shut, her nostrils flaring as she inhaled shakily. "Don't do this to me."

"Do you want me to promise not to touch you? Is that it?"

She opened her eyes. Her lips trembled, but she pressed them together without replying.

"Because I can't promise that," he went on. "I tried. Damn, I tried, but I broke that promise just like all the others." He caught her finger, enclosing her hand in his. "I'm wrong for you, Audra. I have no right to touch you but there's no way in hell I can let you walk out that door."

Her fingers curled into a fist against his palm. "Why, Sam?"

There were so many answers, but none of them was the right one. She would leave eventually. And he'd have to let her go. But he couldn't think of that. Not with the storm raging outside and the fire crackling on the hearth and Audra standing so close he could feel her wet skirt brush his knees and her breast press the back of his knuckles with every breath she took.

He released her hand and grabbed her shoulders. "I can't keep you safe from Fitzpatrick if you leave, but I can't keep you safe from me if you stay."

She tipped back her head. "So?"

"Dammit, Audra!" He yanked her against him and anchored his fingers in her hair. "I'm not made of stone."

"Neither am I. Not stone, not decorator icing that melts in the rain, and not fluffy, mindless pink cotton candy either. So if you're planning on pushing me away again and telling me it's for my own good, then do it now."

"Audra, you—"

"Right now, Sam. Either finish what we started, or let go of me and get out of my way."

His hands tightened. She stared at him defiantly, her gaze sizzling with challenge. Then she lifted her arms and curled her fingers around the back of his neck.

At her touch, his self-control, already stretched too thin, finally snapped. He moved at the same moment she did, lowering his head as she raised up on her toes.

# Chapter 13

The tension of the past weeks exploded in a glittering rush. Their mouths came together with an impact that verged on violent. Sam parted her lips with his tongue, sweeping inside to reclaim the taste that haunted his dreams. Audra met him eagerly, her fingernails digging into his skin under his collar as she tried to pull herself closer. Moving his hands to her waist, he lifted her feet from the floor and molded her to the front of his body.

It wasn't close enough for either of them. He'd waited so long, he had no restraint left. As she hooked her heel behind his calf, he turned around and pressed her back to the door. Freeing his hands, he fumbled with the buttons of her blouse, then swore and grasped the wet fabric in his fists. Cloth ripped, a button flew to the floor...and Sam felt Audra smile against his mouth.

Hard, triumphant desire shot through him. He peeled the blouse from her shoulders and she didn't stop him, she helped him, pulling her arms from the sleeves and unhooking the clasp of her bra. He cupped her breasts, a moan of pure pleasure rumbling in his throat as he felt her damp skin warm and her nipples harden.

Sighing, she clasped her arms around his shoulders and pushed herself more fully into his embrace.

How could he have resisted this long? How could he have thought that he'd be able to deny the need that flared through him? Through both of them? To hell with being noble. They'd come so close to this so many times. What harm would it do if they relieved the tension just this once?

He ran his hands over her possessively, reveling in the soft resiliency of her skin and the feminine weight of her curves...until his fingertips brushed the ridge of puckered skin below her left breast.

He broke off the kiss and looked down. Her skin was flushed, her chest rising and falling unevenly with her rapid breathing. Her breasts were more beautiful than he remembered, perfect firm globes tipped with rose. But under his thumb, at the side of her rib cage, there was a shiny red patch of healing skin.

Fingers shaking, he traced the edge of the bullet wound.

And the desire he felt deepened to something else so swiftly it took his breath away. He couldn't name the feeling—it was unlike anything he'd experienced before.

"It's okay, Sam. It's closed up." Grasping his wrist, Audra lifted his hand and placed it back on her breast.

He raised his gaze to her face. He didn't deserve her forgiveness or her generosity, but that didn't make any difference to how he felt. The urge to give himself to her as openly as she was offering herself to him overcame all reason. Scooping her up in his arms, he carried her to the living room, dragged the blanket from the sofa and lowered her to the floor in front of the fireplace.

Kneeling beside her, he eased off the rest of her clothes, then discarded his own. In the firelight her skin heated to a rosy blush as she reached for him. Her smile shy, her touch sensuous, she traced the contours of his chest, splaying her fingers in a delicate caress as she moved her hands downward. Her gaze followed her hands...and her eyes widened. "Oh my."

Her soft exhalation, her look of wonder, affected him more powerfully than he would have believed possible. She hadn't even touched him where he most wanted—no, *needed*—to feel her and already he was nearing the edge. His blood was pounding, his hands were trembling as if this were his first time. There was no room for thoughts of skill or seduction, only a blind, primal need to make her his.

He came down on top of her, possessing her with his hands and his mouth, giving in to his hunger. She responded hesitantly at first, but soon her sweet body was writhing beneath his. Her lips parted on sounds of pleasure more eloquent than any words could be. She clutched the blanket, tossing her head, tightening her thighs for a breathless, endless moment. Then she shuddered and cried out, her gaze meeting his, her eyes shining with...amazement.

''Oh, Sam,'' she whispered.

He smiled. Giving her pleasure was so deeply gratifying it was almost enough. Almost. He reached for his discarded clothes and took his wallet from the pocket of his jeans, then smoothed on a condom and rolled to his back, pulling her on top of him. ''Your way this time.''

Shaking her hair from her eyes, she braced her hands on his chest to push herself up. ''What?''

Her breasts swayed invitingly with her movement. He reached up to cover them with his palms. ''Take me inside you, Audra.''

''I haven't...'' Her eyes fluttered shut as his fingers squeezed gently. ''But I've never.... Oh, Sam, that feels so good.''

He skimmed his hands past her waist to grasp her hips, and guided her into position.

''Sam, I'm—'' She caught her lower lip between her teeth, arching her back as he pressed her steadily downward. ''Mmm,'' she murmured, wriggling her hips.

At her movement, he tightened his grip, holding her steady as he surged upward. He heard her gasp, her nails curving into his shoulders. She was tight, too tight as she closed around him, but he moved again and the tightness eased. And then she was moving with him, sliding, gasping, tensing...

Sam wrapped his arms around her and held on as they peaked

together. Even after the tremors faded and her body went limp, he wasn't ready to let her go. Clasping one hand over her buttocks, he kept her with him as he rolled them to their sides.

A log fell over in the fireplace, sending a shower of sparks against the iron mesh curtain. Light flared briefly, cutting through the shadows to bathe Audra's face in an orange glow. Slowly she blinked open her eyes and looked at him. "I never..." She paused. "I didn't know it could be like that."

"It's never been like that for me, either," he said quietly, stroking her hair back from her cheek.

And it hadn't. Sex with Audra had been unlike anything he'd known before. Maybe it was because of her uninhibited honesty, so different from the life he faced every day. Maybe it was because they'd waited so long, or because the tension had built too high. Whatever. He was feeling too good to think about that now.

Sam kissed her mouth, her cheeks, her nose, whatever he could reach, then pulled back his head and smiled. "What do you say we go upstairs and do this right?"

"Did I do it wrong?"

Chuckling, he kissed her again, then gently eased away. "I don't want you getting bruises from this floor," he said. He helped her to sit up, draping the blanket around her shoulders. "There's a double bed in the main—" His words cut off on a whispered oath when he saw the bright red smear on her thigh. "Oh, God! I hurt you."

"Not really. Only for a minute. I'm fine, Sam," she said, her hands drawing the edges of the blanket together.

"No, you're bleeding." He wiped off the blood with his fingertips, his gut knotting. "Damn, I should have been more careful. I must have broken open your wound somehow."

"It's not the wound that..." She turned her head away. "I mean, that's fine."

"Audra, let me see."

"No. It's nothing to worry about. I've heard it's to be expected when...this happens."

He grasped her chin and turned her face toward him. "What are you talking about?"

"I thought you knew."

"What? What should I know?"

"That some bleeding is normal when it's the first time."

"The first... Did you say the *first time?*"

"Yes."

He jerked his gaze down to his lap. It was so obvious now that he knew what he was looking at. The blood. The tightness he'd felt. Her sweet, innocent response— "Dammit, Audra! You're a virgin?"

She smiled at him shyly. "Not anymore, Sam."

That much was true. With her tangled hair and swollen lips, and that sensual gleam in her eyes, she didn't look the least bit virginal.

He'd hurt her. He'd taken her innocence. He should feel guilty.

But he didn't. No, instead of remorse, he felt a sharp stab of satisfaction. Primitive, male, possessive satisfaction. No one had touched her before him. No one had heard her cry out or felt her tremble. *She was his.*

And the hell of it was, he knew she'd never be.

As the silence dragged out, Audra's smile faded. She watched an array of expressions flicker across Sam's face—denial, acceptance, regret—until he raked his fingers through his hair and turned away. Without a word, he disposed of the condom and yanked on his jeans and shirt, then walked over to the front door to pick up her blouse.

Well, what had she expected? she asked herself harshly, trying to blink back the tears that threatened. A declaration of love? A fairy-tale romance? She knew better than that. Love wasn't what she'd asked for. It wasn't what either of them wanted, right?

He gathered the rest of her clothes and handed them to her. "I didn't mean to hurt you," he said, his voice low and hoarse. "I hadn't known. I guess I'd assumed that you and Ryan..." He cleared his throat. "I apologize for the pain, Audra."

"I'm all right."

His hands curled into fists as he watched her slip on her torn blouse. "I shouldn't have been so rough."

Rough? He'd been passionate, but he hadn't done anything that she didn't want. She pulled on her damp skirt and pushed herself to her feet. "Stop apologizing, I'm fine."

He stepped back. "The water tank should have heated up by now, if you want to take a bath or anything."

God, she hated this awkwardness. What was the big deal about virginity, anyway? It was inconvenient and embarrassing and it was high time that she was rid of it. She didn't regret its loss. Really, she didn't. How could she? Except for that brief pain, she'd enjoyed every second of it.

Oh, yes. She'd enjoyed it. The way he'd made her feel, the way he'd kissed her and touched her, the way he'd moved, his naked shoulders gleaming in the firelight, his muscles tensing, his gorgeous mouth curving in a sensual smile...

"You were right," Sam said.

"What?"

"This isn't going to work." He picked up the blanket, folded it carefully and put it back on the sofa. "I'll get someone else to stay with you."

She stood where she was, watching him move restlessly around the room. He was doing it again. Hot and cold. Advance and retreat. Five minutes ago they'd been lovers. Now he was trying to push her away and go back to how it had been before. "Was it that bad?"

At her question he whirled around. "No."

"Because I know I probably made some mistakes but—"

"Audra," he said firmly, his gaze steady. "It was the best sex I've had in my life."

His frankness shouldn't fluster her, considering what they'd just done. She drew in a steadying breath. "Then why are you treating me as if you wished this had never happened?"

"Because I do." He started toward her, then stopped and shoved his hands into his pockets. "Because you were a virgin."

"I don't see what difference that should make."

"I knew I was no good for you. Hell, I've gotten you shot and almost run over. And now I've taken—"

"You didn't *take* anything. I gave it."

"You shouldn't have. Not to me."

"Why not? If not you, then who?"

A fierce glint came into his eyes. "Don't ask me that."

"My husband?" she went on, moving closer. "You know I'm never getting married. So why shouldn't it have been you?"

"Audra, you don't understand."

"Then help me understand, Sam. Don't you think you owe me that much?"

A muscle jumped in his cheek as he stared at her. Then on a muttered oath, he closed the distance he'd put between them and caught her by the shoulders. "Your brothers were right to keep me away. They must have realized I wasn't the kind of man for you. We're too different."

He'd said that before. Many times. But something about his tone told her that this time it was more than simply an excuse. The afterglow of their lovemaking, and the bravado that had gotten her this far, gradually gave way to misgiving.

She'd thought she wanted an explanation. Now she wasn't so sure.

For a minute he stood without speaking, his fingers tightening as his expression wavered between vulnerability and defensiveness. Then he exhaled harshly and started to talk. "Remember that story I gave you about my background?"

"That your parents died in a car accident? But you said that wasn't true."

"None of it was true. I was raised in Chicago. I don't know who my father was. Neither did my mother. She never wanted me, but she couldn't afford an abortion. She only kept me around for the welfare money. And that was fine as long as I stayed out of her way and didn't cramp her style."

Shock held her speechless. She couldn't imagine any woman being that cruel to her own child.

"The last time I saw her I was eighteen. She and her latest

man were snorting cocaine in the bedroom. I heard she died a year after that.''

"Oh, Sam," she whispered. "How awful."

He snatched his hands back and crossed his arms. "That was my world, Audra. That's who I am. There weren't any cozy houses in the suburbs or family parties with balloons and barbecues and kids on roller skates. Hell, I never was a kid. I was in and out of juvenile detention centers from the time I was thirteen. By sixteen, I was living on the street. I saw things and did things—" He broke off, his jaw as hard as his gaze.

"But you survived. That's not anything to be ashamed of. You should be proud of how far you've come."

"Proud? Of being a whore's accident?"

She pressed her knuckles to her mouth, the pain in Sam's words going right to her heart.

"Your family wouldn't have let me in the door if they'd known the truth."

As much as she wished she could deny it, she feared he might be right. "You can't be held responsible for the circumstances of your birth."

"Maybe not, but it's part of who I am."

"Who you *were*," she persisted. "Whatever you did, however you lived, you're a good man now. You're decent and kind and you have a responsible job."

"Decent?" He gestured to her torn blouse. "Hell, Audra, I just took your virginity in the middle of the floor. If I had any decency I would have gotten out of your life weeks ago like you'd asked me to."

"But—"

"I've hurt you, and the longer we're together, the worse it's going to get. That's what I've been trying to explain. You're everything that's innocent and good and I have no business touching you. The kind of filth I come from doesn't wash off."

Audra leaned her head against the rim of the bathtub and listened to the lazy dripping of the faucet. Rain pattered quietly against the window, the last remnants of the afternoon's storm. The peaceful quiet should be relaxing. The steaming water should be soothing. But it was going to take more than a hot bath to chase away this chill.

Well, she'd asked for it. She'd wanted to know why Sam kept pushing her away. And now she did.

His childhood was like something out of a Dickens novel. Bleak, cruel and completely loveless. It was little wonder he was so adamant about being on his own.

Compared to what he'd endured, her own complaints about her family's protectiveness seemed incredibly shallow. How lucky she'd been to have grown up with the kind of security and unconditional love she'd always taken for granted. Sure, her family had their faults, but the love was always there, a safety net for her when she fell, a ladder to help her get up again.

Sam had never had anything like that. It was a miracle that he'd lived to adulthood.

She shifted, turning her head toward the darkened window. From the direction of the woodshed came the rhythmic sound of chopping. Sam was at it again. They didn't need any more firewood—the weather was damp, but it wasn't cold. No, his exercise had another purpose entirely. He was using the physical activity as an outlet for his feelings.

Revealing his past couldn't have been easy. He'd only given her a glimpse of his memories, but the pain behind his words was unfathomable. She could picture him out there, alone in the light from the bare lightbulb, swinging the axe over and over, using the power of his muscles to work through the powerlessness he must have felt as a child.

Yes, he'd been unable to change the facts of his birth. For a man as strong and determined as Sam, that's something that would be hard to accept. But why couldn't he accept the fact that he'd overcome his roots? Why couldn't he see that he really was a good, decent person?

She rocked forward and picked up the soap from the edge of the tub, rubbing the bar between her hands to work up a lather.

She didn't care what he said. He *was* good and decent. If he wasn't, he wouldn't be so upset about what had happened this afternoon.

What had happened this afternoon...

Closing her eyes, she spread the soap over her neck and chest. Sex had happened. As the saying went, he'd made a woman out of her. If he was as thoroughly bad as he claimed, he wouldn't have had any conscience pangs afterward. He wouldn't have denied them this pleasure as long as he had.

Her hands dropped to her breasts, skimming over skin that was still sensitive from the memory of his touch. Even now, after hours had passed, the sensations he'd aroused were still there, just beneath the surface.

*It was the best sex I've had in my life.*

Her lips quirked. It was the *only* sex she'd had, so she didn't have anything to use for comparison. Yet it had been pretty darn fantastic. Waves crashing, the earth moving, stars falling...all those cliché metaphors didn't come close to describing what she'd felt in Sam's arms.

But just like a flood or an earthquake or a meteorite strike, the aftermath was a disaster.

Sighing, she splashed water over her face, then continued with her bath. It wasn't only her virginity that had sent Sam into full retreat. It was his unwillingness to get close to anyone. Now that she knew how he'd grown up, it wasn't surprising. Being rejected by his own mother must have scarred him deeply. He'd have had to develop an incredibly tough, self-sufficient shell in order to get through that kind of childhood. Or lack of a childhood.

She'd thought she'd suffered when Sam had rejected her. And she'd handled it by denying her feelings, and then when that didn't work, by trying to push him away. Why hadn't she realized that Sam was doing the same thing? He'd been pushing people away out of self-defense from the time he was a child. Even now, after he'd opened up his past to her, he'd made it clear that he didn't want her sympathy or her pity.

But she didn't pity him, she loved him.

The bar of soap squirted out of her hands and thunked to the floor. Love? She was in love with Sam Tucker? No, she'd settled that before. It was lust. Proximity. Gratitude. Hormones...

God, talk about being in denial. Of course she was in love with him. The feeling had been there all along, but she'd been too busy trying to rationalize it away to recognize it. She'd been too hung up on her pride and her lack of experience and she'd done exactly what Judy had said: she'd been so afraid of trying again that she'd buried her heart.

The chill that had stiffened her muscles melted away. She loved him. She knew it with a certainty that left no more room for doubt. The knowledge was so certain that it must have been drifting around in her subconscious mind for weeks, and now it had finally surfaced.

It was love, all right, but it wasn't the easy, comfortable bond she had with her family, or the idealistic devotion she'd felt for Ryan. No, it was a steady, strong, down-to-earth man-woman love. Why else had she continued to care, despite what she'd been through? Why else had she chosen Sam to be the first and only man to make love to her?

Water surged over the sides of the tub as she grasped the rim and rose to her feet. Her first impulse was to shout it out loud, to run to Sam and throw herself into his arms and tell him how she felt...and then watch him withdraw even further into that shell.

Wrapping a towel around herself she padded to the window. Light shone from the open door of the woodshed. The sound of chopping had been replaced by the whine of a power saw. Lifting her arm, she flattened her palm against the rain-streaked glass.

Sam had never been loved. At some stage of his life, he must have wanted to be. All children wanted to be. But he'd survived by closing off that part of himself. How deep did the emotional scars go? Having never been loved, was he incapable of accepting it? Was he unable to love in return?

She didn't know. He'd been willing enough to accept the physical expression of her feelings. He'd even wanted to do more,

until he'd used the excuse of her virginity in order to go all noble
and aloof again. She understood why he didn't want to get involved or risk commitment.

Yes, but what did *she* want?

That was an easy question. She didn't want to accept the distance between them. She didn't want to complicate her life with
worries about the future or things neither of them could change,
but that didn't stop her from wanting Sam.

Oh, yes. She wanted him.

So, here she was. A woman still tingling from her initiation
into sexual pleasure. Alone on an isolated farm with the man she
loved…a man who would rather chop wood and use power tools
than come to bed with her.

And she had no idea what she was going to do about it.

Sam lifted the shutter he'd repaired last night into place beside
the front window. He was fastening it to the frame when he
caught a blur of movement at the corner of his vision. He whirled
around, the screwdriver clenched in his fist. When he saw it was
Audra, he didn't relax. If anything, the tension he was feeling
grew worse.

She looked fresh-scrubbed and wholesome, as pure as the sunrise he'd watched after his sleepless night on the couch. Evidently
she'd found some of Middleton's clothes—the purple T-shirt she
wore was long enough to pass for a dress. She'd knotted a paisley
tie around her waist and hadn't bothered with shoes…and she was
so beautiful he couldn't look away.

Without a doubt she had the best legs of any woman he'd ever
known. And he liked the way the folds of that T-shirt draped
teasingly around her curves, and the way her hair looked as if it
had been tousled by a lover's hand. But what drew him the stron-
gest was the expression on her face. Part shy, part sensual, the
same way she'd looked when she'd touched him in that gentle
exploration of his body.

How much firewood did he need to split to get her out of his
system? After the way he took her innocence, he shouldn't even

be looking at her. He was nothing but the scum his mother had always called him. No, he was worse. Because instead of the remorse he should be feeling, he still felt that stubborn sense of possessive satisfaction.

And God help him, he wanted to fold her into his arms and kiss her good morning and pretend it wasn't the Fitzpatrick case that was keeping them here together.

"Hi," she said, moving along the porch toward him. She held out one of the mugs she carried. "I made some coffee."

He put down the screwdriver and reached for his shirt, achingly aware of the way her eyes gleamed as her gaze dropped to his chest. "Thanks."

"There isn't much in the way of food here, but I made a peach cobbler if you want some."

As usual, the aroma of her coffee made his mouth water. After yesterday, her love of cooking took on an whole new significance. For a woman as passionate as Audra to remain celibate all these years, she must have used her cooking as an outlet for her sensuality. So it was easy to understand why the mere smell of her baking could arouse him. "Peach cobbler?" he asked as he took the mug she offered.

"I found some biscuit mix and canned peaches in the cupboard with the coffee. I hope Detective Middleton doesn't mind."

"He won't. The stuff's probably left over from the last time we used this place."

"And I, um, borrowed one of his shirts."

"He wouldn't mind that, either." Sam certainly didn't. He backed up to sit on the porch railing and sipped his coffee. For a moment he indulged himself, studying the way the supple cotton fabric molded her as she moved. And he remembered the way his hands and his lips had touched her skin....

The sound of a car engine intruded into his thoughts. He stiffened, preparing to get Audra back into the house, but then he recognized the throaty growl of Bergstrom's Mercury.

When he'd called Xavier last night to explain the situation, Sam had asked him to send out a replacement. That's what Audra had demanded, anyway. For everyone's sake, it was the best thing to do. It had been practically impossible to sleep on the couch, knowing she was only a staircase and a closed door away from him. And now that he knew what he was missing, how could he possibly get through another night, and then another after that...until their time would be up and she'd be out of his life for good.

Swearing under his breath, he pushed away from the railing and headed for the steps. He didn't want to think about his job or this case or what was right and what was wrong. He wanted Audra. And why the hell couldn't Bergstrom have been late?

The moment Sam turned away, Audra took a deep breath and tightened her grip on her mug to keep her hand from shaking. How could he look so good in rumpled clothes and morning stubble? How was she supposed to sip coffee and carry on a polite conversation when what she really wanted to do was kiss him good morning and tell him she loved him? And show him she loved him?

Gravel crunched as a huge, rusty old boat of a car pulled up beside the woodshed. It took a moment for Audra to recognize the tall man who emerged from the car. But then she saw the blond hair and the flash of a toothpaste-ad smile. It was Piers Bergstrom, the policeman who had taken her statement in the hospital. But what would he be doing out here...

Of course. This would be Sam's replacement.

She shouldn't have hesitated. She should have kissed Sam good morning after all.

Bergstrom took two suitcases from the trunk of the car. "So this is how you spend your vacation," he said as he followed Sam to the house. He grinned when he caught sight of Audra. "I admire your dedication, Tucker. Yes, I surely do."

Sam scowled. "Any word on that black sedan?"

"It was stolen, just like you figured." Bergstrom dropped the suitcases on the porch. "Good morning, Miss McPherson. We meet again."

"Hello." She glanced at the suitcases he'd brought, finally recognizing the one with the flowered tapestry pattern. "Is that mine?"

"I called Judy and explained the situation," Sam said. "She took care of packing your clothes."

"You have a charming sister-in-law," Bergstrom put in. "She asked me to pass on her best wishes."

"Thank you for picking up my things," Audra said.

He flashed another toothpaste-ad smile. "It was my pleasure, but personally, I don't think you can improve on what you're wearing."

She tugged on the hem of the T-shirt, feeling suddenly self-conscious. It hadn't bothered her when Sam had looked at her legs like that. "Uh, thanks."

He inhaled deeply, then groaned with exaggerated pleasure. "What is that delicious aroma?"

"Peach cobbler."

"Mmm, I think I'm in love."

Sam glowered. "Did you bring any supplies?"

"I thought you could take care of that," he said, inhaling again. "Do I smell coffee too?"

"You're welcome to have a cup. And help yourself to the cobbler," she said, moving toward her suitcase.

"Aren't you going to join me?" Bergstrom asked.

"No, I think I'll go and change."

"And deprive me of this feast for my eyes? That shirt never looked so good on Middleton."

"Berg," Sam muttered. "Back off."

Bergstrom winked and grabbed Audra's bag before she could reach it. "I'll carry this upstairs for you. Which bedroom are you using?"

"The one with the lock on the door," Sam said. "You'll be staying on the couch."

"Uh-uh," he said, shaking his head. "Not me."

Sam took a step toward him. "I want to talk to you."

"Later."

"Now, Berg."

Audra pulled the suitcase from his hand and opened the screen door. "Excuse me. I'm going to unpack."

As soon as the door swung shut behind her, she heard Bergstrom's voice through the screen. His tone was suddenly all business. "I brought your spare gun, Tucker. It's in the other suitcase."

"Why? What were you doing in my apartment?"

"Hey, how else was I going to pack your stuff?"

"What?"

Audra paused in the hall, twisting around to listen.

"I can't stay," Bergstrom was saying. "I have to be back in the city by noon, so it looks like you're still on bodyguard detail."

"What?"

"While you've been on vacation, the rest of us have been working our little butts off for Xavier. We got a break on that kiddie porn ring case."

There was a brief silence. "That's good news," Sam said.

Did he mean it was good news about the break in the case? Or good news that Bergstrom wouldn't be staying?

What did it matter? The other suitcase contained Sam's clothes. He wouldn't be leaving after all. She'd have more time with him. Audra grabbed the banister, her steps light as she climbed the stairs to the bedroom.

Considering the circumstances, and the threat from Fitzpatrick, she shouldn't be feeling this good. Nothing had really changed. Sam was still keeping himself unreachable. Their association was still temporary. Their parting had merely been postponed, that's all.

She swung the suitcase onto the bed and zipped it open, then frowned when she looked inside. There had to be some mistake. These weren't her clothes. No, wait. There was the blue dress Judy and Geraldine had talked her into buying. And that was the nightgown she wore on really hot nights, but she didn't recognize those shorts or that tank top. She picked them up and held them against her. They appeared to be her size, but the top had such a scooped neckline, and the shorts were so short, she never would have chosen anything like this for herself.

Quickly, she sorted through the rest of the clothes. There was a pair of slim-cut beige jeans, a few flirty little sundresses, makeup and more nightgowns and underwear she didn't recognize. It was all her size, but those scandalous scraps of lace and satin had never been stored in Audra McPherson's dresser drawers, that was for sure.

She dug deeper into the suitcase, suspicion growing. Evidently, her hopelessly romantic, matchmaking sister-in-law had been quick to grasp the potential of the situation. "Judy," she whispered. "What have you done?"

Her hand closed around a rectangular cardboard box. She drew it out, her frown deepening as she turned it over to read the label. Two dozen, extra large. Lubricated. Quality guaranteed. What on earth... Two *dozen? Extra large?*

Well, she'd obviously guessed Sam's size correctly, too. But what on earth did Judy expect her to do with...

Shaking her head, Audra dropped the box on the bed. And for the first time in weeks, she began to laugh.

# Chapter 14

She must be doing something wrong, Audra decided, pressing her hand to her stomach to calm the butterflies. Seduction was supposed to come naturally to a woman in love, wasn't it? Not that she'd had any previous experience, but she had always been a quick study, and she was willing to learn.

It had seemed like a good idea this afternoon. Preparing a romantic, candlelit dinner for two, wearing one of the flirty little dresses Judy had packed, dabbing the perfume in places that made her blush.... God, it had been so long since she'd been on a date, let alone thought about romance, she was a bundle of nerves. Taking a deep breath, she smoothed down her dress and fluffed her hair, then turned around and carried the cheesecake to the table.

Sam was still sitting as stiffly as he had throughout their dinner. He glanced up when she came in, but then he tightened his jaw and lowered his gaze.

"I made some dessert," she said. She was stating the obvious, but she needed to say something to break the silence.

"Looks good."

She sat down across from him. The moment she reached out to pick up the knife, her strap slithered down her arm. Swallowing a sigh, she nudged the strap back on her shoulder. She shouldn't have worn this dress. It looked fine when she was standing, but every time she sat down the snug bodice pushed upward and the narrow straps slid down. How was she supposed to look stylish and attractive when she couldn't even manage to control her clothing?

The candle on the table wavered as a breeze wafted through the window. In the flickering light, the angles of Sam's face looked carved from stone. "You didn't have to go to all this trouble, Audra. I don't expect you to cook for me."

"Oh, I enjoy it." She cut a piece of cake and put it on a plate. And her strap fell down again. Deciding to ignore it, she passed the plate to Sam. "I'm glad that general store had everything on my shopping list."

His hands fisted on the table top. "No problem."

She'd been tempted to add a bottle of wine to the list, but she'd worried it would have been too obvious. Maybe she should have anyway. And she should have tried to tune in a country music station on that radio on the bookshelf. He'd said he liked Garth Brooks. Well, everyone liked Garth Brooks, but...

Why was she so nervous? She hadn't been nervous yesterday. Their lovemaking had been so gloriously spontaneous, she hadn't had time to think of anything else. And this time it would be even better, because she knew she loved him. Pressing her hand to her stomach again, she drew in a deep breath.

His nostrils flared as he dropped his gaze.

She sighed and cut a slice of cheesecake for herself. It had been a challenge to make that dessert with the limited utensils that she'd found in the kitchen, but she'd done her best. "It's cappuccino," she said.

"What?"

She gestured toward his plate. "The cheesecake."

His hand tightened around his fork. With a quick jerk, he lifted a bite to his mouth.

Audra watched for his reaction, remembering how he'd enjoyed testing the fudge sauce with her all those weeks ago. He was a man of strong appetites, and she hoped that by stimulating this one, she'd stimulate another. He chewed slowly, his expression softening as his eyes half closed in pleasure. But then he blinked and set his jaw.

It wasn't working, she decided as they finished their meal in silence. Whoever said that the way to a man's heart was through his stomach?

Maybe she should have waited a few days, let him get accustomed to the idea of trusting her before she threw herself at him. Yet their time here was limited, and she didn't intend to waste a minute of it. It didn't matter if he couldn't return her feelings right away—she loved him enough to accept whatever he was willing to give. She wasn't going to squander another one of their precious nights here listening to him tossing and turning on that sofa while she lay all alone in that double bed.

Did love always make a person so shameless?

She propped her chin on her hands and leaned toward him. "Would you like some coffee?"

His fork clattered to his plate. "For God's sake, Audra, that's enough."

"What?"

"Lean over any more and you're going to fall out of that dress."

She glanced down. The bodice was still in place, although both straps drooped over her arms. "No, it's pretty well stuck."

He rubbed his hands over his face, then stretched his arm across the table and grasped her wrist. "What are you doing, Audra?"

"What do you mean?"

"The perfume, the dress, the black underwear."

She glanced down again. "You've been peeking."

"You've been flaunting."

"Me? I'm not the one who's been parading around half-naked all day. Didn't Bergstrom pack any extra shirts for you?"

"It was hot. I was busy."

"Right. Chopping wood we don't need and playing with your tools."

His lips twitched. "My tools?"

"What were you repairing this time?"

"The frame on the back door." He loosened his grip, rubbing his thumb along her arm. "The meal was delicious, Audra."

"Thank you."

"But I meant what I said. I don't expect you to cook for me while we're here."

"There isn't much else for me to do."

"We could go for a walk tomorrow, as long as we don't go too far from the house."

The gentle caress of his thumb was making her breathless. "That would be nice. What about tonight?"

"What?"

She moistened her lips. "What do you want to do tonight?"

His thumb went still. For an endless minute, he watched her in silence, his eyes gleaming in the candlelight. "You know damn well what I want to do."

"And what's that, Sam?"

"Audra, I've been watching you try to keep that dress on for the past hour. Now I want to peel your clothes off you an inch at a time. Then I want to touch you, from the tips of your dainty little toes to that place on the side of your neck where I can see your pulse racing."

She swallowed hard. Maybe the seduction was working after all. "And then?"

"I want to put my mouth where my hands have been and taste what I've touched."

A tremor tickled through her stomach, not from nervousness any longer but from anticipation. "And then?"

"I want to feel you do the same to me."

Desire slammed through her at the image his words painted. Oh, God. Who was seducing whom?

"You should have left with Bergstrom."

"Did you want me to?"

"Hell, no. But I told you I wouldn't be able to keep you safe from me if you stayed."

"I've been safe for twenty-eight years, Sam. Maybe I don't want to be safe from you."

His gaze intense, he continued to watch her. Then he swore under his breath, laced his fingers with hers and tugged her forward.

She didn't even consider resisting. Smiling, she rose to her feet and moved toward him.

His chair scraped the floor as he pushed back from the table. Drawing her closer, he pulled her onto his lap. "If I were the man you deserved, I wouldn't be doing this," he murmured.

She lifted her hand to his cheek. "But you're the man I want, Sam."

He shook his head. "After what I did yesterday..."

"What *we* did," she corrected.

"I can't promise you anything, Audra. I can't change who I am."

Pressing her fingers to his lips, she stopped his words. "I don't want promises. And I don't want to think about yesterday. Or tomorrow. I'd rather concentrate on tonight."

He nipped the tip of her index finger, his lips curving into a smile as she dropped her hand. With his gaze steady on hers, he moved his hands to her back and lowered her zipper to her waist. One by one, he slid the narrow straps of her dress past her elbows and guided her arms free. Then he grasped the center of the loosened bodice and eased it downward. An inch at a time.

The breeze from the window whispered over her bare skin.

nd she rolled her shoulders with pleasure. Lifting her hand, he started working on the buttons of his shirt. Even if he adn't told her he wanted her to touch him, her own need to eel his skin beneath her palms would have led her to this.

She'd been right the first time—seduction did come naturally o a woman in love. Parting his shirt, she slid her hands inside nd splayed her fingers, greedy for the sensations she remem-ered. She'd never thought much about male beauty, but Sam's ody was truly beautiful. The springy curls in the center of his hest, the taut skin that stretched over his muscles, the silky ine of hair that arrowed temptingly downward...it was all so ew, so different, so...

There were no words to describe what she felt. It wasn't omething that could be expressed rationally. But then, love vasn't rational, was it?

Beneath her hip, she felt Sam swell and harden, and her own ody softened instantly in response. Yet even as she felt herself nelt toward him, she felt a surge of strength. *Her* strength. The ower of her own femininity that she'd hidden away along with er heart. Eagerly, brazenly, she dropped her hand to his waist nd unsnapped the stud of his jeans.

Sam shuddered, his hands unsteady as he traced the edge of er bra until he found the front clasp. The strapless wisp of lack lace fell away easily. He tossed it behind him, then put is hand on her thigh. "Stand up for a second, Audra."

"Mmm?"

"I want to take off the rest of your clothes."

Her eyes widened as she glanced around. "Here?"

"Yeah," he murmured. "Do you mind?"

Did she? In front of the fireplace was one thing, but being aked at a dinner table was so...daring. And deliciously vicked. Her pulse racing, she slid from his lap and let her dress all around her feet.

Groaning, he leaned forward, dragging her against him as he ressed his face between her breasts. His breath hot on her kin, he hooked his fingers in the waistband of her panties and inched them down. When he pulled her back on his lap, instead of having her sit sideways, he guided her leg around his so that she straddled him.

Audra grasped his shoulders, shocked by the intimacy of their position. ''Sam, what—'' Her half-hearted protest cut off on a gasp as she felt his mouth close over her nipple.

And then she couldn't think. All she could do was feel. Sam was doing things to her, *for* her, that she'd never imagined. He took her newly awakened awareness of herself as a woman and showed her there was much more, oh, so very much more to learn.

It was one of those perfect late July days, when the air was alive with the scent of hay and gentle warmth. Somewhere near the top of the apple tree, a robin sang to the afternoon sun. Leaves rustled overhead, dappling the long grass with delicate shifting shadows. Beyond the shelter of the boughs, puffy white clouds danced along the horizon.

Two weeks at the farmhouse had passed like two hours. Or maybe two years. Somehow, Audra's sense of time had altered. Knowing how fleeting it was, she'd tried to pack a lifetime of memories into a handful of days.

The day after tomorrow, this was all going to end. Instead of sitting on a blanket under an apple tree, she'd be sitting in a courtroom across from Larry Fitzpatrick. She'd have to look into the eyes of a man who had killed in cold blood, a man who had tried to kill her. She'd have to face reality.

And then, after the trial was over, she'd have to say goodbye to Sam.

But she wasn't going to think about that. She'd done a pretty good job of shoving it to the back of her mind so far. And she was determined not to waste the short time they had left by wishing she had more.

Lying back on the blanket, she tucked her bag under her head for a pillow and lifted her arm to point at the sky. ''Look, Sam. The one on the left. It's a horse.''

"It's a cloud, Audra."

"Come on, Sam, be a sport. What do you see?"

He turned on his side, levering himself up on his elbow to lean his head on his hand. Instead of looking at the sky, he fixed his gaze on her face. "Freckles."

She rolled her eyes.

"Seven of them. Right...there," he said, tapping the tip of her nose with his finger.

"You're not cooperating."

He trailed his finger along the side of her jaw and down her neck. "Why? Because I'd rather look at you than at a formation of condensed vapor?"

"Thank you. I think."

Leaning over, he kissed her gently, his lips curving into a smile against hers. Then he stretched out crosswise on the blanket and laid his head on her stomach. "Okay, which one's the cow?"

"Horse." She pointed toward the cloud she'd noticed. "Oh. Now it's more like a dragon. See the wings coming out of the back?"

"If you say so." He caught her hand, pulling it to his mouth to nibble her knuckles. "You taste like cinnamon."

"That's from the coffee cake."

"Is there any left?"

"Hang on," she said, stretching her free arm toward the plastic container she'd brought to the orchard with them. She dragged it closer, then picked up a chunk of the cake and dropped it in his mouth.

He closed his eyes in pleasure as he chewed. "You're going to make a fortune when you open up that restaurant if you have this on the menu."

"Thanks. I'll give you a discount when you eat there."

Instead of replying, he went back to nibbling on her fingers.

She knew what was behind his silence. It was because she'd referred to their future, as if they had one, as if she'd see him again, as if he'd still be a part of her life. That was a subject they'd both carefully avoided for the past two weeks. And it had been a wonderful two weeks. She wouldn't have missed it for the world. She just wished...

No. That was a door she didn't want to open. She'd told herself she'd be happy to accept whatever he was willing to give her. And he'd already given her more than she'd imagined.

He'd been a tender, considerate lover. After that deliciously scandalous incident on the chair, it hadn't taken long for him to coax her past her initial hesitancy. Sam made no secret of the delight he took in being the one to teach her the pleasures of sex, and she'd been an eager student—by the end of the first week, they'd tried out every piece of furniture in the house.

And if there wasn't any love in his lovemaking, well, she'd gone into this with her eyes open, hadn't she?

Easing her hand from his, she stroked the stray hair from his forehead, then buried her fingers in the thick, dark locks. She loved this freedom to touch him, and to be touched in return. He was no longer her unattainable fantasy man, the sexy, naked stranger who had burst into her life two months ago. She'd seen past the surface to the sensitive, scarred soul beneath. "Sam?"

"Yeah?"

"Why did you decide to become a cop?"

He rolled his head on her stomach to meet her gaze. "Where did that come from?"

"I was just thinking. Wondering. I was kind of born into the food business."

"And I was born on the wrong side of the law."

It was getting easier for him to talk about his past, she realized. Although he was a long way from resolving his feelings over his childhood, at least he didn't clam up as quickly as he used to. She smiled, toying with the hair that curled behind his ear. "So what made you join the force?"

"I already told you that. Xavier encouraged me."

"How did you meet him?"

"You mean you haven't guessed?"

She paused. "You met him in a professional capacity, right?"

Sam nodded.

"He arrested you for something, didn't he?"

"I stole his car."

"You...stole his car?"

"Tried to." He turned his face back toward the horizon, settling his head more comfortably against her stomach. "I wasn't a very good thief. Xavier caught me before I got the thing in gear."

"What happened?"

"He was working in Juvenile back then. Hauled me in front of a judge that very night, talked her into giving me probation and releasing me into his custody."

"His custody? What does that mean?"

"I was trying to take his car because I wanted somewhere to sleep. He took me home with him, made me wash and wax that old Chevy and mow his lawn before he let me eat."

"Xavier? I can't believe Lieutenant Jones did that. He seems like such a... I don't know. A tough guy."

"Don't get me wrong, it wasn't as if he wanted a kid or any of that sentimental stuff. His wife had died the year before and he wanted to keep busy," he explained. "He was just doing his job."

*Just doing his job.* She lifted one eyebrow. "Now, where have I heard that before?"

"Xavier wasn't like the social workers and do-gooders who used to visit the detention centers and spout all that garbage about us poor misunderstood youth. He expected me to work for my keep. Even back then he was tough. Once when I missed my curfew because I was out hustling pool, he tossed me into a holding cell for the night. Then he decided I had too much time on my hands, so he made taking my high-school equivalency exams another condition of my probation."

"No wonder you decided to become a cop," she said softly. "He was a wonderful role model."

"He was okay. Taught me a lot."

"It sounds like it."

"You know what he gave me when I graduated from the Academy?"

She paused, then shook her head. "No, what?"

His lips curved into a lopsided smile. "That old car I tried to steal."

Audra swallowed hard, trying to get rid of the lump in her throat. Another piece of the puzzle that was Sam had just fallen into place. She looked at his familiar smile, her heart turning over. And she hadn't thought it was possible, but the love she felt for him deepened. "Sam, I..."

The words were there, pushing at her, trying to be said. But she swallowed them along with the emotion. Blinking the moisture from her eyes, she looked at the branches overhead. The apple blossoms had long since given way to the budding fruit, but in her mind she saw the golden outline of another blossom, and the diamond sparkle that should have lasted forever.

Sam turned his head and nudged the underside of her breast with his nose. "What?"

"I..." She drew in a shaky breath. "I'm glad you met someone like Xavier."

"Yeah," he said, grinning. "Even when I'm on my vacation time, this job can have damn good fringe benefits."

"Fringe benefits?" she repeated, struggling to keep her tone as light as his. "Is that what I am to you?"

The glint of teasing faded from his eyes. He sat up and moved closer, bracing his arms on either side of her. "Audra, you are, without a doubt, the best thing that's ever happened to me in my entire life."

Oh, God. Why did that sound like a goodbye? Time was running out, but she didn't want to risk what little they had left by telling him how she felt. He couldn't be pushed. She'd learned that a month ago, during that humiliating confrontation at the Fitzpatrick wedding.

Sam cupped her cheeks in his palms and leaned over to give her a long, achingly tender kiss. Then he drew back, picked up the gun he'd left on the edge of the blanket and tucked it behind his belt. "It's getting late," he said, his voice hoarse. "Time to go."

The phone call came the next morning. Audra heard Sam's voice in the living room and set down the crepe batter, alerted by the concern in his tone. She'd assumed the call was from Piers, who had become their unofficial go-between, keeping them up-to-date with the legal wranglings that were taking place during the lead-up to Fitzpatrick's trial. Those calls were always brief and to the point, and Sam's voice took on what she'd come to think of as his cop tone, distant and curt. But from the sound of it, this call wasn't about official business.

Pausing to take the skillet off the heat, she wiped her hands on a towel and hurried out of the kitchen. He was just setting the receiver back on its cradle when she reached him. "Who was that?"

He rubbed his jaw, his morning growth of whiskers rasping in the silence. "Xavier."

"Oh. Is there a problem with the trial?"

"No. That's progressing right on schedule."

"You sounded worried."

Dropping his hand, he turned to face her. "Your father wanted him to contact you."

She felt her stomach drop. Because of the need for security, no one but Xavier's team knew exactly where she was. Except for a few brief telephone calls to assure them she was fine, she hadn't spoken to anyone in her family for weeks. She hadn't minded—she'd been too wrapped up with Sam to miss them. They knew she'd be back in Chicago by tomorrow, so why would her father want to contact her now?

"Something's wrong, isn't it?" she said. "Is it my mother? What happened?"

He eased the towel from her fingers and clasped her hands in his. "Your mother's fine. Geraldine went into labor last night."

"Finally! She must be so pleased. She'd been dying to see that..." Her words trailed off as she saw the look on Sam's face. "Oh, God. What happened? Is the baby all right?"

"They did an emergency cesarean half an hour ago. The baby's fine, but Geraldine went into shock."

"No," she said, shaking her head. She yanked her hands from his and backed away. "No, not Geraldine."

"They're treating her for it, Audra. I'm sure she'll be fine."

Whirling around, she headed for the door. "I have to be there."

"I'll take you to see her tomorrow on the way to the courthouse."

"No. Now. Tomorrow could be too late."

He strode after her and caught her elbow. "We can't risk taking you back this close to the trial. The security we planned won't cover you if—"

"For God's sake, Sam, don't you understand? I have to be there," she repeated. "My family needs me. And I need them."

"I'm sure the doctors are doing everything possible."

"This isn't about medical treatment. It's about love."

"Your safety is my priority here, Audra." He tightened his grip on her arm. "I can't let you—"

"Love, Sam. Pretending it doesn't exist won't make it go away."

"I don't know what you're talking about."

Her eyes filled with sudden, hot tears. "Maybe you're right. Maybe you don't know what I'm talking about."

"It's my job to protect you until you testify," he went on. "I can't ensure your safety if we go back now."

She wiped her cheeks with the back of her hand. "We're

going to have to go back eventually, Sam. We both know this has to end.''

''Not yet,'' he said, clenching his teeth. ''Not yet. We have another day here.''

Shaking her head, she tried to tug her arm free. ''Sam, let me go.''

The tension in his body tremored through his hand. He stared at her, his hardened jaw and stubbled cheeks making his expression grim. Behind his gaze emotion flashed, a naked spark of raw need.

They'd played out this scene before. She'd demanded to leave, he'd insisted she stay. That argument had ended on a blanket in front of the fireplace. But it hadn't really ended. No, it had only been postponed, glossed over, pushed to the back of her mind.

''All right, Audra,'' he said finally. ''Pack your things. We'll leave in five minutes.''

Yet he didn't let her go. Instead, he pulled her into his arms and held her tight enough to hurt.

# Chapter 15

Constance McPherson engulfed Audra in a tearful embrace the minute she stepped from the elevator. Sam stayed by her side defiantly. He knew he wasn't welcome here, but he wasn't going to leave Audra to face this crisis by herself.

Who was he fooling? She wasn't by herself, she never would be. She had her family, she didn't need him.

"How is she?" Audra asked, pulling back to look into her mother's face.

"There hasn't been any change in the last hour," Constance said. "I guess that's good, in a way. She's holding her own."

Judy joined them, her face pinched with worry. "I know Gerri won't let this beat her. She's got so much to live for."

Audra looked around. "Where's Jake? Is he okay?"

"He's with Geraldine." Constance lifted up her glasses to wipe her eyes on her sleeve. "He hasn't left her side. He loves her so much, I don't know what he'll do if she... Oh, Lord."

"Whatever happens, we'll get through it, Mom," Audra said. "How's the baby?"

Constance sniffed and gave her a watery smile. "He's perfect. An absolute angel."

"Why don't you go and see him," Judy said. "We're on our way to the chapel." She paused as she met Sam's gaze. "I'm glad you're here," she added. For a moment it looked as if she were about to say more, but then she blinked hard and moved away.

As Sam followed Audra down the corridor to the nursery, he noticed John and Christopher among the group of people outside the window. The last time the McPhersons had gathered in a hospital like this, it had been because of Audra. Sam vividly remembered the desperation he'd felt. He hadn't wanted to lose her. She'd been his responsibility. He cared for her.

And yet in a matter of days, he would walk out of her life for good. Once she gave her testimony, his job would be over. Case closed. He'd have no more excuses to stay.

It was inevitable. He'd always lived alone. He thrived on independence. He didn't belong in her world. She deserved better than him. He'd only end up hurting her more.

Damn, it had all seemed so clear two weeks ago. There were reasons, good reasons, why his relationship with Audra shouldn't continue. Sure, the physical thing had been great while it had lasted, but he wasn't cut out for the kind of emotional closeness she wanted.

*If not you, then who?*

His hands tightened into fists as he tried to push that particular thought out of his mind. It was because he'd been her first, that's all. It was natural that he'd feel possessive about her. That's why he couldn't picture another man touching her body or holding her in his arms while she slept. Or greeting her with a morning kiss. Or seeing her smile as she found whimsical creatures in the clouds.

Or standing beside her to dry her tears.

Her chin trembled as she stepped closer to the nursery window. "Oh, Sam," she murmured. "He's beautiful."

He glanced past her. A nurse was handing a red-faced, wrinkled infant to a woman in a rocking chair. "Isn't that one of your sisters-in-law?" he asked.

"Yes, that's Esther," Audra said. "I don't know why she'd be in the nursery."

"We drew straws to see who'd get to feed him," John McPherson explained, moving next to Audra. He gave his daughter a brief hug, then turned to look at Sam. "Detective Tucker."

Sam nodded a cautious greeting. For Audra's sake, he hoped her father wouldn't insist that he leave. Because as long as Audra wanted him, he wasn't going to let anyone drive him away.

But once this job was over...

His mind couldn't seem to get past that.

"I see Lieutenant Jones passed on my message."

"Audra insisted on being here."

"She would. She's always been very devoted to the people she loves." He looked back at his newest grandson. "Jake hasn't named him yet. He's waiting for Geraldine."

"They wanted this baby so much," Audra murmured. "She has to pull through."

"We've got to have faith."

"I know, Dad. It's just that it seems so unfair."

"There aren't any guarantees in life, Audra. Especially when it comes to love and marriage. It's always a risk." His expression grew thoughtful. "Geraldine hadn't told any of us that she was risking her life with this pregnancy."

"What? I didn't know—"

"It seems she hadn't told Jake, either. He's blaming himself, but he shouldn't. She knew very well the chance she was taking."

Sam returned his gaze to the baby. Oblivious to the turmoil his birth had created, the child had relaxed in his aunt's arms and was contentedly emptying his bottle.

And why shouldn't he? The baby was completely innocent.

He couldn't be blamed for his mother's condition. No child could be held responsible for the circumstances of his birth....

Weeks ago, Audra had said those same words to Sam, but there really was no comparison between this child and the baby he had once been. There hadn't been a crowd of relatives anxious to welcome Sam into the world. No one had competed for the chance to hold him. He hadn't been born from love. He hadn't even been given any. It wasn't any mystery why he didn't understand what it was.

Audra reached for his hand. Without hesitation, he laced his fingers with hers, drawing her closer so that she could lean her head on his shoulder.

John met his gaze above Audra's head, his expression as inscrutable as always. Then he looked past him, his face suddenly draining of color. "Jake?"

Keeping a firm hold on Audra, Sam turned around. Jake was walking toward the nursery, his steps unsteady, his shoulders stooped with weariness. For a moment he stared blankly at the people who were gathered in the hall.

Christopher was the first to react. He stepped forward to meet him, grasping his twin by the shoulders. "Jake?"

Jake scrubbed his face with his hand. "I've come for the baby."

"What?"

"My son." His throat worked as he swallowed. "I want to bring him to Geraldine. She's asking for him."

"She's awake?"

"Fifteen minutes ago." Tears ran freely over Jake's cheeks as his face creased into a smile.

Memory reverberated through Sam at the sight of Jake's frank emotion. He recognized that incredible relief—a month ago he'd felt it himself.

"The doctor says she's going to be fine."

Audra sighed and leaned heavily against Sam. "Thank God."

Her brother's grin was ebullient as he moved to the nursery

door. ''And Gerri told me if I didn't get our son down there
in the next thirty seconds, she's going to come and get him
herself.''

''Do you swear to tell the truth, the whole truth and nothing
but the truth?''

Audra rested her left hand on the smooth cover of the Bible
and kept her gaze on Larry Fitzpatrick. ''I do.''

After so many weeks spent worrying about what she'd say,
and so much effort spent ensuring she'd have the chance to
say it, actually testifying proved to be somewhat anticlimactic.
Audra had been warned what to expect, and the cross-
examination was brutally thorough. Yet the memory of that
night was unshakably clear in her mind. All she had to do was
tell the truth.

It wasn't as difficult as she'd thought. Although witnessing
a murder was something she'd never be able to regard dispas-
sionately, by revealing what she saw, at least she'd be able to
achieve some balance in her mind. Fitzpatrick wouldn't escape
justice this time—his carefully crafted public image had been
shattered, and his financial base was crumbling as his money-
laundering network was being shut down. Even some of his
lawyers were rumored to be deserting him, now that his assets
had been frozen.

Marion and her new husband had come to the courtroom.
She looked years older than the bride she'd been a month ago,
and she rarely smiled when she looked at her father, yet beneath her air of disillusionment there was a new hint of
strength. Other rumors had been circulating, hints that Fitzpatrick's daughter was trying to sell her father's estate, not to
keep the money but to donate the proceeds to charity. That
wouldn't surprise Audra—she'd always felt that Marion was a
good person in spite of her roots. After all, she knew of certain
people who had managed to overcome backgrounds that were
far worse.

Yes, everything was working out. Everything was coming to an end. Everything.

"Thank you, Miss McPherson. That will be all."

Holding herself stiffly, she stepped down from the witness stand.

Sam met her in the hall outside the courtroom. The sight of him sent a thrill all the way to her toes, as it always did, but she didn't run to him as she would have two days ago. He looked like a stranger, with his hair freshly combed and his suit neatly pressed. But it was more than his clothes that made her hesitate. He'd been unusually withdrawn since they'd left the hospital yesterday, as if he were concentrating on some internal argument that only he could hear.

"I'll give you a ride," he said.

Although it was only going to prolong the inevitable, she didn't have it in her to object. She let him guide her to where he'd parked his car and sank back against the seat, achingly conscious of how near he was. And how the distance between them was getting greater by the minute.

But this was what they'd agreed on, wasn't it? It was working out exactly as they'd planned. He was going to see Fitzpatrick convicted. She'd get the reward money and be on her way to the complete independence she'd always wanted. She'd known their relationship was temporary. She'd told herself he'd be satisfied with whatever he was willing to give....

No. She wasn't satisfied. After the emotional roller coaster she'd been on for the past few days, there was no way she could simply shut off her feelings. Seeing Jake and Geraldine with their baby had made Audra take another look at her plans for her own life. Although her sister-in-law had been too weak to sit up, and it was painfully obvious that her usual vitality had been drained by her ordeal, the radiance on her face brought a lump to Audra's throat even now.

As her father had said, there were no guarantees. She'd learned that with Ryan. Risk and love. The two always seemed to be intertwined. She loved Sam. Yet she didn't want to risk losing him by telling him she loved him.

What had once been a valid concern now seemed pointless. Worse, it seemed downright cowardly.

They arrived at the apartment building just as the afternoon shadows were lengthening into evening. Sam waited until she'd unlocked her door, then insisted on going inside first to check the place out. "Okay," he said after he'd made a circuit of the rooms. "Everything seems to be just how we left it."

She closed the door behind her and tucked her key back into her purse. "I thought there wouldn't be any problem about my safety once I testified."

"I just wanted to make sure."

"So that's why you wanted to drive me home," she said, striving to keep the pain out of her voice. "You're still just doing your job."

"Audra, I can't forget what happened to you." He slipped his forefinger under the knot of his tie and tugged it loose. "Being at the hospital yesterday, and then listening to you talk about it up there on the stand today was like living through it all over again. I failed to protect you before."

"You can't keep blaming yourself for that. It was my choice to get involved in this case."

He shrugged out of his jacket and tossed it on the back of the sofa. "It wasn't your choice to get shot."

"I thought we'd gotten past all this. But maybe it's better to bring it out in the open instead of pretending it's not there. I've been doing too much of that lately."

"Too much of what?"

"Pushing things to the back of my mind instead of talking about them." She walked up to him and laid her hand on his arm. "Once and for all, Sam, my being shot was an accident."

"If it hadn't been for me—"

"If it hadn't been for you, I might have died," she said firmly.

''No, you've got it wrong. I got you mixed up with this case. *t*'s my fault you were hurt.''

''My family had already agreed to do that catering job before *y*ou told me Fitzpatrick was a criminal. I would have been at *t*hat wedding whether you were or not. Fitzpatrick's meeting *s*till would have taken place. Falco still would have been *k*illed.''

Beneath his sleeve, his muscles hardened into taut ridges. ''You were in the line of fire because you were talking to me.''

''The wedding was over. I would have been counting the *s*upplies and loading the van, so chances are I would have been *o*utside at that particular time anyway.''

''But—''

''Think about it, Sam.'' She tightened her grip. ''You pulled *m*e down. You called the paramedics. If you hadn't been there, *F*itzpatrick might have seen me and made sure not to leave a witness.'' She paused to take a steadying breath. ''Or I might have bled to death before anyone noticed I was missing.''

His breath hissed out. ''No.''

''Yes. You can't look back and change just one thing in the past. There's no way of knowing what else would have happened differently.''

Moving suddenly, he wrapped his arms around her back and pulled her to his chest. ''I can't even think about losing you, Audra.''

''You won't.''

''I don't know how your family does it,'' he went on, pressing his cheek to the side of her head. ''There are so many of you, and you all care about each other. So many things can happen. Like with Jimmy, and Geraldine. And you. When one of you is hurt, you all hurt.''

''That's love, Sam. It's a risk.''

''It's so much easier being alone.''

''I used to believe that.'' She flattened her palms on his chest and lifted her head. ''I swore I'd never again set myself up for the kind of pain and guilt I went through when I loved Ryan. But you know what? I was wrong."

"I don't know anything about love."

She smiled. "Yes, you do."

"Audra..."

"I love you, Sam."

Except for the steady rise and fall of his chest, he didn't move.

"I love you," she repeated. "I know you don't want to hear it, but you've felt it." She pressed her palm over his heart. "No one gives medals for the courage it takes to risk your heart, and love never makes front page news. You live with danger and excitement all the time in your undercover work, but do you know something? Love is the real adventure."

"I've never..."

"It's okay." Moving her hands to the center of his chest, she started undoing his buttons. "I know it's your first time. I'll show you."

He dropped his arms, his body humming with tension. "Audra."

His voice was low and rough, with a new note of resolution she hadn't heard before. She tugged off his tie and tossed it over her shoulder, then parted his shirt and pressed her lips to the base of his throat.

Two weeks ago her boldness would have amazed her. But not now. Taking his hand, she led him into the bedroom.

Dusk had darkened the corners of the room, but there was a glimmer of bronze sunlight at the edge of the curtains. She bypassed the bed and drew him beside the window. "That first time I saw you, this is where you were standing."

"I remember."

She pushed the shirt from his shoulders, running her palms over the sinewy outline of his biceps as she eased the sleeves down his arms. "At first I thought I had to be dreaming."

"You fought like a wildcat."

She reached for his belt, sliding the leather through the

buckle by feel. With an ease that had come from plenty of practice, she lowered his zipper. "You terrified me, but when I realized you didn't mean me any harm, you fascinated me. You made me feel things I didn't want to feel."

Lifting his hand, he leaned toward her but she stepped back and held up her palm. "Wait."

He stared at her, his gaze snapping with barely leashed passion. *"Wait?"*

"I want to do this myself." Hooking her thumbs in his waistband, she eased his pants and his briefs over his hips and down his legs.

He kicked them aside with a quick jerk, then inhaled sharply as she trailed her fingers back up his thighs. "Audra, what are you doing?"

For a heartbeat she paused, drinking in the sight of him. His hard, muscular body was as familiar to her by now as her own, and yet it still had the power to make her breathless. He'd taught her about sex. Now it was her turn. She looked into his eyes, willing him to see the emotion in hers. "I'm making love to you, Sam."

And that's exactly what she did. Without words, using the instincts of her body, she showed him the love she felt. She caressed him with her hands, her nails, her knuckles and her lips. Her own pulse raced in a rhythm to match his as he responded to her touch. The setting sun gleamed on his skin in a caress of its own as he stood motionless, pleasure rippling across his powerful frame.

With a groan that was ripped from the last shreds of his self-control, Sam scooped Audra into his arms and carried her to the bed. Something was breaking loose inside him. Doors that had been firmly shut, that he'd given up trying to open, were cracking wide. It was terrifying and exhilarating, unlike anything he'd felt before.

He wanted to join more than their bodies. This urgency was beyond anything physical, and yet he knew he couldn't wait another second. Hands shaking, he got rid of her clothes and drove himself into her.

He'd thought things would be different once they came back to the city. He'd assumed it was only the temporary isolation of the farmhouse that had allowed him to push aside the hard-learned habits of a lifetime. He'd been wrong.

This wasn't a temporary affair. This wasn't a role or a job or any of those excuses he'd so desperately used to shield himself from the truth. He felt a tremor quiver through her body and he tightened his arms around her, wanting the moment to last. He didn't intend to let her go today. Or tomorrow. Or ever.

Was this love? Was that the name for the feeling that swept over him?

Sealing his mouth to hers, he shook with the force of the release that tore through them both. This time the glow didn't fade. Even as his pulse slowed and his breathing steadied, the warmth stayed with him. He levered himself onto his elbows to look into Audra's face.

Her lips swollen and moist from his kiss, her cheeks flushed, she smiled up at him.

He'd hurt her. But she'd forgiven him.

He was a bastard, an unwanted castoff, but she wanted him. She believed he was good and decent. And dammit, she made him feel as if he could be.

*It was safer to be alone. Less painful.*

*Maybe I don't want to be safe from you.*

"Audra," he whispered. "That was..."

She didn't help him find the words, she simply waited, her faith shining from her eyes.

He smiled. "This love business is still kind of new to me. I think you're going to need to show me again."

# *Epilogue*

"This isn't the way to my restaurant," Audra said, twisting on the seat to look at Sam. "Where are we going?"

His mouth lifted into one of his adorable, lopsided smiles. "We're taking a detour. You've been so busy with your plans for next week's opening, I figured this is the only way I'm going to get you to myself for the evening."

Her lips twitched. "This is kidnapping, Sam."

"So, call a cop," he said, his smile turning into an unrepentant grin.

Laughing, she relaxed and watched him drive. So much had happened in the weeks since the trial had ended, it was still hard to believe how quickly her life could change. Fitzpatrick had been found guilty and was safely behind bars, his criminal network was smashed and the insurance company had come through with its promised reward just in time for Audra to close the deal on the restaurant of her dreams.

And speaking of dreams, her restaurant wasn't the only one that was coming true. Every night she spent with Sam, every morning she awakened in his arms, the love they shared continued to grow. She'd been right. Love was the real adventure.

Sam flicked on his turn signal and turned the car into a familiar driveway. Audra lifted her eyebrows. "This is Christopher's house," she said.

"That's right."

"What are we doing here?"

"Picking up our dinner."

"What? Why?"

"I can't cook," he said, giving her a quick kiss before he opened the car door. "Wait here."

With a sense of unreality, she watched him stride past a pair of catering vans to the kitchen entrance. Esther and Judy must have been watching for him. They handed him a foil-wrapped casserole and several paper bags, then waved cheerfully to Audra as he walked back to the car.

She stared as he placed the food carefully on the back seat. "All right, what's going on?"

"I told you. I can't cook," he said, pulling back onto the street. "So I hired McPherson Catering to provide dinner for us."

"You...hired my family? And Christopher agreed?"

"He passed my call to Esther. Judy happened to be there and helped prepare the meal."

Judging by the aromas that were filling the car, the two women had outdone themselves. "Sorry about Christopher. I hope he wasn't rude."

He lifted his shoulders. "I don't expect him to change his mind about me overnight. Same goes for all your brothers. They have good cause not to welcome me."

"Well, they'd better get used to the idea of us being together," she said firmly. "I won't tolerate—"

"Don't worry." He dropped his hand to her knee. "They're not going to scare me away."

She blew out her breath in a huff. Aside from her brothers'

usual protectiveness, there was probably still some resentment over the way they'd all been fooled by the fake engagement.

Only it had never been a complete fake, had it? Because somewhere along the way she had fallen thoroughly in love with her fiancé.

"What were you on the phone about all afternoon?"

"I was talking to Xavier." He lifted his hand as he changed gears to turn a corner. "I thought you were going over your budget."

"It's done. Were you planning your next assignment?"

He paused. "No, I'm requesting a transfer."

"Why? I thought you liked working with Xavier."

"I did, but he agrees with my decision. I'm going to be working with the Juvenile Crime division." He glanced at her, his expression suddenly serious. "I think I can do some good there."

Oh, he would do some good all right, she thought, remembering the successful way he'd handled Jimmy. Sam's understanding of troubled teenagers came from personal experience—he was an ideal example of how the right help could turn someone's life around. "You'd be a natural," she said.

"Funny, that's just what Xavier said."

As she'd done countless times already, she marvelled at the inner strength it must have taken for Sam to become the man he was. And now that he'd be working with children, there was a chance that eventually he'd be able to come to terms with his own past.

Taking a chance. Risking it all. The idea didn't scare her anymore. Love had its risks, but it had its rewards, too.

Settling more comfortably against the seat, she smiled at Sam as he drove through the sparse evening traffic. Gradually, her smile turned into a puzzled frown when she saw where they were heading. "What are we doing here?"

"Just picking up some supplies," he said, slowing down as he pulled up to the curb in front of her parents' house. "I'll be right back. Your mother said she'd leave everything by the door.''

''But...''

He was already out of the car and moving up the front walk. Audra crossed her arms, watching in amazement as he returned with a small carton, two folding chairs and a table. He stored everything in the trunk, then without another word of explanation, he pulled away.

Three blocks later, he stopped again, this time in the parking lot of her old school. Her mind was clicking over with possibilities as she watched Sam carry everything toward the park beside the schoolyard. She remembered very clearly the last time they'd been here. It had been just before that first dinner with her parents. They had taken a walk toward that willow tree and...

Sam returned and opened her door. ''Come with me.''

He led her across the grass to a table beneath the willow. Audra paused in amazement, her gaze taking in everything, from the snowy white tablecloth to the pair of candles that flickered in the gentle breeze. ''Oh, my God,'' she breathed. ''What's going on?''

He pulled out one of the folding chairs and helped her to her seat. ''We're having a romantic dinner,'' he said.

''But why—''

''Most people only have this opportunity once in their lives.'' He sat across from her and filled her wineglass. ''The last time I did this, I remember thinking it wasn't right, that I should have done it differently.''

Her heart turned over. ''Oh, Sam.''

''But like you said, we can't go back and change the past. From now on, I want to concentrate on our future.''

*Our* future. ''I'd like that, too.''

''Audra, I don't want to measure our time in days. I want more.'' He took her left hand in his and brought it to his lips. ''I want it all. I want everything we pretended to have. A family. A future.''

"So do I, Sam."

One at a time, he kissed each of her fingertips. "I want the right to stand beside you through whatever happens in our lives," he said, his voice as steady as his gaze. "I know how you feel about marriage, but I hope I can change your mind. You don't deserve anything less."

Her eyes filled. "What are you saying?"

He slipped his free hand into his pocket, then gently eased a ring onto her third finger. "I don't want to play a role this time, Audra. I want the real thing."

Drawing in her breath, she looked down at her hand. The candlelight gleamed from a band of gold...that was engraved with a delicate pattern of apple blossoms. "What..." She lifted her gaze to his face. "That's my ring!"

"It's always been yours."

"But how..." She rubbed her thumb across the diamond. "I thought you gave it back."

"Somehow it kept slipping my mind. I think part of me knew all along that I wasn't going to let this end." He smiled. "Well, Audra? Will you marry me?"

"Oh, yes. I'll marry you. On one condition."

"Name it," he said swiftly. "Anything you want."

Leaning across the table, she framed his face in her hands. "This time, Sam, let's not have such a long engagement."

\* \* \* \* \*

# ▼™ SILHOUETTE SENSATION®

## AVAILABLE FROM 22ND OCTOBER 1999

## DANGEROUS TO LOVE  Sally Tyler Hayes

*Heartbreaker*

Sexy spy Dan Reese had been holding Jamie Douglass at arm's length
long enough, and they'd both been ready to unleash their passion when
a traitor in the agency nearly killed Dan. Suddenly he had to fight to
reclaim the man he once was, so that Jamie didn't have to face the
danger alone…

## CLAY YEAGER'S REDEMPTION  Justine Davis

*Trinity Street West*

The dark, rugged loner should have frightened Casey Scott given the
menacing midnight calls she was receiving but, although the sexy
stranger was impossible to ignore, she felt safe in his arms. Would this
ex-cop be able to forget his past and protect his woman?

## CATTLEMAN'S PROMISE  Marilyn Pappano

When Olivia Miles arrived on Guthrie Harris's land, looking for a home
for her twin daughters, she came bearing a deed that said *his* ranch was
*hers!* Forced to make room for the single mum and her children, would
Guthrie rethink his vow never to lose his heart again?

## THE MOTHER OF HIS CHILD  Laurey Bright

Five years after little Kristy was conceived, all of Charisse Lane's
carefully constructed lies came tumbling down. She came face-to-face
with the father of the child she'd raised, and he had no intention of
walking away. Resisting his convenient marriage proposal wasn't going
to be easy…

# AVAILABLE FROM 22ND OCTOBER 1999

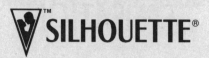

## Intrigue
*Danger, deception and desire*

**McQUAID'S JUSTICE** Carly Bishop
**A LOVER AWAITS** Patricia Rosemoor
**REDHAWK'S HEART** Aimée Thurlo
**TWILIGHT ILLUSIONS** Maggie Shayne

## Special Edition
*Compelling romances packed with emotion*

**THEIR CHILD** Penny Richards
**THE COWGIRL & THE UNEXPECTED WEDDING**
Sherryl Woods
**THE MAJOR AND THE LIBRARIAN** Nikki Benjamin
**THE MILLIONAIRE BACHELOR** Susan Mallery
**THE RANCHER AND THE REDHEAD** Allison Leigh
**JUST WHAT THE DOCTOR ORDERED**
Leigh Greenwood

## Desire
*Provocative, sensual love stories*

**LOVE ME TRUE** Ann Major
**THE DADDY AND THE BABY DOCTOR**
Kristin Morgan
**HER HOLIDAY SECRET** Jennifer Greene
**THE LAW AND GINNY MARLOW** Marie Ferrarella
**THE COWBOY WHO CAME IN FROM THE COLD**
Pamela Macaluso
**HART'S BABY** Christy Lockhart

9910

# 2 FREE

## books and a surprise gift!

We would like to take this opportunity to thank you for reading this Silhouette® book by offering you the chance to take TWO more specially selected titles from the Sensation™ series absolutely FREE! We're also making this offer to introduce you to the benefits of the Reader Service™—

- ★ FREE home delivery
- ★ FREE gifts and competitions
- ★ FREE monthly Newsletter
- ★ Exclusive Reader Service discounts
- ★ Books available before they're in the shops

Accepting these FREE books and gift places you under no obligation to buy, you may cancel at any time, even after receiving your free shipment. Simply complete your details below and return the entire page to the address below. *You don't even need a stamp!*

**YES!** Please send me 2 free Sensation books and a surprise gift. I understand that unless you hear from me, I will receive 4 superb new titles every month for just £2.70 each, postage and packing free. I am under no obligation to purchase any books and may cancel my subscription at any time. The free books and gift will be mine to keep in any case.

S9EA

Ms/Mrs/Miss/Mr ............................Initials................................
BLOCK CAPITALS PLEASE

Surname ........................................................................................

Address ........................................................................................

.....................................................................................................

............................................Postcode..................................

**Send this whole page to:**
**UK: FREEPOST CN81, Croydon, CR9 3WZ**
**EIRE: PO Box 4546, Kilcock, County Kildare (stamp required)**